PRAISE FOR *BLACK NOWHERE*

"*Black Nowhere* is an extremely unsettling thriller that haunted me for weeks. It's a shrewd critique of Silicon Valley startup culture, a brisk FBI procedural, and a chilling look at a very modern form of amorality."
—Dave Eggers, author of *The Circle* and Pulitzer Prize and National Book Award finalist

"*Black Nowhere* is a blast. A gripping thriller with wonderfully nuanced characters. If you haven't been reading Reece Hirsch, it's time to start."
—Lisa Lutz, *New York Times* bestselling author of *The Passenger*

"*Black Nowhere* is a Dark Web *Scarface* for the twenty-first century! Fast, smart, and timely, Hirsch hits all the right notes in this cat-and-mouse page-turner that exposes the false utopia promised by the modern internet. I hope there is much more to come from Special Agent Lisa Tanchik."
—Matthew FitzSimmons, *Wall Street Journal* bestselling author

"Smart, intense, and frighteningly real—I loved this book! Readers who enjoy thrillers with a heavy dose of high-tech computer wizardry will devour Reece Hirsch's gripping new novel. When two of the smartest people on the planet face off in a cat-and-mouse game that might be the end for them both, the outcome is anything but certain."
—Karen Dionne, international bestselling author of *The Marsh King's Daughter*

"A sleek and suspenseful state-of-the-art thriller with crisp writing and engaging characters that has something to say about the way we live now."
—Peter Blauner, author of *Sunrise Highway*

PREVIOUS PRAISE FOR REECE HIRSCH

The Insider

"Regulatory attorney Hirsch's debut thriller has something for everyone. Hirsch's fast-paced, film-ready plot and tough, ambitious characters will keep fans of legal thrillers on the edge of their seats."

—*Publishers Weekly*

"San Francisco, the Russian mob, big business, and very fine legal madness—great stuff . . . from Reece Hirsch, [who] is writing and running with the big boys."

—John Lescroart, *New York Times* bestselling author of *Poison*

"Gripping and gritty . . . All the danger, treachery, and action that make a reader clamor for more are there. Well done."

—Steve Berry, *New York Times* bestselling author of *The Bishop's Pawn*

The Adversary

"Reece Hirsch is both a great stylist and a cunning storyteller, and *The Adversary* is his best work yet. This is a first-rate thriller that grabs you from the first pages and doesn't ever let up. I defy you not to stay up late finishing it."

—David Liss, Edgar Award–winning author of *The Day of Atonement*

"*The Adversary* is a page-turning brew of technology, murder, mayhem, sex, romance, and revenge, spiced with several surprising twists. This is a compelling thriller novel that will appeal to all readers."

—*Tallahassee Democrat*

"*The Adversary* is a satisfying hard-boiled mash of pop novel genres: a cypherpunk, lawyer-detective, conspiracy theory, blow-up-Manhattan thriller with furious pacing and compelling characters and scenarios. Reece Hirsch's second novel is dizzyingly, compulsively readable."

—*Electronic Privacy Information Center Alert*

Intrusion

"With *Intrusion*, Reece Hirsch has written a timely and poignant thriller of international cyberspying while keeping the story a sweaty-palmed thrill ride. Fans of Joseph Finder and Christopher Reich, meet Reece Hirsch!"

—Robert Dugoni, *New York Times* bestselling author of the Tracy Crosswhite series

"*Intrusion* is a cutting-edge, prescient thriller that draws the curtain back on the mysterious, little-understood work of data collection, data mining, and cybercrime. The kind of rare thriller that will change the way you think about everyday life and things you normally take for granted. So read it with the lights on, before someone turns them off from afar."

—Jon Land, *USA Today* bestselling author of *Strong Darkness*

"*Intrusion* is the best cybersecurity thriller I've read this year. Reece Hirsch really knows what he is talking about— and has a talent for making the pages fly. A must read for thriller lovers!"

—Allison Leotta, author of the Anna Curtis series

Surveillance

"Wow. I read *Surveillance* in one fell swoop—absolutely riveting and compelling. It propels Reece Hirsch right to the A-list of the thriller game. Loved every line."

—Ken Bruen, author of *The Guards*

"*Surveillance* involves a dark and dangerous technology that resembles what Will Smith's character went up against in *Enemy of the State* with the feel of Robert Redford dashing between New York and Washington in *Three Days of the Condor*. Those are lofty comparisons, I know, but Hirsch more than measures up thanks to a pair of appealing heroes and the devilish conspiracy in which they find themselves embroiled. The classically structured *Surveillance* delivers on all its promises, relentlessly satisfying in all respects."

—*Providence Journal*

"Snap your cell phone's SIM card in half, stuff a copy of *Surveillance* into your bug-out bag, and make sure you're not followed to your off-grid cabin in the woods, because Reece Hirsch's latest Chris Bruen novel ratchets up the paranoia something fierce."

—Chris Holm, author of *The Killing Kind*

BLACK
NOWHERE

BLACK NOWHERE

REECE HIRSCH

THOMAS & MERCER

Text copyright © 2019 by Reece Hirsch

Published by Thomas & Mercer, Seattle

www.apub.com

Amazon, the Amazon logo, and Thomas & Mercer are trademarks of Amazon.com, Inc., or its affiliates.

ISBN-13: 9781542042918 (hardcover)
ISBN-10: 1542042917 (hardcover)

ISBN-13: 9781542042895 (paperback)
ISBN-10: 1542042895 (paperback)

Cover design by Rex Bonomelli

Printed in the United States of America

First edition

For Kathy

1

It started with an anonymous post on a message board called PillMill, a place where illegal drugs were bought and sold. The message read, If you're looking to score some Oxy at a good price, you need to check out Kyte. It's next level. The message included a link.

FBI special agent Lisa Tanchik was stretched out on the couch in her studio apartment in San Francisco's Potrero Hill neighborhood, laptop on her stomach, her pale complexion made paler by the screen's moonglow. Her shoulder-length black hair was pulled back in a ponytail, and she was wearing a faded FBI Academy sweatshirt. She looked younger than her twenty-seven years. Her laptop bore a sticker for DEF CON, the Las Vegas hacker convention that she had recently attended. A cooling mug of black coffee sat beside her.

Curious, she clicked.

And plummeted down a rabbit hole into a world that never should have existed.

Kyte looked nearly as slick as eBay and featured a well-organized menu of every illegal drug known to man. There were listings for Afghan No. 4 heroin, fish scale Colombian cocaine, hash, LSD, MDMA, synthetic opioids like fentanyl, and a black tar heroin known as the Devil's Licorice. There were black market prescription drugs like

Xanax, Ritalin, and, as promised, OxyContin. Name a drug, and Kyte was selling it. While drugs were the primary product line, Kyte was also selling other illicit goods and contraband, including malware, pirated DVDs, and even guns.

Each drug's listing featured a description detailing the nature of the high (a variety of MDMA was touted as offering "a swoosh of confidence and well-being"). Customers rated products on a five-star system. Afghan No. 4 heroin was apparently a crowd-pleaser, garnering 4.8 out of 5 stars and 154 reviews. There was even a seller's guide that provided helpful instructions on how to vacuum seal and inconspicuously package drug shipments so that they would be invisible to electronic sensors and canine olfactories.

Lisa sat straight up and brought the laptop over to her kitchen table, where she began capturing screenshots. She had to kick aside a cardboard box of her ex-boyfriend's things, which she had assembled for pickup. That box, along with the recycling bin brimming with empty vodka and wine bottles, said more about her present circumstances than she would have liked.

As she scrolled through page after page after page of sellers offering illegal drugs, the enormity of the enterprise began to sink in. Kyte was probably brokering as much drug traffic as the largest crime syndicates.

As a specialist in cybercrime, Lisa was no stranger to the so-called Dark Web. Most upstanding citizens led their online lives exclusively on the "surface web," the home of the mostly legitimate websites that were offered whenever people typed search terms into their favorite web browsers. But a shadowy realm existed beneath that surface, consisting of unindexed websites accessible only by using the Tor Browser, formerly known as the Onion Router. Tor passed internet traffic through at least three different servers before sending it on to its destination, with each relay adding another layer of encryption. Tor allowed persons seeking to operate in secrecy, from criminals to political dissidents, to shield their identities through the browser's strong encryption and use of a cryptocurrency like Bitcoin as a payment method.

And if Kyte provided an anonymous marketplace that was truly beyond the reach of law enforcement, then how long would it be before it wasn't just selling drugs and malware? How long before terrorists began using it to plan and assemble the makings of the next Oklahoma City or 9/11?

Lisa's fingers moved quickly over the keyboard, and within seconds she had created an account on Kyte as Rodrigo, an identity that she had used online many times before. Rodrigo purported to be a midlevel independent drug dealer in his early twenties who was tech savvy, with vague, self-proclaimed connections with Mexican drug cartels.

Although it wasn't part of her officially sanctioned duties, Lisa had made a hobby of lurking on the Dark Web and internet relay chat boards to observe the hackers, cybercriminals, cranks, and miscreants who frequented those shadowy corners of the web—creating an expansive network of contacts in that underworld that she hoped would one day pay off in an investigation. Internet relay chat, or IRC, boards, were online forums where hackers could communicate with relative anonymity. She had a few online personas that she had used consistently over time so that they were recognized in certain quarters and had some history to them. She even maintained a journal so that she could keep their histories and foibles straight. She had created the Rodrigo identity when she had still been a security consultant to the FBI, tracking a hacker who had been selling data obtained from an HMO breach. Rodrigo had proven to be such an engaging and persuasive character that she hadn't had the heart to take him out of circulation when the investigation was done.

After spending the better part of a recent weekend exploring online in her various personas, distracting herself from her fresh breakup, Lisa thought she understood a little bit how someone with multiple personality disorder must feel.

She ultimately concluded that the reason she did what she did online was because she happened to be weirdly adept at it. She was a talented and inventive liar. When someone suffered from clinical depression and relied on alcohol as a coping mechanism, the truth was rarely a good option.

If she was being honest with herself, her use of alter egos was no longer entirely about hunting cybercriminals for the FBI. Lisa felt strangely liberated when she assumed an online persona. She had spent enough time as some of them, like FireStarter, a fourteen-year-old boy from Daly City, that she slipped into being them like an actress reprising a role.

Donning one of her online avatars untethered her from the limitations of her real life, in which her career and social life were less than satisfying. Some people drank or took drugs to achieve that sort of escape, and Lisa figured this outlet was healthier than most.

She chose a listing for a tiny vial of LSD from a seller known as TripMaster and placed the order as Rodrigo, using a PO box that she'd established for this sort of purpose. She promptly received a reply message from the seller: Thanks! Your package will ship in 2–3 business days. If you're taking more than the microdose, we recommend that you find a quiet place with a soothing vibe before ingesting and allow yourself six to seven hours. Happy trails, TripMaster.

Perhaps the package would reveal clues to the identity of TripMaster or the operators of Kyte.

She knew that the FBI would never give an untested field agent such as herself an opportunity to bring down a high-value target like the head of the Sinaloa drug cartel. But based on what she had seen so far, locating and arresting the founder of Kyte would amount to that sort of career-making bust.

This was the opportunity she had been waiting for.

2

First thing the next morning, coffee in hand, Lisa knocked on the door of her boss, Special Agent in Charge Pam Gilbertson. Gilbertson supervised the San Francisco field office and its satellite offices, known as resident agencies. The door was partially open, and even though the workday hadn't officially started yet, Gilbertson was already on the phone.

Gilbertson motioned her inside. Her boss was tall and athletic looking, even at twice Lisa's age. She was legendary in the bureau for leading the investigation and capture of an Atlanta serial bomber. She finished up her call with a curt, "Yes, well, I'm going to reserve judgment on that." Gilbertson hung up the phone and stared at Lisa.

"Special Agent Tanchik, are you aware that I have an open-door policy?"

"Yes, I am. And it is very much appreciated."

"Well, you should know that's just something that I say. It sounds good to some of our colleagues who've been to business school. As you seem to have noticed, my door was open in the literal sense. But in the metaphorical sense, not so much."

"I see." Lisa gave a tight smile and stepped farther into her boss's office.

"What I'm trying to tell you is that I hope you have something pretty damn important to say to me. Otherwise, you should be speaking to your SSA." Lisa's immediate supervisor was Supervisory Special Agent Dan Melcher, who managed her squad.

"I think I do. Have you heard of Kyte?"

"No. What is it?"

"It appears to be a Dark Web marketplace for illegal drugs."

"That doesn't sound unusual."

"What's unusual is the scale of it. It looks like it could be processing hundreds of thousands, maybe even millions, of dollars in transactions."

"Per year?"

"Per month."

Gilbertson frowned. "That can't be right. Show me."

Lisa pulled a handful of papers from her computer bag—printouts of the screenshots she'd taken of Kyte's drug offerings. Gilbertson examined the first page slowly; then her pace quickened as she flipped through the entire stack.

While she was doing that, Lisa, still standing, pulled out her laptop, booted up Tor, and navigated to the Kyte website.

When Gilbertson had finished with the screenshots, she asked, "There's more like this?"

"So much more," Lisa said, sliding the laptop across the desk.

The room was silent except for the clicking of keys as Gilbertson explored the site. Finally she said, "It makes sense now. Last week I saw a report from the Postal Inspection Service that they've seen a huge uptick in the number of parcels they've found containing drugs."

Gilbertson paused, seemingly lost in thought for a moment; Lisa imagined she was working through the jurisdictional and bureaucratic ramifications of this discovery. "Have you told anyone else about this?"

"No."

"Then I want you to prepare a report with everything that you've learned about this . . . Kyte. I'll take it up with the ADIC."

The assistant director in charge, or ADIC (pronounced "a dick"), was Gilbertson's boss and was based in the Los Angeles field office. Every agent in the FBI field office had a joke that turned on the fact that the SAC was just below ADIC. The fact that SAC Gilbertson was a woman only made matters worse.

"Is there anything else I can do?" Lisa asked.

"Just file the report, Tanchik. I'll let you know."

"I'd really like to be assigned to this case."

"There isn't a case yet. And like I said, I'll let you know." After a pause, Gilbertson added, "Good work on this."

Lisa knew this was her cue to leave, but she remained standing in the doorway of the office, tempted to press her case. She'd been working there for four years. Gilbertson had been something of a mentor to her, but Lisa recognized that their relationship going forward was going to be determined by whether she was able to contribute to investigations and produce results.

"Is there something else?" Gilbertson asked.

After a pause, Lisa asked, deadpan, "Would you like this open or closed?"

Gilbertson swiveled in her chair to face her desktop computer, turning her back to Lisa and signaling that the meeting was over. But Lisa suspected that it was also to conceal a smile.

3

Lisa was running late, and it made her stomach churn. She had overslept, the traffic on the 101 from San Francisco to San Jose had been miserable, she was hungover, and she was headed for an all-day meeting that she believed would be pointless. It was also the seventh anniversary of her sister's death, a day that was never easy, even under the best of circumstances.

When she finally arrived at the FBI's San Jose regional office, she took a moment in the parking lot to remove a pint of Smirnoff vodka from the glove compartment and half fill an empty water bottle. She took a long drink from the bottle and a deep breath, left the water bottle in the car's cup holder, and climbed out of her Audi.

Two hours later, she was slouched in the back row of a conference room at a regional interagency meeting of agents from the FBI, Homeland Security, DEA, and the United States Postal Service. It was Lisa's turn to serve as her field office's representative at the meeting. She was trying to stay awake through the dreaded postlunch presentation. A postal inspector from Denver in a JoS. A. Bank suit and a porn-star mustache stood at a podium at the front of the room, flipping PowerPoint slides and speaking in a monotone.

I'm listening to a one-hour presentation by a postal inspector. Kill me now.

Lisa took the exercise a step further.

What would it take to stop those slides from turning?

She recalled some of the cases that she had studied at Quantico, imagining how an all-star lineup of murderers would go about ending the sonorous postal inspector.

Darlene Harding would poison that glass of water on the podium next to him with cyanide.

Old-school Mafia hit man Enrico Iacconi would slip the garrote wire around his neck and gently pull him back from the podium in a slow, trembling dance, the inspector's wavering finger still straining for his laptop to turn just one more slide before he drew his last breath.

Lisa abandoned the exercise. While she was in a black frame of mind, she didn't want to exacerbate matters.

She had been at the FBI for four years and was still looking for the case that would elevate her career. Her first two years had been spent on probation, shadowing a training agent. Part of the problem was that she didn't quite fit the profile of an FBI agent—or any other recognizable profile, for that matter. While the agency talked of a new FBI that was smarter, more nimble, and better able to combat cybercrime, the agents who advanced through the ranks still tended to have a certain keen-eyed, square-jawed look about them.

Lisa was decidedly not that type. She had hated the boot camp aspects of Quantico. Whether male or female, every agent had felt lucky to draw her for an opponent in hand-to-hand drills. Physical training had been a master class in daily ass kicking, and she had usually been on the receiving end. She was five feet six and slender. One guy she had dated had called her "unconventionally beautiful," which she took to mean that her nose was a little too pointed, her lips a little too thin, her demeanor a little too blunt.

She felt like the high school nerd who had her immaculate GPA marred by the required physical education class—except that at the FBI Academy roughly 10 percent of the curriculum was the equivalent of PE.

Ever since she was a kid, Lisa had been drawn to computing and coding. Science was about uncovering the rules that governed our world, but computing was about *writing* the rules, creating entire universes out of zeros and ones. She had earned a full scholarship to George Washington University through the federal CyberCorps program. In exchange, she was expected to use her cyberskills in the service of the federal government. Lisa had ultimately decided that a career as an NSA spook would involve more moral uncertainty than she was comfortable with, but working for the FBI catching cybercriminals seemed to have an appealing clarity.

She had a master's degree in computer science and knew much more about the internet and cybercrime than most of her classmates. She could write an elegant line of code and had the skills necessary to hack most commercial websites, which was admittedly a fairly low bar. But choosing a career in law enforcement over data security was a decision that she sometimes wished she could do over. She had started out with the FBI as a civilian contractor performing computer forensics, but she had changed career paths when she'd started seeing agents take her work product and use it to actually put serious cybercriminals behind bars.

She knew that she could have doubled her government salary at a security consulting firm in the private sector. She also could have opted to be an analyst rather than a special agent, which in many ways would have been an easier and more obvious fit for her—the physical training was far less rigorous. But she couldn't help feeling that if the FBI was going to be truly effective in stopping cybercrime, they needed special agents in the field who understood the technology—geeks with guns.

Still, despite her technical skills, Lisa had yet to receive any of the plum assignments pursuing cyberterrorists and hackers. When it came time to tap a young agent for one of those assignments, her bosses still seemed to feel more comfortable choosing someone who had that FBI-by-way-of-central-casting look—even if they couldn't distinguish a firewall from a fork bomb.

And then there was the Video, which was the first thing in the minds of her colleagues and superiors when her name came up.

Lisa hadn't been on the job long when she had been assigned to a team of agents taking down a counterfeit–credit card operation run by a branch of San Francisco's Russian *mafiya*. The bust had occurred in a large warehouse in the Mission Bay area, and she'd been tasked to hold down one of the building's exits far away from the main action. But when her fellow agents had moved in, a beefy Russian with a shaved head and a Cyrillic neck tattoo had managed to escape the initial arrests.

Of course, he'd come barreling through Lisa's door.

She hadn't heard the footsteps approaching over the sound of gunfire from inside the warehouse, and he had been on her before she could draw her weapon. He probably weighed close to 300 pounds to her 125, and what had ensued resembled a head-on collision between a MINI Cooper and an eighteen-wheeler. The footage (regrettably, a security camera had captured every moment) showed that Lisa had been briefly airborne. A team of agents coming around the side of the building had promptly taken the Russian into custody. But the security camera footage had been replayed in Quantico training sessions and had made her famous in the worst possible way. At least she had stood her ground and tried to tackle the perp at the knees. At least she had done that.

Tired of contemplating the cul-de-sac that was her career, Lisa was about to choose another killer from her case files to make a run at the postal inspector when something he said actually caught her attention.

The postal inspector was talking about Kyte. He was flipping through slides containing screenshots of Kyte's drug listings much like the ones that she had shared with her boss two weeks before.

Why was she just finding out about this now? Why hadn't Gilbertson gotten her involved?

At the end of the presentation, the postal inspector mentioned that there was an interagency task force, dubbed Operation Downdraft, being formed to take down Kyte and the people behind it. Lisa hurried up to the podium after the presentation and made her interest in joining the task force known. She then called Gilbertson to volunteer.

"I'm surprised that I wasn't informed that the Kyte investigation was moving forward," Lisa said. "After all, I was the one who discovered the site."

"You would have been involved if this was purely a bureau matter," Gilbertson said. "But it's an interagency thing now."

"I want to be on the task force."

"No one's been assigned yet, but you sure you want this?" Gilbertson asked. Gilbertson had saved Lisa from washing out of Quantico because she valued her cyberskills. But Lisa had gotten the impression that Gilbertson wasn't going to expend any more political capital protecting her.

"I'm sure."

"You ever been on a task force with other agencies?"

"No."

"I thought not. Everyone spends their time jockeying for position instead of doing investigative work. And if you somehow manage to produce results, you'll end up with footprints on your back from everyone trying to claim credit."

"I know how to use my elbows under the boards," Lisa said. She had learned long ago that the tactical use of sports metaphors seemed to put her colleagues more at ease.

A skeptical pause on the other end of the line.

"All right," Gilbertson said. "It's not like anyone else is lining up for this one."

"Thanks, boss."

"But if I were you, I'd think carefully if this is where you want to put your focus. From here, it doesn't look like something that's going to advance your career. And frankly, you could use a win in your column." Gilbertson probably would have preferred for her to pursue a more modest cyber investigation in which she was more likely to earn sole credit for a conviction.

"I see something here," Lisa said. "I want this one."

Another pause.

"I'm technically supervising this matter for the bureau, but I have other priorities right now. You're going to have to run with this largely on your own—and you'll be judged accordingly."

"I can live with that."

"Then it's yours. But don't say I didn't warn you."

Lisa sat through the remainder of the day's presentations, only listening for one thing—more information about Kyte. She booted up her laptop, but then a DEA agent named Harold Constantine drew her attention to the podium. Constantine, who had an acne-scarred face, a receding, middle-aged hairline, and an unctuous voice, was speculating about the identity of Kyte's founder.

"Whoever created Kyte is a new type of cybercriminal, someone who has the skills of a tech entrepreneur, is as brazen as any cartel kingpin, and is careful and smart enough to hide seemingly beyond the reach of the agencies represented in this room. It's going to be challenging to profile this person because we've never seen anyone quite like him. Or her."

Constantine gripped the podium and leaned into the microphone. "So who is this guy?"

4

Nate Fallon was late for his next Stanford graduate program physics class, Quantum Information: Visions and Emerging Technologies, but he was cool with that. In the multiverse of possible realities, there were versions of himself that made it to the class on time, and others that did not. This just happened to be a reality in which he was late.

Sitting under a tree on the Jordan Quad on a temperate, sunny day, Nate removed his vape pen from the pocket of his yoga pants. He took a hit, admiring the efficiency of the technology. The pipe's battery-powered heating unit blazed for a moment, vaporizing the sativa cannabis oil contained in a clear cylinder screwed into the front of the pipe, generating a perfectly portioned hit of mind-clearing, tension-easing, clarity-producing vapor. Just what he needed to get his head around the phenomenon known as entanglement, in which quantum information may be woven into correlations among multiple qubits.

"Don't start," Hardwick said, taking the pipe from Nate. "When you start talking about qubits, it hurts my brain. And I mean that literally. Computer science is linear. I listen to you talk physics theory for ten minutes, and I feel like my brain is enveloped in a cold fog."

"Maybe it will make you a better coder," Nate offered, gazing up the gnarled trunk of the black oak. "Give you that flash of inspiration."

"Coding isn't about inspiration. It's about focus, precision, speed." Hardwick took a hit from the pipe, drew it deep into his lungs, and exhaled a wisp. "And this is not helping."

"And yet . . . ," Nate said.

"And yet," Hardwick said, nodding, "I do so love getting baked."

Hardwick was twenty-six, a year older than Nate, with short, pale-brown hair and squinty, appraising eyes behind wire frames. While he dressed like a disheveled lab rat, Hardwick always managed to retain a certain professorial demeanor. Nate had known Hardwick since he was eight years old, and Hardwick was his oldest and best friend. In a Palo Alto neighborhood full of professors' kids, he and Nate were always the brightest of the bunch, so they had naturally gravitated to one another. They had both managed to stay close to home by getting admitted to Stanford as undergraduates and then as grad students—Nate in the physics program and Hardwick in computer science.

They had grown up in Silicon Valley in the nineties and had both acquired the virus endemic to that time and place. Nate recognized a similar condition in his friends who had moved to LA and fallen under the spell of the film industry. Down there everyone knew weekend box office grosses. In the Valley, everyone knew whether the latest IPO had met expectations. If you lived in LA, you couldn't help but envy the studio execs and film stars when you glimpsed them behind tinted windows, gliding down Sunset Boulevard in their Range Rovers. If you lived in the Valley, the cool kids were the venture capitalists and entrepreneurs who could sometimes be spotted piloting their humming Teslas into the gleaming, low-slung corporate campuses of Menlo Park, Milpitas, and Cupertino.

Most of their friends from high school and college were working for tech companies. Hardwick had already turned down several lucrative job offers, expressing ambivalence about the tech industry's belief that disruption equals progress. But a programmer as talented and skilled as Hardwick could not resist the siren song of the Valley indefinitely.

They sat quietly for a minute or two, listening to the wind rustle the leaves and feeling the dappled sunlight on their faces.

Finally, Hardwick tapped his watch. "Shouldn't you?"

Nate didn't wear a watch, but he confirmed the time on his smartphone. "I should."

"I should too."

They got up and headed in opposite directions across the quad, Nate to his class and Hardwick to his office hours as a teaching assistant in the Computer Science Department.

Nate entered the physics and astrophysics laboratory and slipped into the classroom ten minutes late, quietly taking his place in the back row. But not quietly enough; the professor looked up from his whiteboard and seemed to make a mental note.

As the other students in the class had already done, Nate opened up a word processing program on his laptop to take notes. But since his back was to the wall and no students were sitting next to him, he also opened up Tor, clicking the desktop icon of a globe with bright-green continents against gray oceans and concentric green circles ensnaring the planet. It looked like the logo of a comic book supervillain.

Nate tried to concentrate on the professor's abstruse discussion of quantum physics, but he became distracted by the alerts that were constantly pinging for him on a dashboard that he had created. The dashboard monitored activity on his hobby, his experiment, and his passion project—the Dark Web marketplace Kyte.

The message board was blowing up because Kyte's drug sales, already robust after six months in business, were apparently going through the roof.

Nate was thrilled at the spike in revenues, but not so much because of the profit that it represented (although that was certainly nice). He was excited because his creation was connecting with people, finding its customer base.

He needed to figure out what was happening, and he couldn't do it in the middle of a lecture hall, surrounded by his classmates.

Nate shut his laptop and crept out of the classroom. Once again, the professor cocked an eyebrow at him, but Nate didn't care. This was more important.

He found a coffee shop across the street from the campus, where he could work unobserved. Nate always sat with his back to the wall like a Wild West gunslinger so that no one could see his laptop screen.

At first he couldn't figure out why Kyte's drug sales were spiking so dramatically. But then he saw that a new arrival in one of the forums had mentioned an article in *Mocker* about Kyte. Kyte was going mainstream—or as mainstream as a site can get when it sells illicit narcotics.

The headline read "The Dark Web's Online Drug Bazaar." Written in *Mocker's* patented snarky prose, the piece touted Kyte as the not-so-secret secret of all of your druggy friends. The story was accompanied by screen grabs showing Kyte's offerings of cocaine, marijuana, and molly.

Sales through the Kyte platform had suddenly doubled to nearly a million dollars a day. Each sale was subject to Kyte's transaction-processing fee of 7 percent, which meant that Nate was now earning approximately $70,000 per day.

He tried running some diagnostics, certain that the figures must be incorrect, but he was unable to detect any malfunction in the dashboard.

He tried another approach, going to the live log of transactions being processed through the site. It showed a constant stream of purchases, at a volume that would support one-million-dollars-a-day sales.

If anything, the sales were increasing.

Kyte had already been a thriving venture. Now it was a monumental success.

Nate ran a hand through his thick brown hair and stretched his long legs out in front of him. He wanted to jump out of his chair, punch the air, laugh and shout, but he knew how foolish that would look in the middle of a crowded coffee shop.

No one would know it by looking at him in his yoga pants and faded, dirty T-shirt, but Nate was suddenly on his way to becoming a newly minted millionaire and the founder of the hottest, fastest-growing start-up in Silicon Valley. Kyte was destined to become the sort of phenomenon, like Facebook or Uber, that would attract press and investors and the *Wall Street Journal*—if it were legal.

In this triumphant moment, Nate recalled his venture's modest beginnings. When he'd first stumbled upon the Dark Web, he'd felt like his hero and role model Steve Jobs must have felt when he'd seen a primitive personal computer for the first time. At the recommendation of a classmate, Nate had purchased some Adderall through a Dark Web site to help him study for an exam. The Adderall had helped him focus all right, and he had seen in a moment of drug-sharpened acuity that the Dark Web's small-time drug sales could be professionalized and conducted at scale through a marketplace—a black market version of eBay. He'd had that rare feeling that everything he was and everything he could be was suddenly available and laid out before him.

His Kyte experiment combined several things that he was passionate about: weed and light hallucinogens, e-commerce, and libertarian thinking. Influenced by his father, Davis, a professor in Stanford's business school, Nate had attempted a couple of low-stakes online businesses—a website selling used video games and an app to track food trucks around the Stanford campus—both of which had failed miserably. When he was honest with himself, he recognized that he had been driven to try again in part to show his father that he could do what Davis could only teach.

Nate thought the name Kyte (as in "higher than a") suited a website that would offer illegal drugs, malware, and other forms of contraband. He had toyed with a few names but had finally settled on a single, elegant syllable. It had the ring of one of those names that became part of the lexicon, like Google or Uber. The site even had a logo (the white outline of a kite against a deep blue background) and a slogan ("Higher").

He hadn't been expecting all that much from Kyte—it was an experiment, mostly. The thesis of this experiment was that it was possible to create a marketplace where people could freely buy and sell whatever they wanted, entirely beyond the reach of government interference or regulation. Nate had gone door to door for Libertarian Party candidates, so the notion of actually creating what libertarians refer to as a "frictionless economy" excited him.

Of course, the FBI and an alphabet soup of government agencies would want to shut down Kyte's sales if the site ever came to their attention—a prospect that, he realized, was now an inevitability after the *Mocker* article. But that was the most thrilling part of the experiment—Nate didn't believe that they'd be able to stop him. In theory, the purchaser of a bag of weed through Kyte would be engaging in a completely anonymous transaction thanks to the multiple layers of encryption offered by Tor and the cryptocurrency Bitcoin. Of course, the purchaser would have to provide a delivery address for the package, but a fake name provided deniability in the unlikely event that the contents of the package were discovered en route.

Nate wanted to laugh out loud, but he was in the middle of a busy coffee shop, and he didn't want to appear deranged. Why had he doubted himself? He should have known that Kyte was going to work. After all, successful online businesses give the public what it wants, and they do it through a seamless user experience. And there was certainly a large segment of the population that wanted drugs. If he could provide those drugs, and other illicit merchandise, efficiently and in a way that protected the consumer's identity, then the opportunities for growth were limitless. He was targeting the same consumers who had made the drug cartels and organized crime families ridiculously wealthy, but he was reaching that market through the internet with far less overhead. There was no criminal bureaucracy, no army of street dealers that needed to be trained and paid and managed, no sketchy face-to-face transactions.

There was only Nate, providing his marketplace to drug consumers all over the world and taking his 7 percent cut of every transaction.

He shut his laptop and got up to order a fancy latte. After all, he could afford it now. He was going to be very, very rich—if he could manage to stay out of jail to enjoy it.

But by the time he sat back down with his coffee, anxiety had crept in. With the stakes now raised, Nate thought about the precautions he had taken early on to make Kyte bulletproof in shielding his IP address—the information that could lead someone straight to his computer. He retraced his steps to the extent that he could, trying to reassure himself that he had not made any fatal coding errors that would expose his identity.

But as he did so, another worry occurred to him: His website wasn't built to process the volume of transactions that he was now getting. It was like trying to run a fire hydrant through a garden hose—the water would flow steadily for a while, but it wouldn't be long before the hose burst from the pressure. He was going to have to immediately hire more coders—and figure out how to do so anonymously—to expand the site's bandwidth. If Kyte crashed and was unavailable for a day or two, he could lose his first-mover advantage. If someone else stepped in with a competing business while his site was upgrading, he might never recover his momentum.

Now that Kyte was a bona fide success, Nate felt emboldened, and about more than just the money. He pulled a scrap of notebook paper from his pants pocket that he had been revising in ballpoint pen over the past two weeks.

He typed up the contents and posted it in the upper right quadrant of Kyte's home page. Prime real estate, but he considered it an important message. The statement read:

KYTE: A MANIFESTO

Welcome to Kyte. I hope you find this site useful, and I hope it enables you to do things you want to do that you can't do anywhere else. I thought it was time to post a few first principles to make my intentions clear.

Be Free. There aren't many free places in this world of Big Data and NSA surveillance, but I want Kyte to be one of them. You can do what you want here, sell what you want here, and there won't be any interference by the government, law enforcement— or me. I believe that the world is a better place when people are free to be themselves, and that's going to be our guiding principle.

Be Private. Freedom is impossible without privacy. Since you're here, you already know about the anonymity that Tor offers. Kyte is going to take that a step further by promising you that we will never attempt to crack Tor to give up your identity, and we will never cooperate with anyone who tries to do that.

Don't Harm Others. While personal freedom is our guiding principle at Kyte, we will not sell goods or services that are inherently intended to harm others, such as bombs or child pornography. We do sell drugs at Kyte, but we believe that is a matter of personal responsibility and personal choice.

We're Better Together. If you have any ideas about how we can make Kyte better, freer, or more protective of your privacy, I want to hear them. Let's make this work. Let's build a community.

But there was still something missing. This manifesto was clearly a personal statement, and it seemed lacking without a name attached to it.

Nate tried out a few alternatives before he settled on—CaptainMal. The name was a tribute to Captain Malcolm Reynolds from Joss Whedon's *Firefly* TV series and the movie *Serenity*. Mal was the scruffy captain of a crew of smugglers aboard a spaceship called Serenity, sort of a Han Solo lightly dusted with libertarian ideology.

To Nate's thinking, *Firefly* was a show that was about how to exist beyond the reach of an authoritarian government, and that mirrored Kyte's mission.

He added the signature "CaptainMal" to the Kyte Manifesto and then posted it to the site. Only after it went live did it occur to him why he was a little uncomfortable with the somewhat grandiloquent gesture of a manifesto. Like Charles Foster Kane announcing his intentions as publisher in the first issue of the *New York Daily Inquirer* in *Citizen Kane*, Nate knew that manifestos had a way of coming back to haunt their authors.

5

When Lisa returned home from the interagency conference to her apartment, she couldn't wait to fire up her computer and learn more about Kyte and its founder. But first, in the lobby, she encountered her neighbors Benny Alomar and Carlos Perez. Benny was a set designer at the American Conservatory Theater, and Carlos was a freelance graphic artist.

"Agent Lisa," Carlos said. "Benny's making his famous paella tonight. Stop by for a bowl later?"

"I'd love to," she said, "but I've got some work to do."

"You can't fight crime on an empty stomach, Agent Lisa," Benny said. "And your mama wouldn't want you eating those microwave dinners."

Lisa smiled. "You've got that right, Benny. Maybe later."

"Don't disappoint us, Agent Lisa," Carlos said. "We hate to be disappointed."

When Lisa got to her apartment and continued her examination of the site, she saw the mission statement suddenly appear on the home page. She read and reread the statement, trying to parse the language and assemble the beginnings of a psychological profile.

Based on the degree of hubris on display, she guessed that the Kyte Manifesto was written by a man. The person behind Kyte was clearly well educated and seemed to see himself as some sort of libertarian incarnation of Steve Jobs. Lisa got the sense that he was young. That would explain the misguided optimism of the manifesto, which sounded like a recent college graduate overly enamored with his own ideas.

Aside from the mission statement, she saw few fingerprints of the site's operator. At first glance, Kyte appeared as blandly corporate and efficient as eBay. Lisa tried a couple of rudimentary hacks but was unable to penetrate the site's firewall. Of course, if it were that easy to sniff out the site's IP address or the identity of the founder, one of her law enforcement peers would have already done it.

Lisa was beginning to like CaptainMal, but it only took a moment to remind herself that, despite all his talk about doing no harm, his site was putting dangerous drugs directly into the hands of anyone who wanted them—whether they were forty-five years old or twelve. He was getting rich off the worst sort of suffering, the kind of suffering that her sister, Jess, had endured for most of her abbreviated life.

Jess had been two years older, and Lisa had always felt that she was shadowing her sister from the discreet distance of those two additional years of maturity—and damage.

She'd joined their high school's Brain Brawl team because Jess had been a member. Her fashion sense as a teenager had come from taking into account the three-year change in styles and then calculating what her sister would have worn.

Lisa had even followed Jess down the dark ladder of the depression that they both seemed to have inherited from their mother. And when Jess had abused alcohol and prescription painkillers in a vain attempt to turn the serotonin tide in her brain, Lisa had tried that too. She would never catch up the years, but for a time she'd made a pretty good attempt to replicate the damage.

One morning Jess's roommate had found her dead in her dorm-room bunk at UC Berkeley, a victim of OxyContin and alcohol. It had been ruled an accidental death, not a suicide, but Lisa knew that when you were in the depths of clinical depression, that line was so thin it was virtually imperceptible.

Jess used to talk with Lisa sometimes about their shared depression. After watching a PBS documentary on Winston Churchill, Jess had adopted his term and started calling it her black dog.

One day when Lisa had caught Jess drinking from a plastic water bottle filled with vodka, Jess had smiled ruefully at her and said, "Sometimes you got to feed the black dog, sis."

She had emptied the last drops onto her tongue and coughed. "If you don't feed him, he'll eat you alive."

With her vodka-filled water bottles, Lisa knew something about self-medication, but she had never descended into full-blown addiction the way her sister had. Maybe her sister's example had scared her off that path. Maybe her black dog just wasn't as fierce as her sister's.

But Lisa understood all too well the destructive path her sister had followed. Depression was like a dark room, a black nowhere. Having a drink was like lighting a match—its flicker helped but only briefly. She knew that you couldn't live your life madly burning through matchbooks—you had to somehow let your eyes adjust and learn to see clearly with the little bit of light that was available to you.

Jess's notion of the black dog had stuck with her. She imagined her own black dog, a chocolate Lab, at her heels, sometimes docile, sometimes growling insistently like an idling engine. When the depression swelled, it seemed to leach all of the color out of the world. She felt as if she were on a planet of her own, laboring in a heavy gravitational field that affected only her, barely able to move, barely able to speak, as the world careened heedlessly, stupidly past at full throttle.

As Lisa pursued her investigation of Kyte and CaptainMal, the black dog remained curled up at her feet, sleeping contentedly. She had learned that the best, and least damaging, way to calm the black dog was by losing herself in her work.

The problem was that in recent months the lack of challenging assignments meant that the black dog had been more insistent than ever. Sometimes it took a few drinks to quiet him down, topped off with sleeping pills at bedtime. Before she knew it, she was telling her supervisor that she was down with the flu and needed to take a sick day. She tried not to take too many of those sorts of sick days, because at a certain point people began to suspect that something else was going on.

But even when she had challenging work to distract her, the black dog never really left her side. When something bad happened, a painful memory resurfaced, or her concentration flagged, the dog was there, snuffling and chuffing, nudging her shin with his wet black nose, demanding attention.

She would lie down on the couch in her apartment, and it would settle contentedly by her side. The one companion that was always, always there.

When the sadness was acute, she could spend a whole day like that, barely moving a muscle, as the shafts of sunlight through the blinds downshifted through the spectrum from glaring sunrise to bloody sunset. On those days she would listen to her phone pinging with emails and texts, so numerous, insistent, and oppressive that she couldn't even begin looking at them.

Treatment for depression was not a disqualifying condition for her FBI training, but she had been required to authorize a medical disclosure from her psychiatrist, who had attested that her condition did not impair her judgment or behavior. If her shrink had known about her issues with alcohol and pills, he might not have rendered that favorable opinion, but she had held that information back in their sessions. Lisa figured that even with the statement from her doctor, she would have been bounced from the academy if the bureau hadn't been anxious to add new recruits with computer skills.

The black dog was as much a part of Lisa as the memory of her sister. She sometimes wished that it wasn't always with her, but she didn't wish too hard. Despite the darkness and debilitating sadness that came with the black dog, it was also something that connected her to Jess.

If she was ever able to send the black dog packing, she feared that the last and most inextricable link to her sister would be severed.

———

Lisa did some trolling on 4chan and other chat boards. Once she started looking for it, she saw chatter about Kyte everywhere on the Dark Web and, increasingly, on the surface web. The new site was clearly providing something that a large segment of the population was looking for— illegal drugs that could be delivered to their doors at a reasonable price and with relative safety.

4chan was the granddaddy of IRC boards, and it had a transgressive, hyperbolic tone all its own. The denizens of 4chan included members of Anonymous and many more who were fascinated by the exploits of the hacker collective. In the gleefully offensive world of 4chan, the smallest difference of opinion was likely to end with an all-caps wish that the offending poster would contract AIDS.

It didn't take long for Lisa to find a thread about Kyte from a poster using the handle SharkB8.

SHARKB8: Have you checked out Kyte?

BOGUS: Dude thinks he's the eBay of drugs.

DJINN: What makes you think it's run by a dude? That's some sexist bullshit.

SHARKB8: Spare me the gender politics, Djinn. Everything is not about that.

DJINN: Who says you get to say what anything's "about," you paternalistic, mansplaining douchepuppet.

SHARKB8: I think Anon needs to hack the shit out of that site and take that greedy, pseudo corporate fuck down.

BOGUS: Yeah, it looks like Walmart, all slick and corporate and shit. That's not what the Dark Web is for. Hack em back to the stone age!

SHARKB8: At least someone should take a botnet and DDOS em.

DJINN: I've been rattling the doorknobs over at Kyte. I'll find something soon.

SHARKB8: Like you have the skills, Djinn . . .

DJINN: Choke on your own vomit and die, SharkB8.

At that point a new user entered the conversation—BotShop. Lisa knew from auditing 4chan that BotShop was a member of the leadership of Anonymous and had access to an exclusive chat board where the collective's inner circle planned its coordinated attacks. Lisa's colleagues at the FBI had a thick dossier on BotShop that linked him to about two dozen corporate website takedowns, mostly of the hacktivist variety.

BOTSHOP: Let's take a deep cleansing breath, people. Anon is well aware of Kyte and we don't endorse hacking the site. Yet.

SHARKB8: Does Anon have its own thing planned?

BOTSHOP: Do you think I would tell you if we did?

SHARKB8: Need to know basis. Got it.

BOTSHOP: Anyone who goes after Kyte on their own is going to find themselves banned from Anon's boards.

DJINN: Understood. No need for threats.

With that, BotShop was gone, and SharkB8, Bogus, and Djinn resumed a bickering conversation about the quality of the malware that was currently available for sale through Kyte. They expressed their general contempt for the so-called script kiddies who bought prepackaged malware rather than writing their own.

As far as Lisa could tell, Kyte had been in operation for no more than six months, but it was already attracting the wrong sort of attention—including her own.

A criminal enterprise as large and brazen as Kyte couldn't last forever. Apart from the FBI, DEA, and nearly every other US law enforcement agency, the site and its founder had to be on the enemy lists of a host of crime families and cartels. The drug sales funneling through Kyte were so substantial that they might even be putting a dent in street sales. It was like the drug cartels were the taxi business and Kyte was Uber—a classic disruptive technology.

Except that people who disrupted the business of the drug cartels tended not to live very long.

6

Nate was suddenly a Bitcoin millionaire—many times over—and he found it intoxicating. It was quite a change for someone who had never owned a suit and who was only able to attend Stanford on the deal offered to the children of faculty members. While there were limitations to what you could buy with Bitcoin, Nate had his eye on a luxury retreat in Binna Burra, Australia, that could be had for a mere $3.5 million BTC. One hundred and thirteen lush acres not far from Byron Bay and one of the world's most beautiful beaches, the retreat had eight bedrooms, six living rooms, seven bathrooms, and extensive gardens with rainforest plants. Room enough to invite his girlfriend, Ali, his best friend, Hardwick, and half a dozen or so of their friends. And as an added bonus for the investment of $3.5 million, he would be immediately granted a permanent Australian visa, which was attractive in the event he needed to flee the US. The only thing that kept him from pulling the trigger on his Binna Burra retreat was the fact that Australia had an extradition treaty with the US.

But there was more to running Kyte than just figuring out where to spend his Bitcoin riches. Seven months after Kyte's launch, Nate's business was experiencing the growing pains of any start-up. Given the volume of drug transactions the site was brokering, he had no doubt that Kyte was attracting serious law enforcement attention, which increased his risk exponentially.

Nate had spent much of the past month eradicating obvious coding glitches and tightening up the site's security. Rewriting the site's coding had been unbelievably stressful, like repairing a jet airplane while it was in the air, but now Kyte was more secure than most major e-commerce sites on the surface web.

He'd been hiring as many new coders and website designers as he could find, locating a lot of them from among Kyte's users. Unlike with most start-ups, however, he was unable to conduct his job interviews in person. None of the new employees that he hired could know his identity. That was the only way that he had a chance of staying out of prison.

If you wanted to work for Kyte, you had to be willing to accept Bitcoin as payment. In some ways it limited the pool of talent that he could draw from, but that was okay. He wasn't looking for the type of employee who showed up to an interview with a résumé and a pressed pair of chinos. There was no dental plan and certainly no stock options.

Nate examined a sample Dark Web site that someone named PeechE had designed to sell bootleg DVDs of new feature films. He wished that he could show the site to Hardwick so that he could evaluate its coding and security, but it would be too obvious that he was up to something sketchy.

Nate hadn't slept in twenty-four hours and hadn't showered in seventy-two. His Stanford classes were an afterthought. Because he was trying to keep Kyte from crashing under the massive torrent of daily transactions, he couldn't stop. When he wasn't vetting new employees, he was forced to do his own coding, shoring up the site's weak points and developing new features.

Some Kyte users who came to the site to buy weed were offended that the site sold guns. In order to address this miniuprising, Nate created a new parallel site called the Armory that was exclusively devoted to selling firearms, everything from Saturday night specials to AK-47s. Nate believed people had a right to buy and sell guns on Kyte under the Second Amendment, but he also understood that offering Glocks side by side with molly was bad customer relations.

Keeping Kyte operating had to be his first priority. This was a once-in-a-lifetime opportunity, but it could disappear overnight. If the site crashed, even for an hour, his customers would start looking elsewhere and competitors would try to step in to take his place. His core customers were, after all, drug addicts— or at least drug enthusiasts. And the one immutable constant was that they were going to keep buying—from someone.

He hoped that Kyte would eventually reach a state of equilibrium where the site was properly built out to handle the transaction flow. He still had no idea when business would plateau. The site was now handling $1.4 million per day in transactions. If current sales trends continued, Kyte would soon be processing sales of a billion dollars a year. Unlike Facebook in its early years, Kyte had no problem monetizing its users. Unlike with some of the early Apple personal computers, Nate had a product that sold itself.

It was ten thirty p.m. on a Wednesday night, and Nate was hunched over his laptop in a coffee shop near the Stanford campus. The student crowd was dispersing, except for a few diehards writing papers to deadlines, who would have to be chased out like barflies at last call. Nate joined the exodus and resumed work at his apartment.

DPain, one of his best distributors, direct messaged him through Kyte with an update on customer shipments. Smaller drug sales through Kyte were shipped directly from seller to buyer, eBay-style. Larger transactions often needed to be brokered through Kyte as dealers learned how to transition their sales to the online market. The incoming product would be delivered in person to DPain or another distributor at one of Kyte's logistics hubs. The bulk product was then repackaged by DPain's crew and shipped out in a variety of inconspicuous boxes that had originally been used for everything from video games to sneakers to coffee beans—for an additional fee. The process involved additional risk for his distributors, but Nate maintained his anonymity and never touched the product.

DPAIN: All of yesterday's orders are out the door. I only got three hours sleep, but it's done.

CAPTMAL: Nice work. How's tomorrow looking?

DPAIN: Stacked. Looks like there's a run on molly. Someone must have slashed prices.

CAPTMAL: Can you get it done?

DPAIN: You know it, boss. But I've gotta admit that this schedule is wearing me down. You know I have a delicate constitution.

DPain wrote about prescription pain meds in Kyte's health-and-wellness forum with a depth of expertise reserved for lifelong chronic-pain sufferers. DPain sometimes referred to himself as *supersize*, with several vertebrae that had herniated under his excessive weight. Nate wasn't sure how DPain managed to move so many packages if his mobility was actually limited. He imagined DPain sprawled in a BarcaLounger like Jabba the Hutt, barking orders to a team of minions that he had recruited into his shipping operation.

DPain had earned his screen name, holding forth in Kyte user forums like a Zen master of barbiturates. He oversaw lab testing of certain products to verify their purity and strength, posting the results. He was a colorful figure on the site and even had a catchphrase he used as a tagline on messages. It was a take on Pacino's heavily accented warning in *Carlito's Way*: "You ready? Here comes DPain!" He was also one of Nate's most conscientious admins, willing to use his home in Missouri as a shipping hub for hundreds of thousands of dollars in illegal drugs per day.

Nate knew much more about DPain than DPain knew about him. When DPain had begun to assume a more prominent role at Kyte, Nate had insisted that he provide a scan of his driver's license as a demonstration of loyalty. In the so-called real world, DPain was Jason Pomeroy of Chillicothe, Missouri, with a wife and two kids.

CAPTMAL: I'm working on bringing on some new hires as we speak. If you can hang on for a few more days at this pace I should be able to give you a break.

DPAIN: Anything for the cause, boss. So who's your best admin?

CAPTMAL: That would be you.

DPAIN: I'm going to remember you said that.

CAPTMAL: I can't talk comp right now.

DPAIN: Ok, boss, but when this crunch is over we're going to need to have that talk.

CAPTMAL: I thought I was making you rich.

DPAIN: I could say the same thing about you, boss. You know what would be really anarcho-capitalist of you? Share the wealth, man.

CAPTMAL: I said I was an anarcho-capitalist, not a socialist. But I take your point.

DPAIN: I hope you do.

CAPTMAL: Just give me a few days to get things under control and we'll talk. Ok?

DPAIN: Ok. You're lovin me now, aren't you?

CAPTMAL: How could I not?

Nate didn't like the tone of the exchange. DPain was valuable, but maybe it was dangerous to become overly reliant on any one admin. He resolved to recruit more staff and decentralize his shipping hubs.

Shortly after he signed off with DPain, the computer pinged with another message. He immediately assumed that it was DPain renewing his pitch for a pay raise, but then he saw that the message was sent through the contact form on Kyte. The sender went by the name El Chingon.

ELCHINGON: Are you the owner of this website?

CAPTMAL: Is there a problem?

ELCHINGON: Yes. You're my problem.

CAPTMAL: If you didn't receive your package, just tell me your order number and I'll make sure the buyer doesn't get paid out of the escrow.

ELCHINGON: This has nothing to do with a package. I have a business proposal.

CAPTMAL: Ok.

ELCHINGON: I'd like to acquire an interest in Kyte.

CAPTMAL: I'm not looking for investors.

ELCHINGON: Don't all start-ups need capital? And when you know who I am, I think you'll understand why you need to listen.

CAPTMAL: So who are you?

ELCHINGON: I'm with the Zeta cartel. Heard of us?

Nate slid his chair back from the computer. He'd thought he had been trading messages with some garden-variety crank, but this could be someone far more dangerous. He considered walking away from the conversation but decided there was no upside to antagonizing a cartel boss, if that was who he was dealing with. Might as well hear him out, especially since Nate's identity was shielded by Tor.

CAPTMAL: Sure. But how do I know that you are who you say?

ELCHINGON: Try ignoring me, and I will prove it to you.

CAPTMAL: I'm listening.

ELCHINGON: You're doing very well with your website.

CAPTMAL: We're doing all right.

ELCHINGON: You're being modest.

CAPTMAL: Kyte is open to anyone. You could sell your product here.

ELCHINGON: What makes you think we don't already sell our product through your site?

CAPTMAL: Then what's the problem? You don't like paying our transaction fee?

ELCHINGON: We don't like paying a cut to anyone, but no, that's not it.

CAPTMAL: So what is the problem?

ELCHINGON: You've made it too easy to sell product.

CAPTMAL: Some kid dealing weed out of his dorm room can't possibly compete with a cartel.

ELCHINGON: But fifty thousand kids in dorm rooms is a different story. It's like what's happened to the newspapers.

CAPTMAL: The newspapers? What are you talking about?

ELCHINGON: Used to be that people got their news from big newspapers. They had the printing presses, broadcast towers, armies of reporters. Now no one cares about that shit. They get the news from their Facebook feed.

CAPTMAL: That's what happens when the barriers to entry come down. That's what technology does.

ELCHINGON: If that's what technology does, then we're going to be the ones doing it. Not you.

CAPTMAL: I'll bet you don't like our seller rating system, either.

ELCHINGON: Our product stands up to anyone's.

CAPTMAL: How about after you've stepped on it a few times to maximize profits?

One feature of Kyte that was revolutionizing the drug trade was the seller rating system, which allowed drug purchasers to comment about the quality of a seller's product and service. If that kid in a dorm room in Santa Barbara had better weed than the Zeta cartel, then the kid's star rating would be higher, and he would get the sale.

ELCHINGON: Trust me, we know how to stay ahead of our competition.

CAPTMAL: Then you should have nothing to worry about. That's just the way the free market works.

ELCHINGON: This market is not free. You're going to find that out.

CAPTMAL: Your problem is that you're still in the product business. That's so twentieth century. Now it's all about the platform. Kyte is a disruptive technology.

ELCHINGON: We should discuss this in person.

CAPTMAL: What kind of idiot do you think I am?

ELCHINGON: I asked politely, gave you the benefit of the doubt. I want you to remember later that I started by speaking to you like a man. But clearly you are just a little bitch hiding behind your encryption.

CAPTMAL: If you knew who I am or where to find me, we wouldn't be sitting around talking about economics and barriers to entry, would we?

ELCHINGON: No, we would not.

CAPTMAL: And what if one of your rival cartels came to you and asked you to just turn over your business, would you do it?

ELCHINGON: You are not me.

CAPTMAL: You know, you don't sound like a drug kingpin.

ELCHINGON: I could say the same of you, my friend. Yet here we are. And what's that supposed to mean, anyway? Am I supposed to be typing in broken English? What kind of racist bullshit is that?

CAPTMAL: Sorry. Not what I meant.

ELCHINGON: Let's just say that we wanted to buy Kyte outright. What would your price be?

Nate hadn't really considered the question before, but he figured that Kyte was one of the most successful young businesses on the internet, with unlimited prospects for growth. The figure needed to be substantial.

CAPTMAL: $1 billion.

ELCHINGON: That is not a serious proposal.

CAPTMAL: I know my business, and I think it is.

ELCHINGON: We're going to find you, capitan. You can count on that. And then you're the one who's going to be disrupted. But if you come forward now—AND I MEAN RIGHT FUCKING NOW—we can talk like businessmen, work something out that will be to our mutual benefit. If we have to find you, that option is off the table.

CAPTMAL: Why should I think that you can find me when the FBI can't?

ELCHINGON: You aren't messing with their livelihood.

CAPTMAL: And yet . . . I'm still here and you're still wherever you are.

ELCHINGON: See you soon, tech boy.

CAPTMAL: I doubt that.

ELCHINGON: I want you to remember this moment when you're sitting in an oil drum with a tire soaked in gasoline around your chest. I want you to remember this moment when I light the match and you start burning.

CAPTMAL: It's been great talking with you, Mr. Chingon. Adios.

Nate signed off and immediately googled the Zeta cartel. The descriptions of their violent practices nearly made him vomit. The tactic El Chingon had referred to was apparently called *necklacing*, and it involved placing a tire drenched in gasoline around someone's chest and arms and lighting it on fire.

He wanted to dismiss the conversation as the work of a prankster, but he couldn't. A prankster wouldn't have spoken as knowingly about his business as El Chingon had. Nate's nerves, already jangled from lack of sleep, were now at DEFCON 1.

He was making so much money from Kyte that it was becoming apparent to the cartels. Now the chum was in the water, and the sharks were circling. He should have known that people would come for him and try to take the site from him. There was simply too much money involved.

But Nate had been living in a private bubble, coding nonstop, eating fast food, and drinking Mountain Dew Code Red. After barely venturing outside for three days, it was easy to forget that there was a world beyond the door of his apartment. And that world was full of people hunting him.

He pulled up Kyte's firewall for the umpteenth time, scanning for any signs of an intrusion. Just the usual assortment of pings and port scans. The barbarians were loosing random arrows that were bouncing off the ramparts of the fortress that surrounded Kyte. The site's security infrastructure was like a homemade bulletproof vest. He was about to learn whether his handiwork could stop live rounds.

Nate lay down on his unmade bed and tried to calm himself. As he replayed his conversation with El Chingon over and over, his heart hammered percussively in his chest like it wanted out.

A knock at the door made him jump. Could the cartel have found him already? Had El Chingon been messaging him while watching his apartment from across the street?

Nate approached the door quietly and listened.

"Nate, I know you're in there!"

Ali.

Nate let out a breath and unlatched the door. Ali gave him a quick kiss and blew past. Nate had been seeing Ali Nunn off and on for nearly a year, and things were at that point where the relationship was likely to become serious, or not. She was pursuing a graduate degree in education at USF, and although her ambitions were very different from his, she was every bit as smart as he was. She was also gorgeous—tall, with long black hair, blue eyes, and freckles. "This place is even more disgusting than usual."

"I guess I've been a little preoccupied," Nate said.

Ali saw Nate's laptop open on the kitchen table and moved toward it. "I'll say. Working on your thesis?"

Shit. His Tor Browser was still open to Kyte's admin dashboard. He lunged past Ali and slapped the laptop shut.

"I hope that wasn't porn," Ali said. "Because—ew."

"No, no. Not porn," Nate said.

Her eyes widened. "Ooh. You were working on that mysterious start-up of yours, weren't you?"

"Yeah, something like that."

"Well," she said, flopping down on the couch, "it's a good thing you got to that laptop in time, because otherwise my plan would have been complete. You know, when we met at that party a year ago, it was all a ruse, a corporate-espionage scheme so that I could steal your intellectual property."

"Lucky you didn't find out anything," Nate said with a grin, leaning down and kissing her on the lips. "Otherwise, I'd have to kill you."

7

Nate sat at the desk in his childhood bedroom, which felt deeply weird. His parents, who lived in Palo Alto near the Stanford campus, had kept his high school memorabilia on the dresser and on the bookcase. There was the second-place trophy topped by a runner in midstride, chest pushed forward and arms outstretched, the gold-paint skin peeling away to reveal the black plastic beneath. There was a poster on the wall for Rage Against the Machine, a band he hadn't listened to in years.

Nate's parents had invited him for a dinner to celebrate the publication of his father's book on Fairchild Semiconductor and the birth of Silicon Valley, and he had decided to spend the night rather than drive back to his apartment. He intended to take advantage of the opportunity to get his laundry done, but being in his parents' house also helped settle his nerves after the previous day's exchange with El Chingon. He told himself that *this* was the world that he inhabited, not a world in which cartel thugs hung flaming tires around the necks of their enemies.

He could hear the buzz of party preparations downstairs, the clink of plates and glasses. The sounds of his parents' voices coordinating as they got the house in order before the guests arrived; he could make out the melody of their banter but not the lyrics.

Nate pulled out his laptop to check on Kyte's sales figures, which were still accelerating like a wheelman after a bank heist. His knees bumped up against the bottom of the drawer of his old, kid-size desk, and he felt that his former self and a new self were in uncomfortably close proximity.

There was a knock at the door.

"Come in," he said.

Nate's mother, Hannah, entered, a tentative look on her face. "Am I interrupting something?"

"No, Mom. Just finishing up some work." He snapped the laptop closed and stood up from the desk. He wasn't worried about anyone opening up the laptop and finding Kyte because the laptop's full-disk encryption activated the instant the clamshell was shut.

"Your father would never let on, but he's really glad that you're here for this. It's a big night for him."

Hannah was a hospital administrator at San Jose Regional Medical Center. She was the pragmatist of the family, the one who kept everything and everyone running. When Nate was born, she had taken several years off from work and, for better or worse, had applied all of her displaced organizational energy to their household.

"Is it time to go downstairs?"

"The guests are starting to arrive. Your sister's here."

Downstairs, the guests were indeed starting to arrive, a late-middle-aged bunch consisting of his father's colleagues from the Stanford business school faculty and neighbors. Everyone was gratefully clutching a first drink, and no one more so than his big sister.

Amanda smiled when she saw him and broke away from a man in a cardigan who was talking at her.

"I like the new 'do," Nate said.

She had a new, short hairstyle that suited her, an attractive brown frame for her quick eyes and the mouth that so easily twisted into a smirk or a smile. Even though they had been competing for parental attention all their lives, he actually still liked her—and that was the secret weapon that made her such a worthy adversary.

She began nodding and smiling, waiting for the punch line.

"It's like . . . remember that barbershop that they used to take us to when we were little? All of the haircuts had names." Nate paused for effect. "Now I could be wrong, but that looks like what they used to call the Chairman."

"It's not the Chairman."

"Did you have to ask for it by name at the beauty parlor?"

"Shut up, doofus. And I go to a salon. Women stopped going to beauty parlors in the sixties."

Satisfied now that he had elicited a "shut up, doofus" from his sister, Nate continued. "How's work? How many countries have you been in since I saw you?"

Amanda was a consultant at Deloitte and was constantly traversing the globe to create flowcharts and project plans for giant corporations. Nate was never quite clear on what his sister was charting or planning, but it all seemed very grown up. Their father clearly approved of her job in a way that never seemed to extend to Nate's entrepreneurial efforts.

He looked her in the eye, finally ready to be sincere. "You seem happy."

"Do I? Well, I guess I am. I met this guy about a year ago. He works for Deloitte too. We spent two weeks at the Grand Hyatt in Tokyo."

"Sounds naughty."

"It was for a project. Separate rooms."

"Is it serious?"

"Definitely getting there. But don't tell Mom or Dad that. I'm still keeping them at bay."

"If Mom breaks out the enhanced interrogation techniques, you know it's all over, right?"

"Seriously. Don't you say a word to her." Amanda drew a deep, punctuating breath and changed the subject. "How about you? How's Stanford?"

"It's good. But I'm also working on a side project."

"What sort of project?"

"Just this start-up thing. Too early stage to talk about."

"Stealth mode, huh?" No matter how blandly she tried to put it, Nate had highly refined sensors to detect his sister's irony.

"Yeah, right."

"Have you seen Dad yet? Big night for him." She pointed to where Davis Fallon was holding court to a gaggle of fellow faculty members, sloshing his gin and tonic as he made a point.

"Come on, let's go congratulate him," Nate said.

"No, we've already had our chat tonight. You go ahead."

But when Davis saw Nate across the room, he excused himself and came straight over. He shook Nate's hand and placed the other hand gingerly on his shoulder. Nate recognized that Davis was still trying to get the balance right when it came to parental affection. Nate knew that his father loved him like he was still thirteen years old, so he always seemed a little uncomfortable limiting his displays to a manly handshake.

"Your mother has been in a good mood all day since she heard you were coming." Davis was tall and good looking, with close-cropped sandy-blond hair that was gracefully graying. He looked the part of an executive from one of his case studies, a demeanor that served him well in the classroom.

But Nate knew that was not who Davis was. His father was profoundly indifferent to money and financial matters—it was a language, like mathematics, that he had neither the interest nor the aptitude to speak. Davis's passions were the personal dynamics, social backdrop, and Shakespearean drama of corporate life, and he had discovered the subject of his career in Robert Noyce, the brilliant engineer who'd helped invent the silicon transistor and become one of the founders of Intel.

"You look good," Davis said.

"Dad, you just saw me week before last. I look the same."

"Well, I'm really glad you could make it tonight. How about that?"

"That works."

"How are classes going?"

"Fine."

"You settled on your thesis yet?"

"No, still looking for the right idea."

"Waiting for the veil to part?"

"Something like that. I saw the *New York Times*. You should have told me that was coming out. I think that's what they call a glowing review."

"Well, I knew Hannah would spread the word. She's my best publicist. If your mother was on Facebook or Twitter, she'd really be dangerous."

"Seriously, you must be really pleased with the reception it's getting."

"I'm trying not to think about it too much."

"Why not?"

"When you're a historian, the real test isn't whether your book makes a bestseller list in the first month. The test is whether it becomes part of the dialogue among teachers, students, other historians. Whether people keep coming back to it to understand that person, that time and place."

"So you're playing the long game. Wish I had that much patience."

"Well, you're young. You're still all hormones and id."

"Thanks, Dad."

"Don't take it personally."

"Mom said that you got a note from Howard Shay." Shay was the founder and CEO of Severin, the world's largest enterprise-software company.

"Yeah, the publisher sent him an advance copy. A lot of the big tech guys look to Noyce as their forbearer. The first start-up and all."

The title of Davis's book was *Robert Noyce: Fairchild Semiconductor, the First Startup, and the Birth of Silicon Valley.* In 1957, Noyce had left Shockley Semiconductor Laboratory with the so-called traitorous eight to found Fairchild Semiconductor, the first maker of silicon transistor chips. They were dubbed traitorous because in those gray-flannel days, men in narrow-lapel suits pledged lifetime allegiance to companies like General Motors, IBM, and Coca-Cola. Instigating a mutiny with your colleagues and starting a competing company was something that just wasn't done—until Noyce.

"Must make you feel pretty good."

"Well, it's not really about me. Guys like Shay are interested in Noyce because they want to trace a line between what he did and what they did. It's legacy building. It's not because they're students of history."

"You ever want to start your own company?"

"I thought about it, once or twice," he said, passing his drink from one hand to the other. "When I was younger. But I like to cook too. That doesn't mean I should open a restaurant. The failure rate is astronomical. You know what it's like now."

Nate winced. No conversation with his dad was complete without a reminder of his failures. Nate longed to tell his father all about Kyte's phenomenal success, but he could not. Because that would make Davis an accomplice, and in any event, there was no way his father would ever approve of such a patently illegal venture.

"But what if you could be that one percent? Wouldn't it be worth the risk? If it meant creating something really substantial?"

Davis's eyes narrowed. "As opposed to what? Writing a biography? Getting tenure?"

"I didn't mean it like that," Nate said, although he kind of did.

"I think successful entrepreneurs like Noyce are an interesting breed. They have to be so single minded. It's practically a pathology."

Nate wondered if that described him. He was nearly a member of that club now. In the on-deck circle of greatness. Nate's start-up was having a better first year than Steve Jobs's because, unlike the early PCs, his product sold itself. Unlike Facebook, Kyte was generating massive revenues from day one.

He wanted so much to brag about that, to make his father see. Instead he said, "I'll bet your friend Shay wouldn't call it a pathology. He'd call it an advantage."

Davis seemed displeased. "You think pathology is the kind of word that's used by someone on the sidelines, don't you?"

"I didn't say that."

"You didn't have to."

In an effort to ease the tension between them, Nate grabbed a couple of plastic champagne flutes from a tray on the dining room table. "Let's toast your book."

He raised his glass, but Davis interrupted.

"No, I'm going to get enough ego boosting tonight. I've got one for you."

Davis looked him in the eye and fought to control a twitch at the corner of his mouth, the tell that he was getting emotional.

"To my brilliant son," he said, "and the great adventure that lies ahead. Whether it's in physics or some new business, I know you're going to set the world on fire."

They both made a motion toward one another like they wanted to hug, but they were holding champagne glasses. It was awkward. Instead they clinked glasses—which were plastic and did not clink.

Later, after Davis had made his charming, self-deprecating address to the gathering and Nate had had enough of the sorts of conversations that a son had with his parents' friends, he traded champagne for Scotch and snuck back upstairs. Remembering all the times he'd climbed these stairs drunk, having downed beers with his high school buddies in parking lots and athletic fields around the Stanford campus, he experienced a phantom pang of teen guilt.

But Nate had much more serious matters to feel guilty about now. He lay down on the bed that he had grown up in, put in the earbuds of his iPhone, and began listening to his Moody playlist on Spotify, easing himself into the aching melancholy of "Resurrection Fern" by Iron & Wine.

His father's word—*pathology*—still rankled him. He was self-aware enough to recognize that he was an *analytical* person, sometimes at the expense of feeling. When he listened to Sam Beam of Iron & Wine or Sufjan Stevens at their most hushed and heartsick, he felt like he was self-administering a transfusion of emotion.

He wondered if everyone questioned themselves the way he sometimes did. It wasn't like he was completely devoid of feelings. He was concerned when his mother was ill, and he was proud of his father when his book was published—but those feelings seemed paler, more anemic than the highs and lows that he observed in others. Most people never saw it because his natural charm and good looks were like a cloak of invisibility. Those appealing qualities made people want to like him, believe that he cared, even love him.

Maybe the fact that Nate doubted and questioned himself like this was a sign that he actually had a richer inner life than others. Now that was a rationalization he could work with.

But the truth was he knew his thought processes were different in some fundamental way from his friends' and family's, not clouded by strong emotions. That difference made him capable of things—maybe terrible things, but perhaps great things too.

His father seemed to think that greatness was only possible with some sort of pathology. If that were the case, then Nate decided that he wanted a full-blown case of it. As Hardwick liked to say, citing an old joke among programmers: "It's not a bug; it's a feature."

8

Lisa quickly realized that commanding the attention of the interagency task force wasn't going to be easy. Today's meeting was at the DEA's DC headquarters, and a bloviating senior DEA agent—Harold Constantine, whom she remembered from the regional interagency meeting—was using his home field advantage to take control of the agenda, doling out assignments to the group and generally running the show.

So far, the task force didn't seem to be making any real headway in tracking down Kyte's founder. Among the agents from the DEA, IRS, Homeland Security, and Secret Service assembled in the room, none of them seemed to have spent any significant amount of time on the Dark Web. After a tedious and unproductive discussion with the NSA about developing a means of cracking Tor encryption, the conversation turned to CaptainMal.

Constantine called up a PowerPoint slide with a screen grab of the Kyte Manifesto. "He seems to fancy himself some sort of libertarian thinker. Any ideas on what the screen name means? Mal could be short for Malcolm. Could mean bad. Captain Bad?"

The team was silent. They had nothing.

After giving everyone a fair opportunity to get there first, Lisa raised her hand.

"I know where the name comes from."

Heads swiveled in her direction.

"Captain Mal is a character from the TV series *Firefly*. And the movie *Serenity*. Captain Malcolm Reynolds."

Constantine screwed up his face. "That's science fiction, right?"

"One of the best sci-fi shows ever. And some of Joss Whedon's best work. Far superior to *Buffy*, in my opinion." Lisa was actually more of a William Gibson girl but didn't want to stray too far off topic.

"*Buffy*?" There were a few chuckles around the room. Constantine shook his head. "I'm not going to ask. But what makes you so certain that you're right?"

"CaptainMal tags some of his posts with a line about the uselessness of governments. It's a direct quote from Captain Mal Reynolds in the pilot episode."

"Well, I guess you're right then. So you think he's a sci-fi geek?"

"I think he's a libertarian. A lot of bloggers believe there's a strong libertarian undercurrent in *Firefly*—a maverick spaceship crew operating beyond the reach of governments. And I wouldn't say they're wrong."

Constantine was silent for a moment, absorbing the information. "That's very good, Tanchik. Thank you. I don't know that it leads us anywhere, but it's helpful in building a profile."

"He's almost certainly a geek too," Lisa added. "*Firefly* was not a popular hit and was cancelled after one season. It was championed in certain geeky quarters by the sort of people who attend Comic-Cons."

"People like you, Special Agent Tanchik?"

No one laughed outright this time, but one agent coughed. She sensed the collective smirk.

What Lisa wanted to say: *Yeah, laugh all you want, asshats. You all know that you wish you'd figured it out.*

What Lisa said: "Well, I didn't sign a petition to bring the show back when it was cancelled. But yes, people like me."

"So the founder of Kyte is a geek," said a DEA agent at the front of the room. "News flash."

More juvenile snickering.

Constantine raised a hand to quiet everyone. "It's more than we knew five minutes ago, isn't it?" He nodded to Lisa. "Okay, that was a good start. Since you have the floor, do you have anything else for us?"

Lisa hadn't planned to present her ideas at this time, so she hesitated for a moment, combing through her thoughts on the case for the most promising angle. Just before Constantine was about to take the spotlight off her, she found it.

"Does anyone know where Kyte is recruiting coders?" Lisa asked.

Constantine looked surprised. "What makes you think that they *are* recruiting?"

"That manifesto that was posted—it definitely sounds like the voice of an individual founder. Look at how many times the word *I* is used in that document."

"Still not seeing your point."

"If CaptainMal launched Kyte on his own or with limited assistance, then he would have quickly found himself in dire need of a good team of coders. Otherwise, I don't see how he could keep up with the need for more bandwidth. I'm sure he didn't expect the site to be so successful so fast."

"So what do you propose? That we look for classified ads seeking experienced coders for a criminal enterprise? Or maybe he just dialed the Geek Squad."

Constantine got no laughs this time. Lisa had their attention.

"Well, he might not be using the classifieds, but I'll bet he's putting out feelers on the Dark Web. Probably contracting out discreet coding assignments and paying in Bitcoin."

Constantine placed his elbows on the podium and leaned forward, like a law professor preparing to nail an unprepared student in a Socratic dialogue. "Assuming for a moment that what you say is true, how would we find out where Kyte is finding its coders?"

"There aren't really all that many sites that would meet his needs."

"How do you know that?"

"Because I've spent some time exploring the Dark Web, and there are a few popular places to go if you're looking to hire coders—the underground version of Stack Overflow. There's Code Black and a few other places."

"Sounds like you know your way around the Dark Web."

"Just doing my job. Know your enemy, right?"

"What do you propose?"

"How about if I check out some of those coding sites and see if I can detect any signs of Kyte? If someone is hiring an army of coders, it should stand out, particularly if he's using a single online identity. If we're lucky, he might even be brazen enough to mention Kyte by name."

"Why would he do that?"

"Because Kyte is like a hot start-up. He'll attract better talent if he uses the name."

Constantine considered for a moment. "I suppose it's worth a shot. Why don't you do that and report back at our next meeting."

Lisa looked down at her papers, careful to conceal how pleased she was to have contributed so significantly.

At the end of the meeting, Constantine approached her. "Thanks for your ideas in there," he said. "We could use more of that initiative if we're going to bring this guy down."

"Thanks," Lisa said. "Just an idea. We'll see if it pans out."

"If you see some indications that you're on the right track, let me know before the next task force meeting. We can work this angle together."

Constantine was hedging his bets. If Lisa's idea produced results, he wanted to position himself to take at least half the credit, if not more.

"Sure," Lisa said, though she had no intention of following through. "Good meeting today."

———

Lisa spent two days combing Dark Web sites where coders offered their services, looking for signs that Kyte was recruiting, but to no avail. Maybe the founder was smart enough to disperse his job search over a number of sites. Maybe Lisa was wrong that he was a solo operator. Or perhaps Kyte had been created by an Anonymous-style collective, and she had misunderstood her adversary.

Without any meaningful leads, she returned to the Kyte website and combed through its voluminous listings for clues.

After a while, she found herself staring at the site's user forum. This was where customers could share suggestions about packaging drugs so that they would avoid detection in the mail or complain about a seller who had shipped baby powder instead of cocaine. Replies were posted by other users or, in some cases, the official-looking admin handle Kyte. If she was right about Kyte's creator, the founder was probably responding to comments personally, at least until he could staff up.

Lisa stared at the Comment page for a while, considering the best approach. She shouldn't just concoct a name from scratch because if the founder was going to trust her at all, he would probably check her out. Lisa needed an identity that had a sustained and consistent presence online.

This was a job for Rodrigo. His purported cartel connections made him intriguing and a little dangerous to others in the online community, but his obvious callow geekiness undercut the threat. Lisa wasn't about to tell Constantine about Rodrigo and the other online identities that she had established on the Dark Web. She had a feeling she would only draw more mockery for it, and she preferred to keep the identities secret because she had engaged in some minor illegalities to establish her bona fides, such as small purchases of drugs and contraband.

RODRIGO: Kyte's service is good, but I think you could improve your stealth shipping. If you're looking for pro tips, let me know.

"Rodrigo" had placed an order for LSD through Kyte and had had it delivered to a drop address in San Francisco. If questioned, she would reference that transaction. It was possible CaptainMal would even examine his user history on the site before replying.

She left Rodrigo's statement hanging, staring at the cursor on her screen.

Ten minutes later, the computer pinged with a response. It was a direct message sent through Kyte.

KYTE: Improve it how?

RODRIGO: Well, you gotta use a little imagination. I once shipped ketamine to a buyer with a letter saying sorry but you didn't win our Pokemon merch giveaway. However, as a consolation prize here's a deck of Pokemon cards. You open up the deck and taped to the back of one of the cards is a packet of ketamine.

KYTE: Not bad.

RODRIGO: If someone decides to turn it inside out, you're screwed, but you should always ship so that when you open up the package there is absolutely nothing that would create suspicion. In fact, you should use something like the Pokemon cards that actually reduces suspicion. No one thinks drug deal when they see Pokemon.

KYTE: I do actually know quite a bit about shipping product. It's kind of my business here.

A pause, while Lisa wondered if she had alienated the Kyte admin.

KYTE: But that's a good tip. We can always do better. Thanks.

RODRIGO: De nada.

KYTE: How do you know so much about packaging drugs?

RODRIGO: I grew up in Mexico City. I have friends who work for the cartels.

KYTE: Do you work for a cartel?

RODRIGO: No, but I swim in their waters.

KYTE: Are you here trolling for me?

RODRIGO: Just offering a little free advice.

KYTE: Thanks, but I've found that there's no such thing.

RODRIGO: Ok, dude. Have it your way. But just know that there are people rooting for you out here. I respect what you've been able to pull off with Kyte.

KYTE: That's nice to hear.

RODRIGO: Stay chill, dude.

Lisa signed off. She knew that she should be the one to walk away from this first conversation. If she stayed online and tried to keep the dialogue going, her counterpart would grow suspicious.

The thing that struck her about the brief conversation was that she had addressed the person as if he were Kyte's founder, complimenting him on what he had been able to pull off. The response ("That's nice to hear") was a tacit acknowledgment that Kyte was the site's founder, and he was operating alone. Maybe Lisa was reading too much into the exchange, but she didn't think so.

The odds were good that she had just had her first direct encounter with the infamous CaptainMal. She knew that making contact directly was the only way to bring him down. Operation Downdraft was not a traditional drug investigation because you couldn't rely on flipping street dealers and midlevel distributors to rat out their boss. None of them would know CaptainMal's IP address, much less his identity. The only way to stop Kyte was by cutting off its head—and that meant going directly after CaptainMal.

Lisa felt like a deep-sea fisherman who'd just had a brief, but sharp, tug on her line.

9

Nate and Ali walked along Ocean Beach at dusk as the warmth of the day receded like the tide. The sun was setting over Golden Gate Park and casting its dying amber light over the broad expanse of sand and ocean. It wasn't the sort of showy, set-the-horizon-on-fire sunset that you got in Southern California, but it was perfect nonetheless. Like Ali.

Nate was in an expansive mood. Kyte was a runaway success, he was making more money than he ever could have imagined, and everything seemed possible. Though he hadn't heard from El Chingon again, the threat still hung over him, growing in his imagination. He had begun having nightmares nearly every night of being burned alive by the Zeta cartel, but he tried to push them out of his mind, dismissing the exchange with El Chingon as the work of a prankster with a sick sense of humor.

"What are you thinking about?" Ali asked.

"I'm just thinking that this is pretty good."

She cocked an eyebrow. "This?"

"Ocean Beach at sunset. You. Mainly you."

"That's sweet, Nate. Are you high?"

"Not yet. Tell me what your day is going to be like tomorrow."

"Well, I've started volunteering at this nonprofit in the Mission. I'm scheduled to do some tutoring in the morning. We'll be making illustrated books."

"I'll bet the kids adore you."

"It's cool to see how their little minds work. They're so serious and wacky at the same time—like puppies."

Ali was completing her master's degree in education at USF. Nate admired her commitment to teaching and, especially, her complete disregard for how poorly teachers were paid. Nate was an idealist of a different sort. He would never put it so crassly to Ali, but he thought that it was much more powerful to touch a few million people with an app than to make a difference in one kid's life in a tutoring session. He knew that any teacher would tell him that the exact opposite was true, and that was why he would never say that to Ali.

Instead, what he said was, "You're going to make a great teacher."

And it was true. Ali had exactly the right mix of clear-eyed pragmatism, compassion, and childlike silliness to connect with kids in a classroom. He could even see her making a great mother someday.

"You've seemed different lately," she said.

"Really? How so?"

"Less angsty. Even though you always try to seem so chill and mellow, I could tell that you weren't satisfied with things."

"Being satisfied is overrated. And that's just normal, right?"

"Of course it is. If you're not angsty at twenty-five, there's something wrong with you."

"So how am I different now?"

"I don't know. You seem more focused somehow. But you've also got this crazy energy. Like last night."

Nate put his arm around Ali's waist, pulled her in close, and kissed her. "That's you. That's just me with you."

Ali caught her breath for a moment after the kiss, and they continued walking.

Eventually Ali said, "So can you tell me about this thing you're working on? Your stealth start-up? I've got a feeling it's got something to do with this change in you."

"Believe me, you don't want to hear about that," Nate said, shaking his head. "Besides, I promised my partners that I wouldn't talk. And I signed an NDA." He felt guilty for lying to Ali, and he wondered if he would ever be able to reconcile his two identities. For tonight, anyway, he was content to remain in between, with a foot in both worlds.

She grabbed his bicep with her hands and shook it lightly. "C'mon, you can't even give me a hint?"

"They have lawyers. Serious lawyers." He'd fended off her questions for now, but he knew she was going to keep asking about his business. He was going to have to be extra careful the next time he brought her to his apartment.

They approached a blazing bonfire with a few figures ringed around it.

"Well, some things don't change," Ali said. "Like that T-shirt. How long have you been wearing it?"

Nate looked down at the faded-yellow shirt, really considering it. "I honestly don't know." He sniffed at his armpit.

As they drew closer to the bonfire, he started casting sideways glances at Ali.

"Wait a second," she finally said. "That's Sarah up ahead at that bonfire. And Jay. And Hardwick! What is this?"

"I figured that if you couldn't make it down to Palo Alto to see your old Stanford friends, then I'd have to bring them to you." Ali had been forced to transfer to University of San Francisco in the wake of her parents' unexpected divorce. For a month or so, she'd lost touch with Nate and her other friends at Stanford while she found an apartment in San Francisco and prepared for classes at USF.

"I see your djembe. And bongos. Oh no, don't tell me—is this one of your drum circles?"

"Oh yes, my little slave to the rhythm. That's exactly what this is."

———

The drum circle had been thrumming for a half hour, and Nate was in a mild trance state, his fingers and the heels of his palms slapping the goatskin of the djembe. He had reached that point where he somehow felt in the moment but outside of it too. As he drummed, he stared into the firepit, which was launching particles skyward that were captured and hurled upward in a gusty breeze, birthing tiny, fiery universes in microcosm against the darkening sky.

They had all known one another from their first year at Stanford in the Stern Hall dorm. They had initially bonded through a shared love of weed, but they had remained friends in part because they were such a disparate group. Nate knew that people so different rarely stuck together after college, but that was all the more reason to appreciate them now.

Sarah would be the one to point out that they really weren't all that diverse—all white, all of middle- to upper-middle-class upbringing, all (with the recent exception of Ali) able to afford Stanford's steep tuition. But in personality and temperament, they couldn't be more different— as different as each player's contribution to the polyrhythmic beat.

Jay (law) pounded his drum, declarative and not at all subtle.

Sarah (psychology) tapped out a pattern that was complex and a little erratic.

Ali's rhythm was light and nimble, a counterpoint dancing around the main theme.

And then there was Hardwick (computer science), barely discernible, his playing more about what was in his head than his fingers. But he was right in the pocket if you listened closely.

Nate knew that he probably seemed to fit the spacey, pot-smoking stereotype of a physics student. It had, after all, been his idea to start a drum circle. But this was not a night to dwell on what made them different. Tonight, as far as Nate was concerned, they were one.

Maybe it was the Ghost Train Haze weed. Yeah, the weed was definitely a big part of the feeling, because he was higher than a satellite.

A *geosynchronous* satellite.

Geosynchronous. What an apt and awesome word. Turning with the earth.

But this feeling was more than just the weed.

Maybe it was the friends who surrounded him, their faces plangent in the flickering bonfire. He could tell that they were feeling it too. They were all feeling it together, and that intensified it.

Yeah, *geosynchronous.*

Ali was on the other side of the firepit from him, her long black hair shining, eyes shining, long legs folded awkwardly beneath her.

When he managed to pry his eyes off Ali, he noticed that Hardwick had a sweaty, uneasy look. His drumming on a set of bongos had grown half hearted, and his eyes were casting about like he was trying to locate some fixed center point in a spinning world. Nate knew that look—Hardwick was about to hurl.

Sure enough, Hardwick stood up and raised an index finger. He seemed about to say something, then reconsidered and lumbered off into the darkness.

Nate rose to follow him, grabbing a beer out of the cooler.

The three remaining drummers staggered to a halt after the two defections.

"Everything okay?" Sarah asked.

"I'm sure Hardwick's fine, but I'm going to check."

"You're a good friend, Nate," Sarah said.

"Why don't you and Hardwick just get a room?" Jay added.

Sarah shot Jay a look and said, "*Must* you always be such a tool?"

Ali smiled and nodded at Nate, telling him to go.

Beyond the firelight of the drum circle, Nate found Hardwick lying stretched faceup on the beach, his hands dug into the sand and his eyes staring up at the night sky like he could be flung up and into it at any moment.

Nate plopped down beside Hardwick. It felt good to stretch his six-foot-two frame after drumming for so long, frozen in position.

Nate handed Hardwick the bottle of beer, planting it in the sand between them. "You okay?"

"Things just got a little spinny there for a minute," Hardwick said. "I thought I was going to lose it, but I'm better now."

"Try some beer," Nate said. "Might help."

Hardwick twisted off the bottle cap and took a careful sip.

"They're going to think I'm a lightweight," Hardwick said.

"They would be right."

Nate reclined on the sand, and they both stared up at the starscape, which was intruded upon by the blinking lights of a passenger plane dotting a line across the sky as it headed south to SFO.

At last Nate asked, "Better now?"

"Yeah. Better."

"You feel like talking?"

"Yeah, I'm fine. It's been a while."

"Yeah, I've been kinda busy." After a pause, Nate added, "You ever been on the Dark Web?"

"Sure, I've downloaded Tor and taken a look around. Some twisted stuff there. Not a place I feel the need to revisit. You?"

"Yeah, I just discovered it a few months back, and it just blows my mind how free it is there."

"Free. That's one word for it."

"It's an actual frictionless economy, completely free of government interference."

"Frictionless economy, huh? I thought you'd outgrown your libertarian phase."

"Not really."

"So what's so great about the Dark Web? Unless you're looking to buy kiddie porn or heroin." Hardwick loved nothing better than an argument—as long as it was an argument about an idea.

"People are free there. Or freer than they are on the surface web."

"Everyone is hiding behind layers of encryption there. Everyone is wearing a mask. You never know who you're dealing with." Hardwick pushed himself up into a sitting position and then dusted the sand from his hands.

"And you do on the other internet? Maybe they're free *because* they're wearing masks." Nate also sat up, warming to the debate.

"Maybe they behave *badly* because they're wearing masks. That's why bank robbers wear them."

"The Dark Web is like any place on the web. There are bad people and good people there. Dissidents go there to organize out of view of repressive regimes."

"I think you have to admit that the Dark Web attracts a disproportionate number of shady characters. But I have to admit that Tor is ingenious from a coding perspective. It solves the problem of privacy."

Nate nodded. "It's the last private place."

They were silent for a moment, watching another passenger plane enter their patch of sky, following the same path south.

Finally, Nate continued, still trying to win the argument, even though he already knew it was destined for a stalemate. "I think the world would be a better place if people could do what they wanted without government interference. What's so wrong about that?"

"That depends on how you feel about people," Hardwick said. "Me? I don't trust 'em to behave decently without a good set of guiding principles—the Constitution, for example—and a strong government to enforce them. I guess in general I just don't like people. Present company excepted, of course."

"Really, Hardwick? You're going to insist on getting all misanthropic even on a night like this?"

"I can tell when you're in one of your cosmic, one-with-the-universe moods. That's one of the things I like about you, Nate—that you're still capable of that."

"So is that a backhanded way of saying I'm naive?"

"Yeah, I guess it is. But it's not a bad thing. In fact, it's kind of a gift. People gravitate to it. That's why you get laid like a rock star and me, not so much. Of course, the fact that you look the way you do also has something to do with it."

"Things have been kinda uneventful recently. What about Janine? You still seeing her?"

"Yeah."

"Is that, 'Yeah, but she's probably going to dump me and I'm not that into her, anyway'? Or is that, 'Yeah, I'm way into her and I don't want to reveal my soft emotional underbelly to you because you're such an asshole'?"

"The latter. Asshole."

They both stared up into the night for a while as Nate waited him out.

Finally, Hardwick added, "Things are actually pretty good with Janine. There, are you happy now?"

"Yes." Then after a beat: "I'm really glad to hear it. Janine is great."

Hardwick began testing his balance, raising himself out of the sand. "We'd better get back to the group. You shouldn't keep a girl like Ali waiting."

As they walked back across the dark beach toward their friends, the sight of the fire swirling up into the night sky brought Nate's thoughts back to the one thing he had been trying to forget. Despite his efforts to distract himself with sex, Ali, friends, weed, beer, and the drum circle, Nate couldn't stop thinking about the mysterious El Chingon and the image of himself sitting in an oil drum with a burning tire around his neck.

10

The post by CaptainMal first appeared on the home page of Kyte, but it was reprinted the next day in ValleyDish (under the headline "O Captain, My Captain!") and then in *Wired* online. From there, it exploded like a fragmentation grenade on Facebook, Twitter, and other social media. It even memed.

It was labeled as an entry from the Kyte Founder's Journal. The unexpurgated version read as follows:

> Silicon Valley is built on a lie, and it's a lie told to the young.
>
> They come to the Valley hoping to become the next Brin, Zuckerberg, or Dorsey, or at least to be a part of building something exciting and new. But the reality is very different. I've seen some of the best, brightest people I know squandering their youth as:
>
> Unpaid interns;
>
> Minimum wage "content generators"; and

Sales associates making hundreds of cold calls a day to make quarterly revenue projections for a buggy software product.

They're grossly underpaid, but they're told that they are receiving invaluable experience, and maybe even some sweet stock options—which more likely than not will be underwater if the company ever goes public. If the company tanks, and even if it doesn't, they walk away after a year or two with very little. But their sweat drives the revenues that enable the company to go public. Note that I said "revenues," not "profits," because the idea that a business should turn a profit seems to have become an outdated concept, so Old Economy.

They take all the risk, those interns and content generators and sales associates, because they bet their twenties and thirties that the jobs will be worth it. And they pay the price, while the founders and the VCs have insulated themselves with their stock ratchets and golden parachutes. That tiny band of insiders typically makes millions, maybe even billions, even if the company crashes and burns.

And what do my peers and classmates get in return? A "fun" workplace painted in preschool primary colors with a tube slide connecting the floors. Branded shirts, hats, and backpacks. A kitchen with a wall of candy dispensers where you can have all of the M&Ms and yogurt-covered almonds you can eat.

Kyte may be illegal, but it's still more honest than most Silicon Valley start-ups. We pay our coders and admins better than many of the Valley's giants. We can't provide health insurance or stock options given the nature of our relationship with the law, but at least we don't pull a bait and switch. You get exactly what we promise you, and you take home real money—or at least real Bitcoin.

Our pirate ship is sailing. I can't tell you how all this will end, but I can promise you an adventure. Let's knock Silicon Valley on its ass and show them what a disruption really looks like. I hope you'll join us.

We will never ask you to work for less money in exchange for a "learning opportunity" or a "fun work environment." And I can promise you that we will never have a fucking candy wall.

11

Walking through the Union Square neighborhood of San Francisco headed for the FBI field office and another interagency task force meeting, Lisa was waiting to cross a busy intersection when she noticed the man standing next to her.

He was beefy, taller than her, with a bearish, full brown beard.

And he was wearing a white wedding dress and veil.

As they waited side by side for the light to change, the man turned to her, tossed back his veil, and said, beaming, "It's my day!"

Lisa loved her city.

———

The members of the interagency task force filed into the conference room and assembled around a long table, all carrying cardboard cups of coffee. They had already been warned away from the office's local brew by one of the resident agents. Looking at the tired faces of her counterparts, Lisa didn't get a sense of urgency.

Constantine cleared his throat to convene the meeting. "Well, I guess you've all seen the press coverage of the so-called Candy Wall

Manifesto. Looks like CaptainMal is trying to turn himself into some sort of Silicon Valley folk hero."

"This guy really annoys the hell out of me," said a DEA agent named Fred Spiegelman. "He's not content to just be a regular scum-sucking drug dealer. First he pretends to be some sort of libertarian philosopher-king. Now he wants to shake his finger at Silicon Valley. The guy just pisses me off."

Constantine leveled a cool gaze at Spiegelman. "I've got an idea. Why don't you channel that anger into generating some leads in this investigation? Other thoughts?"

"He's taking a page from the Steve Jobs playbook," Lisa offered.

Constantine leaned forward on his podium. "How so?"

"The manifesto reminded me of Apple's '1984' television commercial, where Jobs tried to portray his company as a scrappy revolutionary taking down Big Brother IBM."

"Only CaptainMal seems to want to take on the entire tech industry—and the federal government."

"I think CaptainMal understands that branding is important for any business—even an illegal one. Portraying himself as a revolutionary is just good brand strategy."

Constantine seemed skeptical, but that was his default setting. "Well, Agent Tanchik, as long as you have the floor, let's start with you, shall we? Were you able to find any signs that Kyte is staffing up with coders?"

"No luck yet," Lisa said. "I visited several of the biggest Dark Web sites for coders, and I didn't see listings or chatter suggesting that someone was hiring in bulk. Nothing that stood out as unusual."

From the head of the long conference-room table, Constantine tried not to look pleased. "Well, I guess it was worth a try. Are you going to continue to observe those sites?"

"Maybe for another week or two, but I'm not optimistic. Kyte's going to need to expand to handle the increase in volume. If I can't spot him at work now, I doubt I'll be able to spot him later—even if he is hiring there. Maybe he's smart enough to disguise the nature of the business in his job listings, or maybe he knows enough to spread his hiring over multiple sites, or maybe he has another way of recruiting coders."

"Maybe," Constantine said. "I notice you're still using *him* to refer to the founder."

"Just my working assumption."

"Let's not make too many of those—assumptions. Any other news to report from the depths of the Dark Web?"

"No, nothing else." She knew that she should probably mention her possible online encounter with Kyte's founder, but she wasn't ready to do that just yet. First, she couldn't be certain who she'd been dealing with. Second, she wasn't sure that she could trust her task force colleagues to properly develop the lead.

Most importantly, she didn't want the prying eyes of the task force peering over her shoulder, observing her interactions with CaptainMal. What she was attempting was delicate and could be easily ruined if her colleagues started trying to dictate how and what she said to the Kyte admin.

The rest of the meeting passed uneventfully, as various agents trotted out their half-baked theories and information that any Kyte customer could tell you. When the meeting adjourned, the person sitting next to her, an Indian man in his midtwenties, leaned in.

"You should keep at it," he said.

"What, the coder angle?"

"Yeah. It's as promising as anything else we have going right now." He extended a hand. "Sanjay Srinivasan." He was a small man, about five feet six (her eye level), with quick, dark eyes and an amused expression. He was wearing black pants and a patterned light-purple shirt, and he had a better haircut than any other male agent in the room.

"You're IRS, right?"

"Correct."

"You've been quiet so far at these meetings."

"I'm not sure I'd get a lot of respect in this room. All these junior G-men looking to make their names." A chagrined look crossed Sanjay's face. "No offense intended."

Lisa smiled. "None taken."

They both stood about uneasily for a moment before he said, "Just remember that it was the IRS that got Capone."

Now she laughed. "You've used that line before, haven't you?"

"That wasn't the first time. I'll cop to that." He grinned and raised his hands briefly, as if to say, "You got me."

"What are you working on?" she asked.

"Oh, I'm trying out a few theories."

"But you'd rather not share them with me."

Sanjay shrugged noncommittally. "You know how it is. I've got a feeling you're holding a few cards you haven't shown yet."

"Fair enough. You're a bit of a dark horse, aren't you?"

"Dude," he said. "That is so racist."

Lisa did a double take but found Sanjay gazing at her with a slight smile, waiting to see how she'd react.

"Don't call me dude," she said.

As they headed toward the exit, Sanjay added, "Let's do compare notes sometime."

"Deal."

———

Back in her cubicle at the FBI field office, Lisa opened up her laptop and was surprised to find that several new user forums had sprung up on Kyte.

But these forums weren't just dedicated to product reviews of the latest illicit drugs. They were filled with philosophical and surprisingly thoughtful discussions of libertarianism and the significance of Kyte.

One discussion included this pronouncement from CaptainMal himself:

> Kyte is an experiment in a violence-free, coercion-free economy. The government's "war on drugs" is an abject failure because it supposes that the state can control human behavior—and has the right to do so. I reject that assumption. By allowing people to buy and sell whatever they please, we are taking the violence out of the drug trade. And isn't it the violence that law enforcement and governments really object to, anyway? Drug violence comes largely from fights over turf, over money. One drug dealer kills another, FBI agents kill the drug dealer, and innocent citizens get caught in the crossfire.

Lisa had to hand it to CaptainMal. In a few short sentences, he had managed to taunt both federal law enforcement and the cartels. Clearly, he believed that he was beyond the reach of both.

> At Kyte, we offer a simple, efficient, user-friendly transaction experience in which there are no street dealers, no guns, no robberies. And why is that? Sure, there's the distance that is provided by an online transaction, and that creates greater safety. But another way we reduce violence is by empowering the consumer, which is at the heart of any great online service, whether it's Uber or eBay.

When you purchase drugs online at Kyte, you have a voice. You can rate your seller and their product. You can complain to us about poor purity, packaging, or delivery times. And if a seller doesn't meet our community's expectations of quality and service, then they won't be allowed to continue selling through Kyte. If you attempt to buy drugs out on the street, you don't have that degree of accountability from the seller—far from it. This is a peaceful revolution—and we intend to keep it that way.

Despite herself, Lisa was beginning to have a grudging respect for the person behind the handle CaptainMal. She didn't consider herself a libertarian, but there was no denying that Kyte's founder was thoughtful and articulate and had a coherent message. Lisa had never been assigned to any drug cartel cases, but she had heard enough gruesome war stories from her peers. If eliminating the sale of illegal drugs was an impossibility—and it definitely was—then maybe it was better to have someone like CaptainMal controlling the trade rather than the brutal kingpins in Sinaloa and Cali.

But that didn't mean that she bought into CaptainMal's ideological posturing. Sure, Kyte professed that it didn't sell goods that were inherently harmful to others—child pornography, bombs—but it was naive to pretend that heroin, meth, and cocaine weren't inherently harmful. CaptainMal could claim that while these products might lead to self-harm, that was a matter of personal choice—that maximum freedom included the freedom to harm oneself—but that completely ignored the disease of addiction and the harm it inflicted on everyone around the user.

Take Lisa's sister. Jess would have been a devoted Kyte customer. The site would have made it so much easier for her to procure the painkillers that eventually killed her. Kyte's manifesto was essentially a twisted inversion of Google's "Don't be evil," because Kyte was, in fact, deeply evil.

When Lisa thought about her sister, as she often did, one incident stuck in her memory. Jess had been abusing alcohol at the time; she'd been missing classes and apparently hadn't left her dorm room at Berkeley in days. Lisa was only a senior in high school, but she'd skipped class one day to visit Jess and hopefully help her snap out of her spiral. She couldn't understand why her sister, who had attained freedom from their parents and the life that Lisa yearned for, would waste it by drinking herself out of college.

"One day you'll understand," Jess said, sipping from a bottle of vodka-laced orange juice. (Or, rather, orange juice–laced vodka, Lisa guessed from the smell.) "You'll be the new me." With her clumped, stringy hair, Jess looked like she hadn't showered in a week. She seemed to be spending all of her time drinking and binge-watching Netflix.

They had argued bitterly, though later Lisa didn't remember the words. She had been too angry for that. What she remembered was a gesture. After they had both said every hurtful thing they could think of, Jess had dismissed her with a sarcastic grimace, accompanied by a flip of her hand. In that moment, Jess seemed to be saying, "Go ahead and give up on me. That's what you really want to do, anyway."

Every time she remembered that day—every time she thought about Jess—she became more determined to bring down Kyte.

She clicked out of the discussion thread and back to the nested listing of user forums. There was even a Kyte book club, hosted by—who else?—CaptainMal. The reading list was heavy on Austrian economic theory, particularly the libertarian economist Lorenz Mayrhofer. Quotes from Mayrhofer, such as "Real peace among peoples can only exist when the state is abolished," were frequently bandied about in the Kyte forums.

CaptainMal's pronouncements sounded like Mayrhofer punched up for millennials: "Why pay taxes to a state that never gave you anything in return? Put your energies into the black market, where we can help each other."

Opening up her regular internet browser, Lisa placed an order for one of the recommended books, Mayrhofer's *Freedom from the State*, in hopes that it might give her some insight into CaptainMal's thinking. She even considered studying up on libertarian philosophy and then initiating a conversation on the subject with CaptainMal, but she quickly rejected that notion. Attempting to sound like an expert on Austrian economic theory would be a dead giveaway that she was attempting to catfish Kyte's founder. Reaching out directly to CaptainMal would also probably arouse his suspicions.

She settled on a strategy, clicked back into Tor, and started typing a comment as Rodrigo in one of the more libertarian-oriented user forums.

RODRIGO: What is this bullshit? Do you need to have a degree in economics to buy drugs here now?

Lisa didn't have to wait long for a response to this provocation.

HANDSOLO: If you don't like what we have to say here, why don't you just leave? Kyte is about freedom of expression and action. You can't stop us from expressing our views.

RODRIGO: I'm not trying to stop you. I'm just expressing my view that your views are pretentious bullshit.

HANDSOLO: You should take some time to think about what people are saying in this forum before you criticize.

RODRIGO: Let's be straight about what's going on here. We're buying and selling illegal drugs. Stuff that gets you high. Take a little too much and you die. No one who hangs out here is going to cure cancer or win a fucking Nobel Prize.

A new poster joined their exchange—CaptainMal.

CAPTMAL: Hey Rodrigo, it's nice to see you on this forum. I understand that this whole side to Kyte may seem a little off topic for you, but it's important to me. I like to say, Come for the Drugs, Stay for the Philosophy.

RODRIGO: Sorry, but this stuff just sets off my bullshit meter.

CAPTMAL: Yea I get it. I used to feel the same way. How about if we take this conversation over to the customer service forum where we were chatting before? We can leave HandSolo and his friends to continue their discussion.

RODRIGO: Ok.

Lisa moved over to the customer-service forum and typed: You there?

CAPTMAL: I'm here.

RODRIGO: I didn't mean to bust balls.

CAPTMAL: I understand that.

RODRIGO: Can I give you a little friendly advice?

CAPTMAL: Ok.

RODRIGO: You need to tighten your shit up. All of this philosophizing and community building is fine if you like that sort of thing. But it makes you seem soft. I hope you're not actually trusting anybody.

CAPTMAL: What do you mean?

RODRIGO: You can't do this all alone, right? You must have coders, shippers, customer service types.

CAPTMAL: Yea, but I keep them all at a distance. No one knows who I am. No one meets me in person. No one gets my name. No one gets a real IP address.

Lisa had noticed that CaptainMal had a tic of spelling *yeah* as *yea* in his posts.

RODRIGO: Glad to hear it. But I know you must be moving pretty fast to keep the site going. When you move quickly, you make mistakes. Just know that as soon as you make a slip and reveal something about yourself to one of your people, you're giving them leverage. When you do that, they've got something they can sell to law enforcement.

CAPTMAL: Sounds like you're applying for a security job here.

RODRIGO: I've got enough on my plate. But you seem like a good guy, and I don't want to see you fail. Don't take this the wrong way, but you strike me as a little bit naive. That can be a good thing, makes you ambitious. But it can also get you killed or behind bars.

CAPTMAL: I know what I'm doing. I appreciate the sentiment, but that sounds kind of patronizing. Why should I be taking advice from you?

RODRIGO: I'm not going to give you my resume. But it's true— I've never done something as big as what you're doing with Kyte. Not many have. I respect that. But I'm also in a position to know that there are a lot of people out there gunning for you— in every sense of the word.

CAPTMAL: I think I traded messages with one of them recently. Do you actually know anyone in the cartels?

RODRIGO: Like I said, I operate on the fringes. I know they don't like you. I hear them talking. I know what they do to people they don't like. I don't want to see that happen to you.

CAPTMAL: What would you do if you were me?

RODRIGO: Trust no one.

CAPTMAL: Even you?

RODRIGO: Especially me. Didn't I already tell you that I have friends who work for the cartels? What have I actually done to win your trust?

Lisa knew this sort of ploy could backfire, but she felt that CaptainMal was smart enough to already have considered everything that she was saying. She hoped he would appreciate her directness.

CAPTMAL: True. I've gotta go, but you should try reading some Mayrhofer or von Mises. We could talk about it next time.

RODRIGO: If you knew me in the real world, you would know that I am not the kind of guy who reads Austrian libertarian economists.

CAPTMAL: People change. That's one thing I do know.

RODRIGO: Maybe. Later.

12

SAC Gilbertson made a rare appearance in the doorway of Lisa's office and approached her desk.

"Do you know who just called me about the Kyte investigation?" her boss asked.

"Who?"

"The director."

"Regional director?"

"No, the big boss." Meaning *the* FBI director. "This is on his desk now, ever since Senator Brosnahan's press conference." The senator from New York had recently called a press conference, practically trembling with rage, to condemn Kyte and its ability to sell drugs with seeming impunity.

National press or attention from Congress was about the only reason the director ever got involved in what was going on in the field offices. This was big news.

"Does this mean you're taking the case away from me?" Lisa said, dreading the answer.

"Believe me, it was discussed. But no," said Gilbertson, with a note of what almost sounded like sympathy. "I told the director that I thought you were the right agent for this, but you're going to have to start reporting to me on a daily basis."

"Will do."

"And if we don't start seeing progress, we're going to have to revisit the question of whether you're a good fit for this."

"Understood."

Gilbertson began to leave but then turned back, as if the point had not been emphasized enough.

"I hope you appreciate why I got that call from the director. It was because *he* got a call from his boss, the guy in the White House. Who doesn't understand why any teenager can go on the Dark Web and buy drugs as easily as ordering pizza."

"We're going to get CaptainMal."

"Don't tell me," her boss said on her way out the door. "Show me."

13

Nate walked up onto the front porch of a shabby and nondescript ranch house in San Francisco's Richmond District. He checked the scrap of paper in his pocket to make sure he had the correct address from Craigslist. The house had a mangy front yard, peeling paint, and shutters with snaggletooth slats.

He could have afforded a luxe condo in one of the formidable new glass towers in South of Market, the ones with 360-degree views of the bay, but that would have been too flashy. Nate was leaving his off-campus apartment for an under-the-radar arrangement where he wouldn't even turn up on the lease. Although he had no evidence that law enforcement was closing in, Nate felt that Kyte was probably attracting so much scrutiny that it was time to go underground.

He knocked, and a few minutes later, a recently postgraduate-looking guy threw open the door, shirtless and wearing board shorts. "Shane?" he said.

Nate had adopted the name of Shane Price in responding to the ad. He was looking for a cash-only house-sharing arrangement. If a potential landlord asked for ID or payment by check, then he had decided that he would simply walk away.

"That's me."

"Dave." Rather than going for a handshake, Dave leaned in, bumped shoulders, and clapped Nate on the back. "Welcome to Casa de Dave. I think you're going to dig it."

Nate felt a little moist after the bro hug but felt it would be impolite to wipe himself off.

Shirtless was not a particularly good look for Dave. He was pale and doughy, with a wispy growth of chest hair that was as patchy as the lawn out front. Nevertheless, Dave seemed singularly comfortable in his exposed skin. This was one nerd who was clearly missing the negative-body-image gene.

"So you seem pretty normal so far," Dave added. "You never know what you're going to get with a Craigslist ad."

"I'd reserve judgment on that if I were you," Nate said.

Dave started to smile, then stopped when he realized he wasn't sure if Nate was kidding.

They entered a central living room with furniture that looked like it had been scavenged from dorm rooms. There was no central flat-screen TV to exert its gravitational field on the room's layout. Tables and open laptops were scattered about, an indication that the tenants' single-serving viewing habits revolved around their computers.

"He's here!" Dave shouted.

A woman emerged from one of the bedrooms at the rear of the house. She had an elaborate and lovely sleeve of tattoos up her right arm, some sort of leafy nature scene, and that drew Nate's attention first. By the time his eyes worked their way up her arm, he realized that she was leveling a dead-eyed stare at him.

"Nice ink," he said.

"Thanks. I'm Merritt."

"Sit, sit," Dave said, motioning to a couch with caved-in cushions. "Isn't there one more of you?"

"Yeah, Jean-Claude, but he can't make it. He just went through a breakup, and he's sort of wallowing in it. You'll like him, trust me. Just not today."

"Okay," Nate said. "So you guys have a spare room?"

Dave raised a peremptory hand. "I think this is where I say, 'We'll ask the questions here.'"

"Try not to be a dumbass, Dave," Merritt said. "So, Shane, what do you do?"

"Well, I was a physics student at USF"—he'd decided to borrow Ali's school for his new, fake identity—"but I'm taking a break from the program, exploring some options."

"Looking for a job?"

"Yeah, eventually, but I'll probably take a little time off to get my head straight, figure out what comes next."

"If you don't have an income, will you be able to cover the rent?"

"That won't be a problem; I just came into a little money from my grandmother. But that's why I was looking for a house-sharing deal. I want to make it last while I sort things out. Keep my overhead low. So how about you two? What do you do?"

"I'm working on a sci-fi novel. Old-school, Heinlein-influenced stuff. Merritt is in a band."

"No offense, but—what do you do for *money*?"

"We're baristas at Z Coffee. But we try not to be defined by that."

Nate nodded. He understood why they needed his extra rent. "So—any other questions?"

"Are you a smoker?" Merritt asked.

"Not tobacco."

"Good answer," Dave said.

"Do you have anyone you'll be bringing over here?" This from Merritt.

"Probably not," Nate said. "Not at the moment. No."

"Sounds like our man Shane is having relationship issues," Dave said. "That's a subject I happen to be an expert in. If you move in here, my door is always open for mentorship, counseling, whatev—" Dave stopped. "She's rolling her eyes, isn't she?"

"Maybe a little bit," Nate said, smiling at Merritt, who continued to respond with a prison-hard gaze.

"So we're all single at the moment," Dave said. "Bad for our sex lives, but good for house *esprit de corps*. It's kinda nice when everybody hangs out and isn't so caught up in their relationships. For a while, anyway."

"Speak for yourself," Merritt said. "I think it's called being a loser."

"So . . . can I take a look at the room?"

Dave rose. "Sure, sure, right over here."

He led Nate over to a room that was only slightly bigger than a penitentiary cell, with a futon and a window looking out on a tiny backyard.

Nate saw Dave and Merritt exchange a look, then nod at one another. "Do you have first month's rent as a deposit?" Dave asked.

Nate pulled out his wallet and handed over six hundred dollars.

Dave took it gleefully. "Welcome to Casa de Dave."

"Who gave you naming rights?" Merritt asked. Even she seemed to have lightened up at the sight of his cash.

"I lived here first. Casa de Dave has a rich history."

Merritt shrugged.

"What about Jean-Claude?" Nate asked. "Do I need to meet him?"

"We have a quorum," Dave said. "The matter is approved. And besides, Jean-Claude is in no emotional state right now to make this sort of decision. We have to let our boy heal. The wounds are still fresh." He made a swiping-claw motion with his hand for emphasis.

"When do you want to move in?" Merritt asked, leaning against the wall.

"How about tonight? I can go get my stuff now and be right back."

"A man of few possessions. You're very Zen, aren't you, Shane?"

"Thanks, Dave," Nate said, trying to avoid a delayed response to his new alias. "I try to be."

As Nate recrossed the front yard, he paused before the picket fence that bordered the sidewalk and gazed back at the house. The new headquarters of Kyte. It didn't look at all like the year's fastest-growing tech start-up, and it certainly didn't look like the hub of a criminal empire.

It was perfect.

For a moment he considered recruiting Dave and Merritt into his business. He sensed that his new housemates would probably jump at the opportunity to make the kind of money that he could offer, and it would be fun to have more of a team around him. Running things by himself was often lonely—and stressful.

But he instantly recognized that for the bad idea it was. Recruiting Dave and Merritt, or heartsick Jean-Claude, was the sort of mistake that would land him in prison. He was going to have to continue to maintain OPSEC (operational security), relying upon his virtual workforce of coders and shippers to perform their piecework without ever knowing his identity. That had a certain romance to it too.

The tech entrepreneur as lone outlaw.

That was a new kind of romantic figure that hadn't been seen before, in a land where the new, new thing was worshipped.

Even the name he had adopted, CaptainMal, sounded vaguely piratical.

Every start-up had to have a creation myth, and as creation myths went, that was a pretty sexy one.

14

CAPTMAL: Hey, Rodrigo. I see you're logged on.

RODRIGO: Yeah, I'm here. You can't sleep either?

CAPTMAL: Not lately. Too much to do.

RODRIGO: I hear you. Don't you have a girl?

CAPTMAL: I do, sort of. But this whole Kyte thing has been taking all my time. I haven't seen her in a couple of weeks.

RODRIGO: That shit will not stand, dude. If you want to keep her, you got to make some time.

CAPTMAL: How about you? You got someone?

RODRIGO: I got LOTS of someones. Keeping it light. Young man gotta rumble. I don't want anyone slowing me down right now.

CAPTMAL: You may have a point there.

RODRIGO: So if you're not getting any, what do you do to relax? Smoke a little of that weed you're so good at selling?

CAPTMAL: Yea, but not as much as you might think given my business. I drum.

RODRIGO: You mean like Keith Moon?

CAPTMAL: No, I play the djembe.

RODRIGO: I don't know what that is, but I'm googling it.

A moment later:

RODRIGO: You're a hippie drum circle dude! That was NOT how I pictured you. I hope you don't have those nasty white boy dreadlocks.

CAPTMAL: No dreadlocks.

RODRIGO: Good, I'm so relieved to hear that, man.

CAPTMAL: But I do yoga.

RODRIGO: Now you're just playing with me.

CAPTMAL: No, really. It's very relaxing. Centers you.

RODRIGO: Yeah, you seem really centered, Captain.

CAPTMAL: You're just in a giving me shit kind of mood tonight, aren't you?

RODRIGO: I only do it with my friends. Take it as a compliment.

CAPTMAL: So how about you? What do you do— aside from dealing drugs and hanging with your cartel buddies?

RODRIGO: I work out. Lift weights. And I work in my sketchbook.

CAPTMAL: An artist!

RODRIGO: Not really but it relaxes me. Actually, I'm not bad.

CAPTMAL: What sort of subjects?

RODRIGO: Just nature and shit. The desert.

CAPTMAL: Send me a photo of one.

RODRIGO: Not going to happen, Captain. My sketchbook is just for me.

CAPTMAL: Sounds like we both lead double lives. I guess you don't show your stuff to your cartel friends either.

RODRIGO: You gotta be hard where I live, man.

CAPTMAL: You sound pretty tough to me.

RODRIGO: Yeah, maybe to you, you djembe playing, yoga pants wearing pussy! I know this one guy who's killed so many people that you look him in the eye and it feels like you just lost a piece of your soul. People like that aren't like you and me, Captain. We do what we do, but we'll always be who we are.

CAPTMAL: I like that. Well said.

RODRIGO: Thank you. Now try to get some sleep. Later.

Lisa considered whether she could establish similar connections with some of the other key players at Kyte, those who were most active in the user forums and seemed to speak on behalf of the site. Those were the people most likely to have clues to CaptainMal's identity.

She closed her laptop and listened to a car's tires hiss on wet pavement outside her apartment building. Whoever and wherever CaptainMal was, they had shared an odd sort of intimacy in the middle of the night, bathed in the glow of their screens. And even though she was not Rodrigo, and he most likely was not really his CaptainMal persona, she had to admit that it was easier to converse with him than almost anyone else that she currently knew. Lisa didn't want to spend too long dwelling upon that sad fact.

And she could tell that he liked her too—in a laconic, dude-to-dude sort of way. She suspected that, like her, CaptainMal knew that people's truest selves were only revealed when they were telling lies.

15

December 8

Nate was sitting at a table in the West Portal Branch of the San Francisco Public Library, checking up on Kyte. He noticed a message directed to the Kyte admin address from El Chingon, which read, Do you hear the footsteps, puta? I'm getting closer all the time. It had been more than four months since the last message from El Chingon, and he had nearly convinced himself that it had been nothing more than a very convincing prank.

Nate's eyes darted around the quiet library, but he saw only the usual cadre of students there for the Wi-Fi and seniors reading newspapers. El Chingon was probably no closer to finding him and was just trying to rattle him. If that was the strategy, then it was working.

Nate's phone pinged with a text. It was from Ali and read, Free for dinner? I know you're busy but . . .

He welcomed being pulled back into his former life, where no one wanted him dead. In his head, Nate completed Ali's sentence—"I know you're busy, but"—with "I'm going to leave your preoccupied ass if you don't start putting some energy into this relationship."

Ali had been trying to connect with him for the past two weeks and had expressed consternation when she'd learned that he had moved out of his student apartment. He knew that if he didn't do something soon, she would move on. And who could blame her? He was so busy keeping up with the endless demands of running Kyte that something had to give—and that something was Ali. Maybe Rodrigo was right about keeping things light.

Kyte was running smoothly that night, so he decided that a gesture was in order. He replied to Ali's text: How about if I pick you up at 7:30?

The reply: Ok. I'm shocked, but pleased. How should I dress?

Something nice—but not too nice. Wear pants.

You too.

Nate decided that it was time to spend a little of the money that he had banked.

———

While Nate couldn't engage in flashy purchases for fear of drawing the attention of law enforcement, there were still a few ways that he could discreetly enjoy his new wealth.

He rumbled up in front of Ali's apartment building in Noe Valley at seven thirty on a vintage Ducati motorcycle—a 450 Scrambler from 1969, with a silver teardrop gas tank. For once, he was on time. He had rented the Ducati for the night from one of his rich Stanford friends. His friend was trying to sustain a lavish lifestyle on a tight family allowance, which meant that he was willing to part with his treasured bike for a night for the right price.

And the price had been very right.

He texted Ali and she came downstairs, a smile of surprise mingled with trepidation when she saw him on the bike. She was wearing black pants and a silvery blouse open at the neck. Her long black hair was pulled back.

"Where did this come from?"

"Borrowed from a friend."

"And you know how to ride it?"

"Climb on back and find out."

Ali made a show of thinking about it. "Not the response I was looking for, but okay." Nate handed her a black helmet. Ali swung her leg over the bike and put her arms around him from behind. As he kick-started the bike and took off down the street, she tightened her grip. Nate liked the feeling and thought that all dates should begin with a motorcycle ride. Riding a bike was the perfect combination of a moderate pulse-quickener and pleasing intimacy. He figured that any date that began with a motorcycle ride was automatically 75 percent more likely to end in sex.

"Where are we going?" Ali asked, speaking almost directly into his ear.

"It's a surprise."

"You're lucky I'm not a prima donna about my hair."

"You look amazing."

"You know that you can't make up for two weeks of ignoring me with one night."

"But I can try, right?"

A long pause, as the wind whipped around and over them. "You can try."

Nate couldn't turn around to look at her, but he sensed that she was smiling. It was probably a small, grudging smile, but a smile nonetheless.

They climbed the on-ramp onto the 80 and were soon cruising over the lower deck of the Bay Bridge in light traffic. Cars passing over segments of the bridge made an insistent *whoom-whoom* sound. Nate felt Ali turn to look backward at the San Francisco skyline behind them. He glanced in the side-view mirror and caught the sunset glowing in the office towers of the Financial District, turning San Francisco into a city of umber.

"So we're going to Berkeley?" Ali asked.

"You'll see."

They motored on through the East Bay, past Berkeley, Albany, and El Cerrito, past the oil refineries of Richmond, over the Carquinez Bridge and into Napa Valley.

Now they had left the suburban and industrial sprawl behind and were on a two-lane blacktop through the valley. There wasn't much traffic, so Nate opened it up, accelerating until the blooming mustard fields on either side of them became yellow blurs in the moonlight. It got the desired response as Ali tightened her grip around his chest.

Nate veered off Highway 29, Napa Valley's main thoroughfare, onto the Silverado Trail, which wound through the woodsy countryside past wineries that gripped the rolling hillsides and spread out into the fields. He leaned into the curves a little but not too aggressively. He wasn't that good a rider, and the goal was not to terrify Ali.

Ali hadn't said anything in quite a while, and he took that as a sign that she was enjoying the ride. The moonlight silvered the fields of twisting grapevines, the rolling hills, and the ancient oaks that loomed over the narrow road. A ride like this could have been chilly, but the temperature was a perfect sixty-five degrees.

Nate left the Silverado Trail and cut over to Yountville on a side road that passed two more wineries. He pulled up in front of an old stone house with a blue wooden door and windows that glowed with candlelight. The brass plaque by the door read THE FRENCH LAUNDRY.

Ali didn't get off the bike immediately. "You're kidding, right?"

"Our reservation is at eight. I took that little detour down the Silverado Trail so we wouldn't arrive early and have to wait."

"How did you get a reservation? I hear you have to call two months in advance, and then you're lucky if you get something."

"I found a foodie blog where people offer reservations they can't keep. I had to win a bidding war, but I got the reservation."

"This place is superexpensive. You really don't have to do this. I'm not that fancy."

"I've had a little good fortune lately, so I've got this."

"This has already been a lovely evening. I'd be fine with getting a burger at Taylor's Refresher."

"They do make a great burger, but not tonight. Now do you want to keep debating this, or do you want to go inside?"

Ali swung her leg off the bike. She was smiling now, and there wasn't anything grudging about it.

They opened the blue door and entered a relatively small dining room bathed in buttery candlelight. They were escorted to a table covered in white linen. Atop the menus were wooden laundry pins bearing the name of the restaurant.

Small plates began to arrive as part of the multicourse tasting menu, each one more amazing and surprising than the last.

Ali spooned some kind of mousse from a glass into her mouth and rolled her eyes. "Oh my god. What is this?"

Nate consulted the menu. "Sabayon of pearl tapioca with poached Malpeque oysters and caviar. So that means you like it, right?"

"*Like* isn't the word. I want to marry it, buy a house in Marin, and have its children. A boy and a girl. Henry and Miranda."

"So that's a yes."

Ali stared at him for a moment and then asked, "What's that?"

Nate picked up a tiny brown ice cream cone that was filled with something diced and glossy crimson. He bit into it. The red stuff was salmon tartare, and the combination of textures (crunchy and smooth) and flavors (salty and sweet) was unlike anything he had ever tasted. Nate was hardly a foodie. He still ate the way he had eaten as an undergrad—pizza and burgers were his two essential food groups. He had brought Ali to the French Laundry solely because he knew it would impress her—and he knew that he needed to impress her. As the waitstaff brought and whisked away one astonishing plate after another, Nate began to appreciate for the first time that a meal could be a kind of performance art.

Nate and Ali spent the first hour murmuring contentedly to each other and occasionally exchanging "Can you believe this?" glances with the young couple at the adjoining table.

Dinner at the French Laundry was a carefully orchestrated three- to four-hour experience. They were just an hour in when Nate's cell phone pinged with an incoming text. It was the burner phone that he kept with him so that his inner circle of Kyte admins could reach him in an emergency. Ali was curiously examining three tiny cups of soup that had been set before her, and he couldn't tell if she'd heard the ping.

He was anxious about leaving Kyte on autopilot for the evening, and he knew that if someone was texting him on the burner phone it must be important. However, he knew that anything that drew his attention away from Ali would defeat the purpose of the evening.

After about ten minutes, Nate excused himself and went to the bathroom. Once inside, he checked the text. It was from DPain, and it read: We need to talk. No more texts. Call me.

Ignoring DPain's request, Nate texted back.

CAPTMAL: I'm in the middle of something. Tomorrow.

DPAIN: Now. Or you'll be sorry.

CAPTMAL: What does that mean?

DPAIN: Call me and find out.

Nate dialed the number that he had for DPain, which was also undoubtedly a burner.

"Okay. What's this about?"

"Let me ask you a question. Actually, it's not a question. It's a statement. I think I've been an important member of the Kyte team."

"Sure, you've been doing a great job. But what's so urgent?"

"I deserve a promotion. You should make me a partner."

"You've been doing excellent work, and I appreciate that, I truly do. But let's be clear about this—there is no path to promotion at Kyte."

"I'm taking risks doing what I'm doing. I handle a lot of product—at my house. Where my family lives!"

"And you're well paid for that. But I'm not taking on partners. I have plenty of other people handling admin and logistics. You're valuable—but you're not invaluable."

"Do you mean Twoey or Alex7? I ship twice the product they do."

"You don't know everyone I'm working with or how much product they handle."

"So we contribute our work, and you reap the profits?"

"That's the way it works when you create a business. You've been paid more than fairly for everything that you've done. I'd be happy to discuss bumping up your rate, though—on Monday."

"I don't think you understand, man. I'm not asking. I have a list of more than fifty thousand user shipping addresses. If you don't give me what I want, I'm going to give them to law enforcement."

Nate was stunned speechless for a moment. He knew that he needed to be very careful in his response.

"I'm glad you brought this up, and I fully intend to recognize your contribution. Obviously, this is catching me by surprise. I'm out at dinner with someone right now. Can we discuss this in the next day or two?"

"You've said that before, and nothing happened. This time, I need an answer in two days."

"I need a week."

The moment stretched as DPain considered.

"Tell me you won't do anything before we've spoken again," Nate said.

Finally: "One week. No more."

"Sure. I just need time to absorb this and get some numbers together. We'll talk in a day or two."

"So we have a deal? It's just a matter of settling on numbers, right?"

"Right."

Nate knew he didn't have a choice.

"You're not going to regret this, partner."

Nate hung up. He wasn't sure what he was going to do, but if he wouldn't let a Mexican drug cartel threaten him, then he certainly wasn't going to allow an addled stoner like DPain to get the best of him. The problem was that DPain had some real leverage to bargain with. The FBI would love to get its hands on that list of user shipping addresses. It might or might not lead to his arrest, but it would certainly cause irreparable damage to Kyte's reputation. When word spread that buying through Kyte wasn't safe, his users would move on to other means of procuring their drugs.

Nate splashed water on his face, then gripped the sides of the sink and tried to meet his gaze in the mirror. First, he needed to log on at Kyte and take steps to limit DPain's access rights to user data. He finally steadied himself—then remembered that Ali was waiting for him in the dining room.

As he returned to the table, he could see her staring at him impatiently. The candlelit room that had seemed so warm and intimate when he left now felt cloying and claustrophobic.

As soon as he sat down, she said, "I know what you were doing in there. I heard that text come in."

"I did take a look at the phone while I was in there. Is that so wrong?"

Ali sighed. "I don't expect you to give up whatever it is that you're doing, this stealth start-up. But after barely seeing you for two months, I was hoping that we could just spend an evening together." She waved her hand to indicate the restaurant. "All this, don't get me wrong—it's wonderful and I love it. But it's not necessary."

He reached across the table and clasped her hand. "I don't want to screw this up, Ali, but an emergency has come up at work. A real emergency."

"What sort of emergency? Are you okay?"

"Yeah, yeah, it'll be okay—I hope. But it's serious, and I have to deal with it."

"So what are you saying? Do you need to leave?"

Nate ran a hand through his hair. "I can't spend two and a half more hours here. I have to get back to the city now."

"Can you tell me what's going on?"

"I wish I could, but I can't."

Ali carefully placed her napkin on the table. "I think I liked it better when you lied to me and made up lame stories. At least that demonstrated a certain amount of effort."

"I don't want to lie to you."

"You may not be lying to me, but you're holding something back that's clearly important. And when you hold something back that's that big, it makes everything else a lie."

"I'm still the same person I was when we met sophomore year."

Ali shook her head. "No, something's happening to you. At first I thought I liked it, but now I don't think I do." She stared down at her plate. "I'll sign an NDA if that's what it takes to have an honest conversation with you."

Nate stared back at her. "I'm sorry. I don't know what else to say."

Ali didn't get angry; she just looked hurt and disappointed, which made him feel even worse.

"You know, someday you're going to look back on this thing that you're doing—whatever it is—and realize it wasn't as important as you thought it was."

"Believe me, Ali. It is important, the most important thing that I've done with my life. Can you please just trust me on that?"

"I can see that you think that," she said. "And I can also see that you think I'm less important. At least I'll give you credit for not trying to bullshit me about that."

"That's not—" Nate began.

"No, don't," Ali said. "This is where I talk. I'm young, but that doesn't mean that I have time to waste waiting for someone to change, to love me more. Or to start loving me. I know I'm going to make bad decisions in my twenties, and maybe you were one of them. But I promised myself that if I made a mistake I wouldn't just keep repeating it out of inertia."

"Ali, I'm doing something that takes nearly everything I've got. If I fail because I didn't try hard enough, didn't want it enough, then I don't think I'll be able to forgive myself—or anyone who held me back." He'd started off trying to choose his words carefully—to not risk revealing too much—but he realized he'd said exactly what he felt.

Ali looked down and fiddled with the heavy, elegant silverware, avoiding eye contact. "I can't say I understand because you're still so cryptic about what you're up to."

"Someday I'll be able to tell you."

She shook her head. "I'm afraid that's not good enough. But you should know something that I learned by watching my father." She finally met his gaze. "He thought that he could pack his heart away in dry ice until later in life when he had time for it. But by the time he finally decided to use it, it was atrophied, a freezer-burned, piss-poor excuse for a heart. Nobody really wanted it at that point—certainly not me."

Ali stood up from the table, startling a waiter who hovered expectantly behind her. In response to Nate's look, she said, "You wanted to go, right? Then let's go."

As soon as Ali rose, their waiter, a young man with a placid face and short blond hair, stepped in with a look of concern. "Is something wrong?"

"Everything was wonderful," Nate said. "But something has come up, and we have to leave."

"Of course. I'm very sorry to hear that. Please have a seat, and we'll prepare the bill." The waiter cast a quick glance around the dining room. He didn't want anyone to think that someone was questioning the food or service. A dinner at the French Laundry involved casting a kind of spell over the diners, and Nate and Ali couldn't be allowed to break that spell.

Outside in the parking lot, Nate said, "We didn't actually get that much to eat in there. Would you like to grab that burger at Taylor's Refresher on the way back?" He made the offer even though he was dying to get to his computer.

"Please just take me home," Ali said.

As they drove back through Napa Valley on the Ducati, taking the direct route this time, Nate thought about what Ali had said, that he would one day realize that Kyte wasn't really so important. He turned that over for a while and decided that she was wrong. The world was full of people. There would always be relationships and maybe even people to love. Who was to say that Ali was the one? Or that there was such a thing as the one.

But Nate was certain he would *never* again be presented with another opportunity like Kyte. There was a reason why they called a paradigm-shifting, disruptive start-up a unicorn. They were about that rare, but Nate had managed to create one. It was the sort of game-changing business that his father only wrote about in his Stanford B-school case studies.

And best of all, it was his. He didn't have to share Kyte with a venture capital fund, shareholders, or a board of directors. No one was going to tell him that he needed to step aside because he needed the "adult supervision" of a gray-haired, veteran CEO.

Ali was a special girl and he truly cared for her, but she was no unicorn.

As they sped down the long straightaway of Highway 29, slicing the warm night air like a 435 cc carbon fiber knife, he realized that he had to let her go. Judging by the way she had just looked at him in the parking lot of the restaurant, he might no longer have a choice in the matter. It was going to require all of his concentration and effort to keep Kyte going—and keep himself out of jail. A relationship would only compromise that concentration.

Eventually, Nate convinced himself that the breakup was for Ali's own good. She was better off keeping her distance from him. Otherwise she might get dragged in as a conspirator if he were arrested. Of course, that line of reasoning came a bit later, during the rationalization portion of his internal dialogue.

It was a long ride back into the city from Napa. The moonlight was still silvery, the mustard fields were still blooming, the temperature was still mild, and the Ducati still hugged the road like a champ.

But Ali wasn't holding on to him as tightly as before.

16

Lisa stared out the front passenger-side window of the SUV at the flat landscape gliding past, rolling farmland dotted with scattered patches of dirty snow, just outside Chillicothe, Missouri. She was a city girl, and she always found it difficult to imagine how people managed to live with all the space and quiet. She figured that sort of life must do something to you. And whatever that was, she hoped it was never done to her.

She was in the car with five male agents who were all suited up with tactical vests under their blue FBI windbreakers. In the trunk was a battering ram for the front door.

The vest applied a pressure to her chest that felt like the beginnings of an anxiety attack. She was tense because she had never led a tactical team before. She had only been part of a tactical unit once previously, and that had ended ignominiously with the Video. This time would be different. After all, they were there because *her* work had led to identifying Jason "DPain" Pomeroy as a primary distributor of drug shipments for Kyte.

Lisa had been reading Kyte's community forums for several weeks. There, someone known as DPain held forth on the nuances of pain meds like a wine connoisseur parsing the relative merits of the 1961 Chateau Latour and the 1953 Petrus. DPain had made the dumb mistake of posting a photo of some product that still contained embedded geolocation data, and it was as simple as that. Being a good investigator was often just a matter of steadily watching until someone made the inevitable slip. They had identified DPain's house from the geotag and, with the help of US Postal Service inspectors, had confirmed at least a dozen parcels containing high-quality heroin, cocaine, and meth delivered to that address.

She glanced at Don Nazarian, who was keeping up a running commentary while he drove. The other agents seemed to be making a show of their nonchalance. Or maybe they really were that much at ease. They had stopped for egg-and-sausage biscuits and hash browns at McDonald's, and the air in the cabin was thick with grease.

Nazarian was on a roll. "You know, no one really knows how they're going to respond in a high-pressure situation until the moment arrives. Several years back, I was pursuing a team of bank robbers, and they had just added a new member to their crew. I'm sure he rehearsed his one line over and over, but when he got there in front of the bank teller, you know what he said?"

Lisa wondered if this story was implicitly directed at her—no one else chimed in. Because Nazarian seemed to be waiting for a response, she finally said, "No, I don't know what he said."

"This is a fuckup, mothersticker!"

The other agents in the back seat laughed like this was one they had heard before.

After the laughing and throat clearing subsided, Nazarian turned the topic toward their upcoming bust. "Judging by his driver's license, our suspect seems to be a big fella. Three twenty-five. Six feet."

"Yeah, so?"

"So if you have to draw down on him, I wouldn't rely on one shot. Big boy like that might take two, three slugs to bring him down. Little thing like you, you don't want to go mano a mano."

Nazarian was referring to the Video, and everyone in the car knew it.

"Duly noted," she said. "Good thing you're going through the door first."

"Oh, am I? I thought you'd save that for yourself."

"See, that would not be an appropriate use of resources. I'm not expendable to this investigation. But you are."

One of the agents in the back snickered, but Nazarian was unfazed. "You've never shot anyone, have you?"

"I've certainly wanted to," Lisa replied. "In fact, I want to right now."

This drew laughs from everyone in the back seat, and Nazarian smiled, but Lisa could see that he was smoldering.

"There it is," she said, gazing at the distant, Monopoly-size house on the horizon. They were speeding down the long, straight highway, but the house didn't seem to be getting much closer.

Lisa squinted into the hazy, white sunlight glaring off the patchy snow. "If we can see them from this far away, then they might see us too."

———

Jason "DPain" Pomeroy was no logistics expert, but he could tell when his little team wasn't operating at peak efficiency. The late afternoon was the most dangerous time, and things were beginning to slip. The first warning sign was when his wife, Pam, opened a Coors tallboy as she packaged shipments of coke and molly into empty video game boxes. The room was warm, and the winter sunlight pouring through the dining room window didn't help matters. Pam rolled the can of beer across her forehead, then took the moisture from the outside of the can and rubbed it into her jeans.

"Pammy, what time do you think it is?"

"I don't know, Jason. Around five, right?"

"It's only four ten. A little early to be drinking, don't you think?"

"Just a beer. What's your problem?"

Jason gestured to indicate their living room, which was dominated by stacks of brown-paper packages containing a pharmacopeia of illegal drugs.

"We're going to make quota today."

"Not at the rate we're going, Pam. And I want to be done on time so we can watch the finale of *The Voice*."

Pam stood. "All right, Team Jason, I'll put the beer in the refrigerator until we're done. Satisfied?"

"Thank you. You see, Pam, when you lose your focus, it affects everyone. The little ones take their cues from you."

Jason nodded at their two offspring, who did not appear to be taking cues from anyone. Fifteen-year-old Jason Jr., a skinny kid in a Slipknot T-shirt with hair dyed jet black, was sitting cross-legged on the floor in a patch of pale sunlight, reading a comic. Thirteen-year-old Monica had the earbuds of her smartphone in and was staring into space. They were both wearing latex gloves to avoid a contact high.

"You got what you wanted, so spare me the lecture," Pam said. She snapped her fingers at the children, and they grudgingly resumed their packaging.

Jason felt a pain at the base of his spine as sharp as a prison shiv. He popped a Percocet and washed it down with Diet Coke. The doctors called it pain management. As if his kind of pain could be managed.

"And yet you get to take those all day long," she added, her eyes on her package, hands moving.

"That's different, and you know it. I have a medical condition."

"Yeah, it's called addiction."

"*You* try getting around with two herniated disks."

Pammy/Pam/Pamela. His wife was like one of those three-sided dice from a board game. Pammy was the girl that he had married ten years ago, a gimlet-eyed Ozarks girl who thought she saw through everyone's bullshit. That was 150 pounds ago—his, not hers. Back then she had wanted to become a store manager at Walmart. It had taken her a few years to figure out that big-box retail wasn't going to be her ticket out of the backcountry. Fortunately for Jason, it had taken her several more to realize that Jason wasn't going to get it done, either, but by that time they had a family to raise.

On her good days, she was Pam—semiresponsible mother and Team DPain's accountant and partner in crime. Smarter than he was when she applied herself.

Pamela was his name for her when she got all chippy and dissatisfied with her lot in life, like she was at the moment. Every day with her was a roll of the dice, and he never knew which face of that three-sided die he would get. Sometimes he thought he could see them all there in a single moment, like one of those weathered highway billboards out on US 65, where the sign was tattering to reveal the old ads layered underneath.

In other words, she was the love of his life.

Jason felt a keen sense of pride watching his family, his crew, back in gear and working away like a bunch of Keebler elves, bringing sweet highs and pain relief to Kyte's customers. He also felt a twinge of guilt knowing that what they were doing was illegal and could put them all in jail, but the money was good, and the guilt, like his chronic back pain, could be managed.

He was anxious about the threat that he had made to CaptainMal the day before, but he felt it had been necessary to get him and his family what they deserved. But it troubled him that CaptainMal knew where he lived and he didn't know the same about his boss.

Jason started when he heard a sound outside.

He had his recliner positioned near the window so that he could spot anyone approaching. He pulled the curtain open and surveyed the driveway, which was empty. No tire tracks or footprints in the new snow, which made the Midwest landscape even more blank and featureless. They lived in a single-story brick house on the outskirts of Chillicothe. There were no other residences in sight, and they were just a couple hundred yards from the longest, straightest, flattest stretch of highway in north central Missouri.

"You hear that?" Jason asked.

"No. Probably the mailman."

Jason peeked through the curtains again. "Too early. And there's no truck."

Pam returned to her package. "You know, I think those pain meds are starting to—"

She didn't get to finish the sentence, because at that moment the door exploded off its hinges, and two agents in FBI windbreakers stormed in, dropping the red battering ram with a thud on the laminate floor.

"FBI. Everybody put your hands in the air," said a young female agent who strode through the door after the two men carrying the ram. "You're all under arrest."

The Pomeroys all complied, except for Monica, who didn't catch the instruction until she yanked out her earbuds.

More agents came through the door, a total of six. They dispersed through the room, making sure that each family member was unarmed and that no one touched the product that was everywhere. Then a couple of agents crept into the back rooms of the house, crouched, guns out.

From the back of the house came five shouts of "Clear!"

The house was accounted for, and he could see the team of agents uncoil a bit, knowing that no one was going to come blasting out of a back bedroom.

The woman agent addressed Jason and Pam. "Just based on what's in plain sight here, I'd say you're looking at at least twenty years in a federal prison."

"Not us," said Junior. "We're juvie."

"You know, I hear juvenile detention facilities are really great these days. You and your sister are going to love it there."

"Do you have a search warrant?" Jason asked.

"We do. You want to see it?"

Jason nodded. The agent produced the warrant, and he studied it for a moment, but his eyes were pinballing so much that he couldn't actually read it. It looked official enough, though.

"Okay, then," said the agent. She added, "Do you prefer Jason or DPain?"

"Jason is fine. And who's DPain?"

"Right. Okay, Jason. If you're willing to listen to what we have to say, I think you'll find that there's a way out of this mess for you—and your family."

For a beat or two, he just stared at the baby agent, trying to decide just how dumb it would be to open his mouth. She didn't look like an alpha dog, but the other agents deferred to her. The FBI's Geek Squad seemed to be in charge of the case.

"Do you have a badge?" He wanted to slow things down, give himself time to think.

She flashed a badge that read SPECIAL AGENT LISA TANCHIK.

"You don't look like an FBI agent."

"Yeah, well, you probably watch too much TV. This is what we look like now."

"You don't look like them," he said, nodding at her square-jawed colleagues.

"Let's stay on point here, Jason."

"I don't have to talk to you."

"No, you don't. That is absolutely correct." She read him his rights, ending with, "You do have the right to an attorney, but I wouldn't recommend it."

"And why is that?" Jason tried out a snarky grin, but he knew that it was probably a horrible, sickly thing to behold. He was scared, and he wasn't a good enough actor to disguise that fact.

Agent Tanchik gestured to the hallway. "Why don't we speak in private?"

"I don't get around so good," Jason said. "Bad back. Two herniated disks."

"I'm sorry to hear that," she said without conviction.

"I guess there's no harm in listening. Pam, kids, why don't you go in back for a minute?"

Pam, Monica, and Junior rose and went down the hallway to the master bedroom, two agents in tow to make sure they didn't flush anything down a toilet.

Monica cast a look back at him like she was being led to the gas chamber.

"It's okay, honey," Jason called out to her. "I'm not going to say anything. I'm just going to see what they have to say."

"Don't do anything stupid," Pam said.

Jason straightened up in his recliner, sending an electric stab up his spine. "It's going to be okay."

Pam delivered a look that could have stripped paint. "Uh-huh."

Then she caught his eye and seemed to read his mind, as only she could do. "Okay," she added, softer.

They waited while the family filed out, and Jason watched Special Agent Tanchik taking in their living room—plastic flowers in a vase, worn couches, the makings of white-bread peanut-butter-and-jelly sandwiches left out on the kitchen countertop, a lone fly lapping the kitchen before settling on a dirty plate. It wasn't hard to spot the recent purchases they had made with the influx of Kyte money—a sixty-inch plasma TV, an Xbox, and the new Dodge pickup in the driveway. He could see her reducing him and his family to some flyover-state stereotype.

But what could he say, really? This was their life.

At least they weren't cooking meth.

Just shipping it.

Once everyone else was out of the room, Tanchik said, "You know, you're luckier than you think, Jason."

"Oh yeah? Why is that?"

"Because you have something we want. Something that could make a big dent in your sentence."

"What's that?"

"We know that you're operating a shipping hub for Kyte. The person we want is the guy in charge—CaptainMal. You give him up, and your situation is going to start looking a lot better."

Jason knew that he should stop talking at this point, ask for a lawyer. But he was so nervous, and the agent already seemed to know so much. He just couldn't stop the words from pouring out. "I don't know his real name. And he uses proxy servers for everything."

"But you're in touch with him?"

"Nearly every day."

"Good." The agent sat down on the ottoman next to him. "Now you're going to have to decide if you want me to be your friend—or not."

"If there's one thing that I know for sure, it's that you are not my friend."

The agent nodded gently and smiled. "That's true, Jason, but I don't have to be your enemy. We could work together on this thing."

"You're offering a deal?"

"It's a little too soon for that. But what if we didn't confiscate your drugs and let you keep working awhile longer? It would be on the condition that you help us take down CaptainMal. You would get to stay with your family. We wouldn't put your wife in prison and your kids in juvenile detention facilities. Your family won't have to see you in handcuffs when they come back out here."

"We're all going to need witness protection."

She cocked an eyebrow. "You really think that's necessary?"

"I already threatened him once. You really think he's not going to be willing to do whatever he needs to do to shut me up? He's got so much money, and I know him."

The agent seemed really interested now. "How did you threaten him?"

"I wanted a piece of the action, so I told him I was going to expose the mailing addresses of Kyte's users if he didn't cut me in."

"How did he take that?"

"He said he'd give me what I wanted if I gave him a week to work things out. I think he may have just been buying some time."

"So when is he supposed to get back to you?"

"Friday."

"Excuse me." Tanchik left the room.

He heard a muffled conversation as the agents conferred.

When Tanchik returned, she seemed resolved. "We're going to take you back to our offices now, and you should probably call your lawyer when we get there."

"My lawyer? You think I have a lawyer?"

"Well, you should think about getting one. I think we're going to be able to offer you a deal."

"So there would be no charges against me or my family?"

"I'm going to see what I can do, but I can guarantee you that things are going to go much better for you, and especially your family, if you cooperate."

Jason could feel the beads of sweat on his forehead. He desperately wanted another Oxy.

"So what exactly do you want from me? Just tell me."

"We want you to keep the pressure on Mal."

"You want me to keep pressing for a cut of the profits?"

"That's right. Press him hard, and keep threatening to disclose the addresses."

"And if I help you catch him, do you think then I could keep some of the money?"

Tanchik gave a disappointed sigh. "No, Jason, there's no scenario here in which you get to keep the money."

"My family's got expenses."

From the kitchen, Nazarian muttered to his partner, "Those loaves of Wonder Bread and jars of peanut butter don't buy themselves, do they?"

Tanchik scowled but otherwise ignored the remark.

"We can get you some spending money and a place to stay, but your old life is over now. You get that, right?"

Jason felt the room grow close around him. He desperately wanted an Oxy, but he knew there was no cure for this pain.

17

After the fiasco of a night out with Ali at the French Laundry, Nate awoke in his apartment thinking of one thing—how he should respond to DPain's threat. He still held out some hope of preserving his relationship with Ali, but that would have to wait. If DPain publicly exposed the addresses of Kyte users, then his business, the little empire that he had created, would vanish overnight. Nate had limited DPain's access rights as soon as he had gotten to his laptop the night before, but the damage had already been done.

His venture was at that delicate juncture faced by all promising start-ups, when perception was as important as reality. In fact, perception was reality. And DPain could not be allowed to damage that perception.

There were competitors waiting in the wings to step in if Kyte faltered. Nate had just seen a YouTube cartoon video promoting a site called Planetary. "Meet Jack," the voiceover had said. "Jack is sad because he is out of tasty bud. Jack goes to Planetary and orders prime bud. Said bud is delivered securely and anonymously to Jack's house. Jack is happy—and *totally baked*." He had to admit that it was kind of cute.

Kyte had quickly built a solid reputation as the Dark Web's eBay of drug sales—but that reputation was entirely dependent on the guarantee of anonymity for its users. If DPain released the user addresses, the customers who loved him now would immediately take their business to Planetary or some other upstart.

The only answer seemed to be to give DPain what he wanted, make him a partner. But Nate did not bargain with terrorists, not when that meant giving away equity in his creation. Kyte couldn't exist in its current form without his inspiration, his vision. In other hands, it would have been nothing more than a grubby bazaar for drugs and other illicit goods. But Nate had framed the site in such a way that it was becoming more than that. Kyte was a raised middle finger to the very notion of government authority.

He messaged DPain to let him know that he was working on an offer. There was no response, which was odd. DPain usually responded to him instantly, particularly when it was about money.

Nate wondered if the request for partnership had been some sort of stalling tactic while DPain made plans to steal Kyte's product and start his own competing site. He wondered how big a crew DPain was working with in his shipping operation and whether they might also be part of the insurrection. Nate finally dismissed his speculation as paranoia. DPain was a follower (albeit a demanding one), not a leader. Nate needed to remain calm and work the problem.

There had to be an alternative to capitulating to DPain's demands. Nate felt the need to speak with Rodrigo, although he couldn't yet admit even to himself what he had in mind.

Nate posted a query in one of the Kyte forums that Rodrigo frequented. An hour later, Rodrigo replied, and Nate invited him to direct message through Kyte.

RODRIGO: Que paso, Mal?

CAPTMAL: I have a real problem.

RODRIGO: Speak to me.

CAPTMAL: Remember when you warned me about an insider turning on me? It's happened.

RODRIGO: What's the damage?

CAPTMAL: None—yet. One of my admins is threatening to publish the addresses of 50,000 users.

RODRIGO: That's bad.

CAPTMAL: Yea.

RODRIGO: What does he want?

CAPTMAL: He wants a piece of the profits. He wants to be my partner.

RODRIGO: Fuck that. What did you say?

CAPTMAL: I told him I'd think about it. What else was I going to say? I needed to buy some time or the addresses would be out there now. I needed to discuss this with someone I trust.

A pause as Nate stared at the cursor, wondering if he had scared Rodrigo off.

RODRIGO: Don't take this the wrong way, man, but why trust me?

CAPTMAL: This sounds funny but I trust you because you're nobody. You don't know who I really am, you're not in my real life. But I still think I've got a sense of who you are. Know what I mean?

RODRIGO: Yeah, I think I do. Do you know the AFK identity of this person?

CAPTMAL: Yea, I made him show me a copy of his driver's license. He uses his house as one of our primary shipping hubs.

RODRIGO: Does he know where you live?

CAPTMAL: No.

RODRIGO: At least you've got that going for you. Have you decided what you're going to do?

CAPTMAL: Not exactly. You said you knew people in the cartels, right?

Nate couldn't believe that he was taking the conversation in this direction, but he hadn't asked the question yet. There was still time to deflect, veer away. He wondered if Rodrigo had already guessed where this was headed.

RODRIGO: Most of the guys I grew up with are hooked up with one of the cartels. Either that or they're dead.

CAPTMAL: Are your friends all in Mexico, or do you know people like that in the States?

RODRIGO: Some of them are over here. I live in the Bay Area now. What are you asking me, Mal?

CAPTMAL: I guess I'm asking if you could have someone beat up this guy who's causing me problems.

RODRIGO: I think I could help with that, if that's what you really want. Is that what you really want?

CAPTMAL: I think so. I just want him to understand that this is not a game. The privacy of our users is vital to my business. If he carries out his threat, he could hurt a lot of people who've placed their trust in me. I can't allow that. I won't allow it.

RODRIGO: Do you think a beatdown would work with this guy?

CAPTMAL: I think so. Probably.

RODRIGO: Is this about protecting customer privacy or is it about protecting yourself? Nothing wrong with either reason.

CAPTMAL: To be honest, it's both.

RODRIGO: Fair enough. Like I said, no reason why you should allow this douchebag to ruin your business.

CAPTMAL: Would you do this thing yourself?

RODRIGO: No, but I know how to get it done. You'll have to pay me in bitcoin and I'll pay the contractor.

CAPTMAL: How much?

RODRIGO: The contractor sets the price and I'll let you know.

CAPTMAL: How badly will he be hurt?

RODRIGO: How bad do you want him hurt?

CAPTMAL: I want something that will make him go away and never mess with me again. I'd be fine with sending him to the ER, but I don't want to put him in a coma or lay him up in traction for six months. Can I just have a leg or an arm broken?

RODRIGO: This isn't like ordering takeout.

CAPTMAL: Just tell me what to do. I've never done this before.

RODRIGO: Clearly.

CAPTMAL: Have you done this before?

RODRIGO: I know how it's done. That's all you need to know.

CAPTMAL: Ok.

RODRIGO: He might go to law enforcement. You can never really be certain how someone is going to react to that sort of thing. You sure he doesn't have a way to tip the FBI to your location?

CAPTMAL: Yes, I'm sure.

RODRIGO: Good. Because if you're not secure, then I'm not secure. And neither is the guy that I'm going to hire.

CAPTMAL: I've worked too hard to let all this slip away.

RODRIGO: Send me his home address and I'll be in touch when I've lined up the contractor.

CAPTMAL: I'll get it for you. Be back in a minute.

Nate retrieved DPain's home address from a journal he kept for Kyte business. As he did that, he thought about Rodrigo's question, wondering if a beatdown would be enough to dissuade DPain from his extortion scheme.

He sat back down at his computer and paused for what seemed like five minutes before resuming at the keyboard. The thought that had come to mind was so powerful that he had to let it strike him like a gong, let the vibrations ripple through him until all of the fear and anxiety and guilt had died down to a low reverb, and he was left with a cold fact.

Nate began typing.

CAPTMAL: What would it cost to change that order from beat up to murder?

———

Lisa shut her laptop and stared at the hulking figure of Jason "DPain" Pomeroy. Pomeroy was sitting across from her in an interview room in the FBI's San Francisco field office, sipping a coffee and studiously pulling apart a cinnamon roll as he waited to be interrogated about his role in Kyte, blissfully unaware that a hit had just been ordered on him.

She continued to stare as her mind reeled at this mind-bogglingly lucky break in the case.

At last DPain took notice of her stare.

"What?" he said.

18

After the exchange in which CaptainMal had ordered the hit on Pomeroy, Lisa had left the interview room for a while to figure out her strategy and let him stew. Pomeroy sat fidgeting in a chair that was too small for his girth. Observing through the one-way mirror, Lisa thought he looked like a hermit crab trying to retreat into a shell that was several sizes too small.

Finally, she reentered the room, giving the door a hard shove so that it banged to announce her arrival.

Pomeroy stabbed a finger at her. "I'm gonna need to see my deal in writing."

"It's coming, Jason. But I need to know that we're on the same page here."

"We totally are."

"Not feeling any residual loyalty to Mal?"

"No. Fuck him. My loyalty's to my family."

"Good. Because he's not being very loyal to you, Jason. Far from it."

"What do you mean?"

"Mal ordered a hit on you. He wants you dead."

Lisa could see the progression of thoughts on his face. First, fear at the notion that someone was coming for him. Then relief that he was secure in FBI custody where no killer could reach him.

"How do you know that?"

"Because Mal asked *me* to take you out."

"What?"

When Pomeroy flinched, Lisa realized immediately that she should have prefaced that statement. For one brief, illogical moment, DPain seemed to think that she was about to pull out a gun and off him.

"I think I could have said that better. He didn't *know* he was trading messages with an FBI agent."

It took Pomeroy a moment to understand what she was saying, but then he unclenched. "That's some crazy shit."

Lisa smiled despite herself. "I know, right?"

"Who did he think he was talking to?"

"A guy named Rodrigo."

"Isn't that entrapment?"

"Leave that to the lawyers, Jason. You should be pleased. You've got him rattled."

"Good. That dude should have paid me."

"You like walking around in the sunshine as a free man, right? Seeing your family?"

"Well, yeah."

"We're going to help you keep that, but only if you work with us."

"How much did it cost to order the hit on me?"

"Forty thousand down, another forty when the job is done."

Pomeroy nodded appreciatively. "So what do you need me to do?"

"Well, first we need you to keep overseeing the shipments of Kyte product. Mal can't know that you've flipped." Lisa had moved all of the drugs and the Kyte customer lists confiscated from Pomeroy's Missouri home to an FBI-owned warehouse south of Market, where DPain had continued to supervise the shipments for the past three days, using his standard techniques to disguise their contents.

"Haven't I done everything you've asked?"

"But we still don't have everything we need to bring down Mal," Lisa said. She considered a few ways to put her proposition to Pomeroy, but she knew that none of them sounded good.

"Just say it."

"Fine. We've decided that you're going to have to die."

Pomeroy stared at her, dumbfounded.

"Yeah, that's right, Jason. And I'm the one who's going to have to kill you."

19

December 12

While making a rare appearance at the physics building to turn in an extension request on his graduate thesis, Nate ran into Hardwick, who was even more animated than usual.

"I heard that you and Ali broke up. What the fuck, man?"

He wasn't ready to have this conversation with Hardwick, but then again, when would he be? He continued walking outside to the quad, and Hardwick followed, blinking in the sun.

"You need to fix this, dude. You don't just throw away a girl like Ali. Of course, she was way too good for you, but that's how all the best relationships are."

"And how would you know about that?" Nate regretted the shitty remark as soon as it was out of his mouth. He liked Janine, Hardwick's girlfriend. In fact, it was the sort of college relationship where all their friends could see them as a forty-year married couple after the second date.

Thankfully, Hardwick brushed it off. "The woman is always the better person, and over time, she makes the man less of a douche."

"Are you calling me a douche?"

"Well, yeah, you are a bit of a dick. Ali was just beginning to civilize you, but your douche nature is strong. It's like one of those antibiotics-resistant superbugs."

"My douche nature?" Nate wanted to be annoyed, but he was already starting to smile.

"I'm here to tell you, as your friend, that you're making a big mistake. It may not be too late to fix this, but you're going to have to step up now."

"She broke up with me."

"Yeah, right. I can see the way you've been acting lately. If I were a little more sensitive, I'd think you were trying to tank our friendship too."

"I've just been a little busy."

"I've seen you busy. What you are now is obsessed. I just don't know what it is that you're finding so fascinating. You shooting heroin or something?"

"No, of course not."

"Well, I came by your apartment to have this conversation and found that you'd moved. I left you a voice mail, but of course, you didn't return it."

"I've been busy. And I found a new place."

"Obviously. Look, I'm not your parent—"

"I'm glad we got that straight," Nate broke in. "Because you were starting to sound a lot like my mom."

"It's this start-up that you're working on, isn't it?"

"Like I said, I've been busy."

"Okay." Hardwick nodded, holding up his hands. "You don't have to tell me what this super top secret project is. That's fine. But this isn't the first of your little forays into e-commerce."

"This is different," Nate said. They were standing next to a bench outside the physics building, but they were both too worked up to sit down.

"But you felt the same way about the video game site and the food truck site, right? Where are they now?"

"I'm telling you this is different."

"I appreciate that you feel that way. I'm just saying that it may not be so. Ali, however, is the real deal. I hate to see you do something you're going to regret."

"You know what I would regret?"

"What's that?"

"I would regret allowing people like you and Ali to stand in my way. I've got a shot at doing something. Something that's not easy. And if my personal life takes some hits during this period of my life, then that's just the way it's got to be."

"Okay, buddy. Good luck with that."

Hardwick turned to leave.

"Thanks, friend," Nate said to Hardwick's back as he walked away across the quad and into a throng of students, rejoining a world that seemed very distant to Nate now.

20

Lisa decided that if DPain's death was going to be believable, she would need the help of a professional makeup artist, and the San Francisco Film Society helped her find one.

Holly Davis showed up at the FBI's field office on Golden Gate Avenue, carrying her makeup kit in a cloth bag. She had reddish-brown hair and fair skin and was wearing jeans and a dark-green T-shirt with an indecipherable faded logo. Her résumé as a makeup artist included several independent films shot around the Bay Area. Holly looked like someone who would fit in perfectly on the set of an indie.

"I hope I can tell this story later," she said when Lisa greeted her in the lobby. "Because I've got a feeling this is going to make a really good story."

"That kind of depends on how it ends."

She nodded. "Understood."

Lisa led Holly back to the interview room where Pomeroy was laying into a breakfast from Carl's Jr.

"Enjoying your last meal?"

"Ha ha," he replied. "You have no idea how stressful this is for me. I eat my feelings, and I have a lot of feelings right now."

Lisa introduced Holly, and she unpacked her makeup kit on the metal table.

"So what are you looking for?" she asked Lisa. "You want a double-tap shot to the head? A gut shot? I can do anything you want. I just worked *Bad Fellas*, a crime flick, so I've mastered all the basic gunshot wounds."

Lisa considered a moment, savoring the options. "Let's go with the head shot. What do you think, Jason?"

"Just make it quick, please."

Holly smiled, starting to get into it. "Oh, I promise you won't feel a thing."

"That's not what I meant," Pomeroy said. "And I'm glad you're both finding this so amusing."

Holly grinned at Lisa, and she grinned back.

"When we're done here, you're going to have to go into hiding while we play this out with CaptainMal. We'll put you up in a safe house that we use for people going into witness protection."

"Can my family visit?"

"No, they cannot. But this shouldn't last too long." Changing the subject, Lisa turned to Holly and said, "We should shoot the photo someplace that looks like a residence. Everything here at the office is a little too institutional."

"My place isn't far from here," Holly said.

"Does it look like someplace where he would live?"

Holly studied Pomeroy for a moment. "I've got a corner with an old couch that should work just fine."

"I'm still here, guys," DPain interjected.

They walked three blocks to Holly's apartment off of Polk Street. It was small but nicely furnished. The kitchen counter was covered with takeout cartons.

The first thing Holly did was pick up the cartons and toss them into the trash can underneath the kitchen sink. "I wasn't expecting visitors," she said.

When she was done, Holly pointed to a slightly shabby sofa in one corner of the room. "I was thinking over there. We could lay him out on the floor next to the couch."

Lisa tried to picture Pomeroy's bloody body sprawled on the floor. "Yeah, I think that would work nicely."

Holly went to the nearby window and adjusted the blinds to let some sunlight in on the patch of floor where the body would be. "What do you think about the lighting?"

"Let's leave the blinds closed and use the iPhone's flash. More lurid that way."

Holly sat Pomeroy down at her kitchen table and got to work. She decided to go with a gunshot to the back of the skull because it was easier to fake convincingly, with the gore and brain matter obscured by matted, bloody hair.

After about a half hour of prep work, DPain looked like a dead man walking. Holly had given him a bit of subtle pallor consistent with blood loss, and the back of his skull was a bloody mess.

"Is that a bit of brain matter there?" Lisa asked.

"Yes, it is," Holly said, proud of her work.

"What do you use for that?"

"I start with oatmeal, but then I mix it with my own special concoction."

"Ah, the secret sauce."

"Can we get this over with?" Pomeroy asked, annoyed by their instant camaraderie.

"Okay, get down on the floor," Holly said. "But be careful not to let your head brush the carpet. You don't want to mess it up."

DPain eased himself out of the chair and onto the floor, grimacing with pain. "This isn't easy for me, you know."

"Let your arms fall loose," Lisa said. "And turn your face toward me a little."

Lisa and Holly examined the scene.

Holly crossed her arms and stepped back for a better view. "That looks pretty good, if I do say so myself."

"Agreed," Lisa said. "Jason, you can close your eyes now."

Lisa held up her phone and captured the mock crime scene with the flare of the flash. Then a few more shots from slightly different angles so that she would have a few options.

"Now let's try a few with the eyes open," Lisa said. "Try staring blankly at that chair over there."

More flashes.

She examined the shots on the screen of her phone, with Holly looking over her shoulder. The gory images sobered Lisa up in an instant, and she no longer felt like joking about their photo shoot. They were trying to catch someone who was willing to pay to end another person's life.

During her training at Quantico, she had studied a wide array of cases involving homicide, but the essence of the act always remained a mystery to her. Sure, she understood self-defense and crimes of passion, when anger and impulse took over in a blinding synaptic explosion. But the perpetrators of premeditated murder were something else entirely.

Could this Mal character be so deluded as to believe that he was ordering this hit to preserve a community rather than to save himself? Lisa vowed that someday she was going to gaze at Mal from the other side of a sheet of prison plexiglass and judge for herself.

Lisa finally returned to the moment and saw that Holly was waiting for her verdict. "I think we've got it, don't you?"

Holly nodded.

"Can you help me up now?" Pomeroy asked. "My back is killing me."

Holly and Lisa turned to stare at him, both performing the necessary mental adjustment.

21

Lisa must have studied the photo depicting DPain's death a hundred times, searching for any detail that looked staged. By adjusting the privacy settings on her iPhone, she had ensured that the photo would not include a geotag. When she was convinced that the photo was flawless, she went online to give Mal the news. She was lying on the bed in her apartment with her laptop. The only lights on in the room were the laptop screen and the TV with the sound off, which was showing an episode of *The Wire*, something to help her get into character as Rodrigo. She had the window open, and a breeze lifted the thin curtains and let the cool San Francisco night inside.

Lisa pinged Mal using Kyte's secure messaging.

RODRIGO: You there?

After a five-minute wait, the response arrived.

CAPTMAL: I'm here. Is it done?

RODRIGO: Done.

CAPTMAL: Do you have proof? A photo?

She attached the bloody photo of DPain.

RODRIGO: Here you go.

There was a lengthy pause. Mal was obviously studying the gruesome photo. Was he feeling horror, relief . . . or nothing at all?

CAPTMAL: You saw the body yourself?

RODRIGO: No, I hired someone to do it. But what more do you want?

CAPTMAL: The contractor worked alone?

RODRIGO: Yes. How much do you really want to know?

CAPTMAL: No, I trust you. I just need to know how many people know about all this.

RODRIGO: Just you, me, and the contractor. He works solo, and he's not talking.

CAPTMAL: Does that mean he's dead?

RODRIGO: I mean that even I don't know his real identity. And there's no incentive for him to ever open his mouth about this.

CAPTMAL: Unless he gets arrested.

RODRIGO: Even if that happened, he has no clue to your identity. With me, he knows what I look like, but that's about it.

CAPTMAL: What have I done?

RODRIGO: Dude. Don't do that. You know what you did, and you know that it had to be done. He was coming after your business. You don't bargain with terrorists, right?

CAPTMAL: Yea, you're right. I had no choice.

RODRIGO: Remember who had your back on this.

CAPTMAL: I owe you, Rodrigo. I'll always be grateful for what you've done here.

RODRIGO: De nada, Mal. I added my finder's fee on top of the contractor's price, so I got paid. But you've gotta know that this won't be the last time.

CAPTMAL: What do you mean?

RODRIGO: Don't be naive, man. You know the business you're in. You can say all you want about frictionless economies, libertarianism, and Ludwig von what's his name. But you're in the drug business, my friend. As long as you're making the kind of money that you must be making, there will be people coming at you. But if you come at the king, you best not miss.

CAPTMAL: I wanted to remove all that violence from the drug trade, just make it a simple, clean business transaction.

RODRIGO: And I love that you think like that, Captain. I do believe that Kyte is a safe—or safer—place for your customers to buy drugs. But it's never going to be safe for you. You know what they say—heavy is the head that wears the crown.

CAPTMAL: I guess I need you on my team then, don't I?

RODRIGO: You need someone like me, anyway. There are plenty of people who could have done what I did.

CAPTMAL: But none that I trust. You don't do what we just did with someone you don't trust.

RODRIGO: Thanks, man. Someday maybe we'll get to have a beer together, or smoke a joint, and talk about all this shit face to face.

Lisa felt that she was taking a chance. If Mal thought she was trying to initiate an in-person meeting so soon after the "hit," he might think that he was being set up. There was a risk that Mal would simply disengage and disappear into the recesses of the Dark Web. She also worried that the Shakespeare reference was a little out of character for Rodrigo.

CAPTMAL: I don't think that's ever going to happen. Just taking your own advice.

RODRIGO: Yeah, of course you're right. Quick learner.

CAPTMAL: I have to be, don't I?

With that, Mal signed off. Lisa stared at her screen for a long time, recognizing that she had just achieved a huge breakthrough in the case. She now had evidence that could convict Mal of attempted murder for hire, which could carry a life sentence. Of course, the fact that there was no actual murder victim would be a mitigating factor.

Her exchanges with Mal could not have been clearer. It was a smoking gun—but it still wasn't entirely clear who was pulling the trigger. A jury would see messages attributed to an online personage known as CaptainMal, but what did that really mean? She still didn't have the identity of the person who controlled that account. And what if there was more than one person with access? She needed more, much more, to establish a connection to a real person who existed outside the Dark Web's hall of mirrors.

But even though it might not hold up in court yet, Lisa thought she was beginning to know her adversary. She recognized Mal's voice when he was trading messages with her. CaptainMal disguised his self-interest behind lip service idealism, and he always felt the need to believe that he was a good person no matter the consequences of his actions. Lisa recognized those aspects of CaptainMal's personality all too well.

———

Nate sat with his back to the wall in a quiet coffee shop in Dogpatch, staring at the photo on his laptop. When he had commissioned the hit through Rodrigo, it had been as easy as ordering a pair of sandals from Zappos.com, but seeing the end result was different. He was half-surprised that the people at the adjoining tables didn't hear the clangor of his thoughts and turn to stare at him.

Nate knew that a sense of unreality was not a defense. He had known exactly what he was doing, but it seemed now as if the decision had been made more by his online avatar CaptainMal than by his AFK persona Nate Fallon. Nate/Mal had analyzed the predicament with logic and detachment and concluded that DPain's death was necessary to preserve Kyte and protect the anonymity of its users. He would do it again if he had to because it was the only solution outside of walking away from the business, from the person that he had become, and from the world that he had created.

But no matter how convinced he was of the justice of his action, there was something about killing someone that didn't respond to logic or reason. It was the first haywire cell of a new cancer inside him—still tiny, but dividing, dividing, dividing.

He clicked the image to enlarge it, until his vision filled with the black hole at the back of Jason Pomeroy's skull. Nate wanted to retch.

He stumbled up from the table, with the groaning scrape of a chair on the floor, and now the denizens of the coffee shop actually did turn to stare.

Nate ran out into the cool night air, which carried undernotes of the ocean's salt rot. He walked a few steps and felt that his head might be clearing, but then he convulsed and threw up into the tiny island of shrubbery that bordered the sidewalk, bracing himself with one hand against a slender, barren tree.

22

December 13

Nate awoke to shafts of sunlight streaming through the blinds of his bedroom window, like golden lances not-so-gently probing the most painful recesses of his sodden brain. After seeing the bloody photos of DPain's corpse, he'd been desperately in need of something to stop his reeling thoughts, and he had temporarily found it at the Rickshaw Stop the night before.

He had drunk until he was sick, sardined before the stage in a writhing throng as a punky band thrashed and wailed. It had been too loud to speak to anyone, and he hadn't wanted to. Clubs like the Rickshaw afforded the comfort of tribal communion without any of the messy human interaction. He didn't remember much about the night, but he did recall being buffeted by the dialed-to-eleven roar of the speakers, so loud that he literally hadn't been able to hear himself think—precisely the desired effect.

Nate couldn't remember how he had gotten home, but he figured that he must have called an Uber, the drunk's savior. With Uber, you didn't have to know where you were, and you didn't have to have any money in your wallet; all you had to do was launch the geolocation pin like a flare and await rescue.

He was relieved that there was no one else sleeping in his bed in the morning, although that might have capped off the previous night's quest for oblivion.

A knock at the door, and then the perennially shirtless Dave leaned inside. Nate didn't understand how Dave managed to remain pale as a grub despite his exhibitionism.

"Shane?"

"Go away," Nate said.

"Rough night?"

"You could say that."

"I hope you didn't, like, *do* anything."

"What's that supposed to mean?" Now Nate looked up at Dave, who wore an expression of genuine concern.

"There are two guys here to see you. They say they're from the Department of Homeland Security. They showed us a photo of you."

Apparently there was no mistaking the look of horror and guilt that was his response to that statement.

"Dude. What *did* you do last night?" Dave said.

Was it possible that they already knew that he had ordered DPain's murder?

Nate considered climbing out the window of his bedroom and running, but he knew that strategy wouldn't get him very far.

For starters, he didn't think he could run ten yards in his current condition without vomiting. If his criminal career was about to come to an end, he decided that he didn't want to go out like some pixelated miscreant from an episode of *Cops*—half-clothed, vomit spattered, and tased senseless. No, he would face up to whatever was awaiting him at the door with some semblance of dignity.

Nate pulled on a T-shirt and cargo shorts and went to the door in his bare feet. As he crossed the living room, Dave, Merritt, and Jean-Claude all watched him with rapt attention like they were watching someone line up his skateboard for some epic fail on YouTube.

After taking a moment to steady himself, Nate opened the door to find two agents fidgeting in their dark suits on an unseasonably warm day.

"Are you Daniel Winslow?" The agent was a hulking man with an acne-scarred face that wore a scowl like he owned it.

"No. My name is Nathan Fallon." Nate knew that he had to use his real name because the agents were going to request identification.

They flashed badges. "We're with Homeland Security. I'm Agent Robert Tombs, and this is Agent Javier Esparza." The badges looked real, and so did their grim expressions.

"What can I do for you?"

Agent Tombs stared at him for a long moment, making Nate wonder how much he knew. Then he reached into an envelope he was carrying and removed a bundle of documents.

"Do these look familiar?" he asked as he handed them over.

Nate took the package and sifted through nearly a dozen fake passports and driver's licenses that he had ordered through Kyte from professional forgers. None of them bore the names Nate Fallon or Shane Price, but they all included the same photo of Nate. The primary purpose of the passports was to afford him a host of new identities that he could use to covertly rent servers to accommodate Kyte's expansion. A passport was generally required to rent servers in another country. After the threat from the Zeta cartel, he had also decided that he needed to be ready to run at a moment's notice, and the fake passports would give him some options. The Canadian, UK, and Costa Rican passports looked very convincing, complete with digital watermarks, faded passport stamps, and worn covers.

"I've never seen these before."

"Really? Because that certainly looks like your photo."

"Sure, that's me, but I didn't order these documents. Someone must be pranking me. That photo was taken from my college student directory."

"Could we see your driver's license, please?" Tombs asked.

"Give me a second, and I'll get it," Nate said, returning to his room to get his wallet.

When Nate returned, Esparza examined the driver's license. "Your housemates seem to know you by another name—Shane Price. Why is that?"

"Just a way of giving myself a fresh start. It's kind of a joke. There's nothing illegal about that, is there?"

"No." Esparza shook his head. "But it's pretty suspicious, Nate. I have to say that. It's pretty suspicious." He paused, then added, "You know, we're actually not looking to give you a hard time here. We're more interested in catching the professional forgers who sell these fake passports."

"Because that sort of service is very popular with terrorists," Tombs added. "You a terrorist?"

"No, sir."

"Kid doesn't look like a terrorist," Esparza said.

"No, he doesn't," Tombs said with impeccable timing, like they had used this patter before. "But you never know, do you?"

"Nope. You never know."

The agents' banter was having the opposite of its desired effect, and Nate's panic began to subside. They had simply blundered upon him, and they clearly had no idea who he was or his connection to Kyte.

"You know, anyone can order this sort of thing on the Dark Web through a site like Kyte," Nate said.

"What's Kyte?"

"It's sort of like eBay, except people sell illegal stuff there." It pained Nate to put it so simplistically, but he needed to remain in character.

He saw the two agents exchange looks. Nate was certain now that they were really just there about the fake passports. But his mention of Kyte had caught their attention, and they were going to make a note of it.

"Sounds like something we should look into," Tombs said.

"Do you have any plans to leave the country?" Esparza asked.

"No. Like I said, these documents must be someone's idea of a joke."

"That's a pretty elaborate joke," Agent Esparza said. "Not just anyone would do something like this. And it would have cost some money to buy documents that look this convincing. I know the work of a pro when I see it. Surely you have some idea of who might be behind this."

"No, not really."

"You don't look so well," Agent Tombs said. "Would you like to sit down? We could talk inside."

"I'm fine right here. A little too much partying last night. That's not a crime, is it?"

Esparza tilted his head as if to get a better look at him. "That depends on the party."

"I wish I could help you, but I really have no idea who did this. And I really do need to drink some water and get some more sleep."

"Have you ever purchased through Kyte before?" Tombs asked.

Nate paused and said it slowly. "I've never used Kyte. Like I said, somebody else did this."

"It was an innocent question."

Nate responded with a skeptical pause. "Do you really have to dress like that? You must be hot standing out there. They should let you wear shorts—like mail carriers."

"So you gonna give us a break and let us come inside?" Agent Tombs asked.

"I'm burnin' up in this sun," Esparza affirmed.

"I'm happy to cooperate in any way I can—if you've got a search warrant." When there was no response, he added, "Do you have a warrant?"

Although the combination of the hangover and abject panic made it difficult to organize his thoughts, Nate tried to perform a quick mental inventory of anything in his room that might reveal that he was the operator of Kyte.

There was nothing but his laptop, and that was turned off and secured with strong encryption. He reminded himself that, now more than ever, he must *never* step away from his laptop when it was on and he was working on Kyte business.

"Nope, no warrant," Esparza responded.

"What do you do for a living, Nate?" Tombs asked blandly.

"I'm taking a break from school. Considering my options."

"What school?"

"Berkeley. English literature."

"Hmm," Tombs said. "You plan on teaching?"

"Maybe. Haven't decided yet."

"Check out the brain on this one," Esparza added. "Someone that smart should know better than to buy forged documents on the internet."

"The Dark Web," Tombs corrected.

"Whatever."

Nate shifted tiredly from foot to foot and put a hand on the doorframe to prop himself up. "Okay, then," he said. "Is there anything else I can do for you, Agents?"

Agents Tombs and Esparza exchanged glances.

"No, that'll be all for now," Tombs said. "We'll just keep these," he added, holding up the forged passports and IDs. "If you have any plans to leave the country, we're going to expect you to contact us. Here's my card."

"Oh," Esparza added. "We'd like to get your email address in case we have a follow-up."

Nate reeled off a fake email address. "Have a good day, Agents."

As they walked down the front walk to their car, he heard Esparza mutter to Tombs, "He's a cocky little prick, isn't he?"

Nate tried to parse the remark. Was it simply a comment on their immediate encounter (in which he had indeed been a cocky prick), or did it reflect a more extensive knowledge of who he was and what he was up to? He knew that he was going to endlessly replay the conversation, looking for clues to the agents' intentions.

Even under the best interpretation of what had just happened, this was not a good thing. He wondered how long it would take them to figure out that he had given them a fake email address. Probably not long.

When Nate returned to the living room, Dave stood up from the couch. "Shane, man, what did they want?"

"Just a misunderstanding. No big thing."

"What sort of misunderstanding?"

"I don't even exactly know. They just asked me a bunch of questions and realized they were talking to the wrong guy. I'll give you a play-by-play later over dinner. Right now, I need to get some more sleep. My head is fucking splitting."

"Okay, dude. You want a beer, hair of the dog?"

"Thanks, man. I'm just going to grab a bottle of water from the fridge. Hydration. Best hangover cure."

Nate set the alarm on his phone and slept restlessly for another hour. He figured that in a worst-case scenario, he had a few hours before the DHS agents decided to return with a search warrant.

When he woke, his head was down to a mild throb. Nate grabbed his djembe and his laptop and headed for the door. Aside from a few toiletries, shorts, and T-shirts, they were pretty much the sole possessions he had brought with him to the apartment, cementing his housemates' Zen image of him.

Nate almost made it out of the house without being spotted, but Dave appeared from the kitchen just as he was opening the front door.

"Where you headed?"

Nate lifted the djembe. "The park. It's a beautiful day. Thought I'd drum a bit, get right with the universe."

"I hear you, man. Let's talk at dinner tonight. I'd like to hear about your conversation with those agents."

"Sure, Dave," Nate said. "But it was really no big deal."

Nate walked out of the apartment into the sunny afternoon, knowing that he would never return. He was going to need a new apartment and a new name.

He resolved that it was also time to set a date for leaving the US. Though the DHS agents were essentially clueless, he could sense that his pursuers were drawing closer. He would miss his family and friends and the Bay Area, but he could operate Kyte just as effectively from some nonextraditable foreign refuge.

Nobody said the outlaw life was going to be easy.

23

January 6

"Big weekend planned?"

Special Agent Jon Amis waited for an answer, clearly hoping Lisa would say no. Jon was a cybercrimes investigator who had been a year ahead of her at Quantico. For a few weeks, she'd watched him edging up to asking her out like a diver flexing his toes on the edge of the board, but he wasn't quite ready to take the plunge without some encouragement on her part.

For now, that was okay, because Lisa had other things on her mind—like bringing down the country's biggest drug dealer. Judging by the number of listings on Kyte, she estimated that revenues might be approaching $2 to $2.5 million per day. If she was correct, Kyte might soon reach annual revenues of $1 billion.

"Yeah, big weekend. I'm actually pretty slammed," she said.

"Still working the Kyte case?"

"My obsession."

"You know, sometimes it helps to take a break, have a couple of drinks. Lets the synapses reset."

"I'm afraid that's not how I work," Lisa said, smiling to soften the blow.

"Relentless—I respect that," Jon said, taking a step back. "Good luck. That captain guy doesn't stand a chance."

"Thanks. Have a nice weekend, Jon."

"You too." He paused before turning to leave. "Just so we're clear, when I mentioned going for drinks, that was me asking you out."

"Yeah, I think I got that."

He nodded slowly. "Good. Because I'd like to try that again sometime. Soon."

"Yeah, you should do that."

Jon nodded again and left the office tamping down a grin. She got the feeling that he was going to engage in some sort of fist-pumping celebration of guyness outside in the hallway, and that made her smile.

Lisa loved the quiet of the weekends in the big office on Golden Gate Avenue because there were no distractions from coworkers, no questions. Just all Kyte, all the time. She took her laptop into the office of one of the directors, one who would never show up on a weekend, because she liked to see the sunset over the Marina District and watch the city lights come up on Van Ness through the floor-to-ceiling windows.

The building's air-conditioning shut down with an exhausted sigh, and she knew the weekend had officially begun. She changed into a T-shirt and shorts and brought out a small cooler filled with ice, vitaminwaters, and a fried chicken sandwich from Bakesale Betty. There was also a water bottle full of vodka, but since she'd become consumed with the Kyte investigation, she had found less need for that.

Lisa was a believer in grinding. She knew that most cases were not broken by Holmesian flashes of deductive insight but rather by simply showing up every day and remaining obsessively observant. CaptainMal had to have made mistakes, and he was probably still making them. It was inevitable because Kyte was such a large operation and because Mal's posts were increasingly showing signs of the strain.

Take, for example, this comment from Mal in a Kyte forum:

Every day that Kyte remains in operation, we make the world a freer place. Of course, there are forces of corporate and governmental oppression aligned against us. But even if LE succeeds in stopping me, they can't kill the idea. Pretty soon there won't be any going back to the old paradigm. Because once people get a taste of true freedom, they won't accept anything less.

There was the latest iteration of Mal's online persona condensed into four short sentences—hubris, paranoia, grandiosity, and idealism—with a touch of the martyr, a new element. By *LE*, Mal meant *law enforcement*.

Lisa's remark to Jon was not hyperbole—she had become obsessed with the Kyte case, so much so that she spent nearly all of her spare time sitting before her laptop prowling the Dark Web site and other sites that referenced it. Even when she had visited her parents in Pasadena for the holidays, it had been difficult to separate her from her laptop. She was the first into the office and the last one out, and when she went home, she took her laptop and continued the hunt. Lisa even brought the laptop with her to restaurants when she ate out. In any event, it reduced the low-grade social embarrassment of dining alone.

Working so hard also had the ancillary benefit of keeping her black dog at bay. As she tapped away at her computer, her face close to the big monitor, the black dog lay curled quietly at her feet, his tail occasionally thumping the floor, just to let her know that he was still there.

Lisa was reading a Reddit thread about Kyte when she noticed one post in particular:

Has anyone noticed that Kyte's IP address is leaking? It glitched out when I entered my password incorrectly. Mal better tighten that shit up.

That meant that Kyte's IP address, which showed the internet location of the server that hosted the site, was visible under certain conditions.

The Reddit post was dated a week ago, and Lisa figured that Mal had probably already seen it and patched the vulnerability, if it had existed at all. Still, it was worth a shot. The Kyte network was a thicket of proxy-server IP addresses and usernames that led nowhere. In order to truly make the case against CaptainMal, she needed to locate Kyte's server, which could be anywhere among the hundreds of millions of computers in the world.

As the river of headlights coursed down Van Ness through the dusk and into the night, Lisa sat at her laptop by the window, punching in false usernames and passwords. Sometimes, courtesy of DPain, she had a real username for which she entered a wrong password. The idea was to keep punching buttons on the site, hoping that the imperfection in the site's coding mentioned in the Reddit string was real and would reveal itself. She used some common freeware to record the IP addresses that communicated with her laptop as she went through the process.

Real username. Incorrect password.

Nothing. The Kyte website displayed a screen with the message **Incorrect Username or Password**. No address showed for the page in the IP address logger.

She repeated the process.

Incorrect username. Incorrect password.

Nothing.

Lisa stood up, stretched, stared at the passing cars. She took a swig of vitaminwater and started to question how she had chosen to spend her Friday night.

The black dog stirred and scratched itself.

Then she sat back down at the laptop.

Incorrect username. Real password.

Repeat.

Repeat.

Repeat.

Nothing.

Nothing.

Nothing.

And then—something.

This time, she was staring at Kyte's CAPTCHA screen, which was used to differentiate human registrants from bots, and not the incorrect username or password page.

And this time, most importantly, an IP address displayed in the logging software.

Kyte's IP address was usually masked, but as the Reddit poster had predicted, it had leaked out through a coding glitch in response to the incorrect user ID/password combination.

With this series of numbers, she should be able to find the physical location of the server that hosted Kyte and its data.

She called the FBI's computer forensic unit at Quantico and asked for help tracing the computer associated with Kyte's IP address.

An hour later, she got a call back from Quantico.

"Well, where's the server located?" she asked.

"My boss wants to know if this is for a terrorism investigation."

"No. Why?"

"It's international. Located outside the US."

"Where?"

"I'm supposed to find out what investigation this is for."

"Tell your boss this is for the Kyte cybercrime investigation. Operation Downdraft. It's an interagency task force. Am I going to have to speak with your boss?"

"Who's *your* boss?"

"I'm my own boss on this. You already have my ID number. I think it's time for you to tell me what I need to know."

After a beat, the analyst said, "Iceland. Reykjavík. The Thor Data Center."

"Thank you."

"But you're going to need letters rogatory if you want to—"

Lisa had already hung up on him.

She felt like she had just discovered a vampire's daytime resting place. Now she had to go there, open up the crypt, and drive the stake in.

24

Brian Hardwick had sensed for a while that something was up with Nate. The breakup with Ali had been a sign, but it was neither the first nor the last. Nate had become secretive, full of cryptic comments, no longer the chill dude of old.

And when Nate had started offering him premium fees for his help with coding over the past few weeks, Hardwick had wondered if Nate might be into something illegal. Nate assured him that he had simply secured some angel money for his "stealth start-up," but Hardwick was not convinced.

Hardwick knew that "stealth start-up" was usually Valley-speak for "bullshit pipe dream," but the good money that Nate was paying his staff was coming from somewhere.

He had insisted that Nate meet him at their usual spot, the Sand Hill Road Starbucks, before he would deliver his latest coding assignment. The coffee shop, located in an inauspicious strip mall dominated by a Safeway supermarket, was just down the road from the Valley's most powerful venture capital firms. By virtue of its location, this Starbucks was a waiting room, a clubhouse, and a makeshift office for a host of would-be Silicon Valley entrepreneurs. But for most of them, it was mainly a waiting room.

Hardwick wanted the chance to ask Nate a few questions face to face. When they were communicating by email, Hardwick always got the sense that he was getting about a tenth of Nate's multitasking focus.

When Nate strode through the door in a rumpled hoodie with a backpack slung over his shoulder, he had an energized, off-kilter look in his eye that Hardwick recognized. It was the look of someone who'd been up studying for an exam for several nights straight. That look was usually soon followed by a crash and two days in a hibernating stupor.

"Hardwick." Nate smiled, and for a moment he looked like the mellow, charming guy Hardwick had known since they were eight. Hardwick rose, and Nate clapped him on the back.

"Good to see you, man," Hardwick said. "I apologize for my little ransom tactic, but I just wanted to see if you still really existed. I was starting to think that I was just chatting with some sort of Natebot."

"Sorry if I've been a little absent lately."

"It's okay. I was just a little concerned about you. It's usually not like you to be so hyperintense."

Nate dropped his backpack and sat down. "Well, maybe that's been part of my problem."

"How are things with Ali? I hate seeing you guys broken up."

"I don't think we're going to be getting back together. I really care about her, and I always will, but she just came along at the wrong time in my life."

"Because you're obsessed with this start-up of yours, right?"

"Yeah, pretty much."

"So how's that going? Still stealthy?"

"Still stealthy, but definitely making strides. I've never been this excited about a project—"

"But you still can't tell me what it is?"

"You should have seen the NDA that the investors made me sign."

"Judging from the pieces I've worked on, like the customer portal, it's clearly an e-commerce site."

"I'm not going to play twenty questions with you."

Hardwick leaned forward, putting his elbows on the table and trying to catch Nate squarely in the eye. "So you're telling me that there's nothing illegal going on here?"

Nate gazed steadily back at him. "This is legit. Totally. I wouldn't have gotten you involved otherwise."

"Okay, then." Hardwick reached into his right pants pocket, removed a flash drive, and slid it across the table. "Here's the coding for the customer-service portal. It's pretty immaculate, if I do say so myself."

In his left pants pocket, Hardwick had a duplicate copy of the coding, with one critical difference. The coding that Hardwick had chosen to supply to Nate contained his "calling card." As was his practice when he was proud of his work, Hardwick had included his cell phone number in the code.

He had decided that if Nate told him that the project he was working on was legit, then he could use it as an advertisement for his coding skills. If the site was as big time as Nate represented, then during beta testing the coding would be examined by people who knew what they were doing. They would recognize that he did quality work and hopefully give him a call directly for a new assignment. He'd embedded his cell number in the HTML code of the page that Nate's website would produce in response to malware, which was likely to be deployed when a potential investor was testing the site.

Hardwick had held himself apart from the Silicon Valley hustle for too long. Nate wasn't the only one who had aspirations.

This was his way of putting himself in the game.

25

Lisa gazed out the window of the Boeing 777 as it descended on an overcast day into Keflavik International Airport. The clouds reflected off the surface of the Atlantic, hazy smudges that resembled submerged islands. Reykjavík was a small city by US standards, not so very far removed from its fishing-village origins. The city didn't sprawl into an endless expanse of suburbs and strip malls; not far beyond the city limits, the glacial landscape resumed.

She was anxious to get to the data center that housed Kyte's servers. There was no doubt in her mind that the server held the key to the case. Every day that Kyte continued to operate was another day in which overdoses and addictions were delivered in innocuous brown-paper packages to thousands of doorsteps by US mail. Of course, if she were honest with herself, she had to concede that career advancement was also part of her motivation.

Lisa was accompanied on the trip by Jeff Sakey, a DEA agent who seemed primarily interested in ensuring, on behalf of his boss, Constantine, that his agency shared in the glory if the trip proved productive. He had slept through most of the flight, and they had only exchanged a few dozen words so far.

When they had claimed their bags, Sakey said, "The hotel is just a few miles from the airport. Taxi should have us there in fifteen minutes."

"It's only noon here. There's still time to meet with the Icelandic prosecutor and the attaché from the US embassy and make it to the data center before it closes."

"Okay," Sakey said, "but we'll be cutting it close. You know the data center *isn't* near the airport. It's out in the country somewhere. On some fjord or glacier or whatnot."

"Yeah, I know. But I want to take custody of that server as soon as possible. We should be able to make it before the administrators leave for the day."

"You think that server isn't going to be there tomorrow?"

"I know the data center agreed to cooperate with us, but I'm not sure what they would do if Mal suddenly decided to shut down the account and delete the data. Their primary allegiance is to their customers."

"And you really think that could happen at any time?"

"Yes, I do. If I were Mal, I'd be paranoid as hell."

Sakey ran a hand through his hair. "Don't you get jet lagged?"

"I won't be able to sleep until we have control of that server. But if you'd rather check in to the hotel, I'm happy to do this on my own."

Sakey sighed. "No, let's go."

They met with the Icelandic prosecutor and the US embassy attaché at an immaculate brick courthouse in the center of the city, where the letters rogatory were accepted without any objection or complication. A couple of officers from the Reykjavík police force were dispatched to ensure cooperation at the data center.

Lisa and Sakey drove their rental car along the waterfront, a view of Mount Esja looming on the other side of Faxa Bay, and past the red-roofed houses in the center of town. The small city had a distinctively Scandinavian vibe, with its spotless sidewalks, clapboard Lutheran churches, and neat storefronts selling wool sweaters and puffin dolls.

Soon they were outside the city and passing through a desolate landscape dotted with patches of snow. Beyond Reykjavík, the countryside seemed raw and unfinished, a geological work in progress. Lisa drove down a long, straight two-lane road that ran through a vast expanse of lichen-covered rocks, without a tree in sight. The vast emptiness made the mountains in the distance ahead of them even more elemental and imposing, like an illustration from a Tolkien book.

The unnervingly lunar vistas got Sakey talking to fill the silence. "I know two things about Iceland," he said. "There's Björk. And this is where Fischer played Spassky for the world chess championship. That was '72. You probably weren't even alive then."

"I'm familiar," Lisa said.

"Yeah, but if you didn't live through it, you can't imagine what a big deal it was. Height of the Cold War. Everyone was playing chess, reading chess books. Can you imagine that? Now they're all playing video games."

"Yeah, these kids today . . ."

"You mock, but it really was a different time. People were genuinely afraid of the Russians. Fischer was like our superhero, taking on this archvillain Spassky. Too bad he turned out to be nuts."

"If you read your comics carefully, I think you'd know that most superheroes are not right in the head."

Sakey considered that statement and nodded.

After about an hour of driving through the craggy, desolate landscape, they topped the crest of a hill and were greeted by an incongruous sight—the brilliantly lit, gleaming expanse of the Thor Data Center, which consisted of a series of modular, hangarlike buildings fronted by a glowing glass cube that was the foyer.

What sort of data center had a foyer that looked like a luxury car showroom?

The facility seemed startlingly out of place, like a spaceship touched down on an otherwise lifeless planet. The sensor-activated glass front doors gasped open as Lisa and Sakey approached, hurrying to get out of the cold. Darkness had fallen, and the temperature seemed to be plummeting by the minute.

Somehow, the Icelandic cops had managed to get there first, as evidenced by the patrol car parked out front.

On the other side of the doors, Lisa and Sakey found themselves standing in a vast and brilliantly lit atrium with polished gray-marble floors. The reception desk looked tiny on the opposite side of the lobby. A blonde woman in a skirt and suit jacket advanced toward them with purposeful strides.

"I'm Benna Gunnarsdottir, managing director of the facility," she said, extending a hand to Lisa. "I was expecting you tomorrow, until the officers arrived." She nodded at the two uniformed police, both with full beards, who looked like a couple of bored Vikings who would rather be pillaging. "Your plane arrived today, right?"

"That's right," Lisa said. "We wanted to take possession of the server as soon as possible."

Gunnarsdottir glanced at her watch. "Well, we don't have a lot of time before we're closed for public access."

"We're not the public," Lisa reminded her.

"Yes, right. Well, we'd better get going. This way."

She turned and walked away, black, flat-soled sneakers squeaking on the marble floor, no doubt required due to electrical hazards.

As they waited for guest passes to be issued at the reception desk, Lisa could see that it was reinforced against explosives. If she were a corporate customer, she wasn't sure if such measures would have been reassuring or concerning.

With passes in hand, Gunnarsdottir led them through a battery of high-tech security measures, including biometric scanners, keypads requiring passwords, and multiple mantraps where the door had to lock behind visitors before they could pass through the next one.

Eventually, they stepped through a final set of secure doors and entered the server farm, a gridiron-size room filled with six-foot-high metal cases housing servers containing terabytes of data.

They continued walking through room after frigid room filled with blinking blue lights and brushed chrome. "Here in Iceland, we're uniquely suited to provide data-center services," Gunnarsdottir said, launching into a practiced sales pitch, seemingly out of force of habit. Lisa was fine with that as long as it didn't slow her down.

"Iceland is equidistant between the US and Europe, which maximizes transmission speeds. We're also economical because we use Iceland's natural geothermal energy to power the centers, as well as natural cooling."

"Natural cooling—what does that mean?" Sakey asked.

"Cooling down the servers is one of the most expensive aspects of operating a data center like this," Gunnarsdottir said. "Since Iceland's temperatures are frigid much of the year, our walls are open to let the air in, serving as a natural—and inexpensive—coolant. Of course, we use a series of filters to remove all impurities before the air reaches the servers." She pointed to the floor they were walking on, which was filled with holes. "That's for cooling."

"Impressive," Sakey said. Lisa turned to stare at him, trying to tell if he was flirting with the facility director.

Gunnarsdottir finally stopped before a brushed-chrome cabinet about the size of a large refrigerator that looked like every other cabinet they had passed.

"Well, this is it," she said.

"We'll want the entire server imaged as of today."

"There's no need for that."

"Why not?"

Gunnarsdottir opened up the cabinet to reveal the servers with their flashing blue lights. She grabbed a brushed-steel handle and removed a blade server, a sleek gray box about the size of a doormat. "This particular account comes with a mirror drive. It's all right here. We maintain a duplicate of everything as part of our disaster recovery plan."

Gunnarsdottir handed the blade drive to Lisa.

"So I'm holding Kyte in my hand right now."

"That's right. The past six months of activity, anyway."

"I'd like to take the mirror drive with us tonight."

"Not a problem."

"Can you install another mirror drive to capture activity going forward?"

"Yes, we'll replace the mirror blade tonight."

"Wait a second," Sakey said. "Why don't we take both copies of the server and shut down Kyte?"

"Because he's going to have backup servers," Lisa said as she examined the drive. "There might be a momentary disruption, but CaptainMal would quickly have the site back up and running—and then he would know how close we are."

"And this way we can keep going back to get new copies of the latest site activity."

"Right." Lisa nodded.

Lisa turned to the facility director. "Would it be possible to connect the drive here so that we can take a quick look to see what we have?"

"Certainly. One of our support staff can set you up."

Gunnarsdottir hailed a tech on their way back to the entrance and deposited Lisa and Sakey in a small office where the contents of Kyte's server were displayed on a desktop computer. The two Icelandic police officers returned to their patrol car for the drive back to Reykjavík, their task completed.

Lisa opened the server file and saw—nothing but a jumble of meaningless words, numbers, and symbols.

She looked up at Gunnarsdottir in alarm. "It's encrypted. I can't see a thing."

"Oh, right," she said, handing her a slip of paper. "You need this password. Sorry."

Lisa typed in the password, and an instant later there before her on the screen was the coding for the site, as well as a record of thousands of transactions dating back six months. The earliest iterations of Kyte had been stored on another server.

"This is it," Lisa said. "This is Kyte. Right here in front of us."

While the server did not reveal the contents of transactions or mailing addresses, it did show shipment dates, dollar amounts, and IP addresses. And she knew that somewhere in the jumble of numbers and coding would be the signs pointing to Mal himself and the IP address that he was using to run his criminal empire.

She couldn't stop scrolling through the server's data. Sakey finally coughed, and she noticed that he was peering over her shoulder.

"You can't review six months of transaction activity tonight. Time to get back to Reykjavík."

"He's in here," Lisa said.

"Well, maybe so, but he'll still be in there tomorrow."

Reluctantly, Lisa disconnected the server and placed it in a large canvas bag. They walked back out through the Thor center's gleaming foyer into the absolute darkness of the Icelandic hinterland.

As the lights of Reykjavík began to show on the horizon, Lisa felt that the city wasn't the only thing that was coming into view.

CaptainMal's days were numbered.

26

After combing the Kyte website for clues to the identity of its operator, Guillermo Torres had developed a grudging admiration for his adversary. The coding wasn't immaculate, but it was good enough, and it seemed to be improving. More importantly, the site's founder had managed not to succumb to the obvious security lapses that were endemic to legitimate e-commerce sites.

That was why Guillermo was stunned when he noticed the calling card.

It was clearly a phone number, plainly embedded in the code without any masking or hashing. A 650 area code—Silicon Valley.

At first he assumed that it must be a prank.

Or maybe Kyte's operator had cribbed the code from another source without realizing that it contained the phone number.

It was not unusual for coders to leave a signature of some sort to claim credit for a sweet segment of coding. But it was rare for the calling card to include such a direct link to the coder's identity and rarer still on an illegal Dark Web site. Usually a coder or hacker would just leave their online alias as a signature, mainly to claim credit among friends.

As soon as his initial surprise wore off, Guillermo began wishing that he had never found the number. He had been enlisted by the Zeta cartel, also known as La Compañia, to hack the Kyte website, and he was afraid that the Zetas would torture and kill whomever the phone number belonged to, even if they had no genuine connection to the site.

Given that this calling card was so astoundingly obvious, he couldn't reasonably claim that he hadn't seen it. The Zetas had hired other hackers to test Kyte's digital defenses. They would find the number if he didn't, and they would know if he turned a blind eye. He had no choice but to tell his boss.

If the Zetas believed that he had held out on them, he would be swiftly and gruesomely dead. It was well known that the Zetas didn't just kill you—they made a production out of it.

Guillermo had never thought he would end up working for the Zetas. Of course, working for the Zetas in Nuevo Laredo was a little like working for General Motors in Detroit. Since many of his classmates from school and kids from his neighborhood were now Zeta soldiers, the notion was not inherently improbable. Guillermo had just never considered himself a particularly promising recruit. After all, the Zs were known as a paramilitary force that was originally formed by commandos from the Mexican Army who'd deserted to serve as the enforcement arm of the Gulf Cartel. Skinny and asthmatic, Guillermo was no one's idea of a soldier.

But as the cartel's criminal enterprise grew more sophisticated and diversified, they needed more than just dead-eyed *sicarios*. They needed hackers and cybersecurity consultants to play offense and defense. The Zs might be brutal killers, but they weren't stupid. They knew where the money was in the digital economy, and they set about recruiting the talent necessary to steal it.

When the moment came, it wasn't really like being offered employment but more like being drafted into military service. A Zeta soldier had shown up in the classroom of Professor Pablo Gutierrez, his computer science professor at the Universidad Autónoma de Tamaulipas, and asked him who his best students were. Guillermo knew that was how it had happened because his professor had called him after the encounter, giving him the opportunity to run.

"I'm sorry to have given them your name, Guillermo, but if I hadn't provided names, they would have killed me." The professor maintained a scrupulously formal facade in the classroom, but now he'd sounded unnervingly unguarded, barely containing the quaver in his voice.

"I understand, Professor. You had no choice. I am, after all, your best student."

"This is not a game, Guillermo. You know what the Zetas are. I know that you're smart enough to take this opportunity to run."

"If I disappear, won't they think you tipped me off?"

"There's no need to worry about that. Someone will be foolish enough to take the work."

Guillermo had left town for a few days, but he wasn't prepared to take up permanent residence across the border. He had a girlfriend and family in Nuevo Laredo, and he wasn't about to leave his entire life behind. He had hoped that when he returned a week later, the Zetas would have filled their quota and moved on.

But they had not moved on. A Zeta lieutenant had told his father that if Guillermo didn't report when he returned, they would be back at the end of the month. The threat was implicit.

So Guillermo had gone to work for the Zetas in a dusty, nearly vacant office park on the outskirts of Nuevo Laredo. When he'd been working toward his degree in computer science, he had dreamed of a job at one of the tech giants across the border. He had watched movies like *The Social Network* and seen what those gleaming, kindergarten-bright workplaces looked like—tech heaven. He had even spoken with a couple of his peers who had landed jobs in Silicon Valley. They told stories of Bring Your Dog to Work Day and kitchens that had a wall dispensing every kind of candy and breakfast cereal imaginable.

The Zetas did not place much emphasis on creating a fun workplace.

His coworkers were scattered around the open office. There were plenty of empty desks left over from the brokerage firm that had formerly occupied the space. Each worker was an island, maintaining a distance of at least a couple of desks from their coworkers. No one wanted to seem distracted or be seen socializing.

The room was largely silent except for the patter of fingers on keyboards, which sounded at times to him like the chittering of locusts descending. They didn't talk much about their assignments, but he had gleaned that some of them were engaged in garden-variety cybercrime, such as phishing scams and hacking retailer credit card terminals that hadn't yet adopted the chip-and-PIN system.

Several more were, like him, dedicated to hacking and bringing down Kyte. He knew this because one colleague had taped to his cubicle a crude drawing of a kite in red-ballpoint flames, crashing.

Ever since he had been recruited by the Zetas, Guillermo had feared that eventually he would be faced with a choice that could lead to someone's death. When he found the phone number buried in Kyte's code, he knew that moment had arrived.

Guillermo stood up from his monitor and went to his supervisor, a midlevel thug who tried to act like he was overseeing their work even though he had absolutely no coding experience. When he wasn't drinking beer and watching soccer, Javier studied them through the glass window of his office, situated along one wall of the open main room where Guillermo and the other computer science conscripts worked.

"I found something," Guillermo said.

"Yeah?" Javier kept one eye on the penalty kick on the TV. "What's that?"

"A phone number."

At this, Javier turned to give Guillermo his full attention. "Whose phone number?"

"I don't know, but I think it belongs to someone who works for Kyte. It was embedded in the code. Like a signature."

"Now why the fuck would somebody do that?"

"I don't know. It's some sort of mistake. They probably didn't know what they were doing."

"Let's have it."

Guillermo produced a scrap of paper with the phone number scrawled in pen.

He handed it over to Javier, who examined it and then laid it flat on the desk in front of him, pressing the wrinkles out of the paper with a forefinger.

"Aren't you going to dial it?" Guillermo asked.

"You do that, they're just going to run," Javier replied. "You think we don't know how to trace a phone number through the police, get an address?"

"He may have nothing to do with Kyte. It could be some code that they lifted from someplace else."

Javier took a swig of beer, eyeing him over the raised bottle. "What makes you think it's a he?"

"I just assumed," Guillermo said. "I mean, look around. We're all dudes here. Except for Mariela, of course." He nodded to the lone female in the workplace, one of his former classmates from the university.

"You're thinking too much about this, *pendejo*." He held up the scrap of paper. "You aren't feeling sorry for this poor bastard, are you?"

Guillermo knew he needed to be very careful now. "No."

"And you would never call this number yourself, would you, Guillermo? To warn him?"

"No."

"That's good. Because when we find him, he's going to talk. He's going to tell us everything. They always do. And we'll know if you make that call."

"I wouldn't do that," Guillermo said, even though he had been considering it.

"You need to stop asking questions now, *pendejo*. Get back to work. You don't want to know the answers, anyway."

When Guillermo returned to his desk, the sound of fingers on keyboards seemed to grow louder, the infestation of insects becoming an all-consuming plague. He put in his earbuds and cranked up his music, Café Tacvba, but it failed to drown out the sound in his head.

27

January 16

The message from FrostyImp, one of Kyte's programming experts, was alarming and to the point: Servers crashed. Kyte under attack from hackers. Demanding $10K in bitcoin to go away. I'm working the problem. Instructions?

Nate typed out a response. Shut everything down. Secure the site and restore operation as soon as possible.

Pay the ransom?

No. I have to board a plane in two hours. If this isn't resolved by then, I'm going to be trusting you to get this under control.

Nate was packing a bag in his new apartment share on Capp Street in San Francisco's South of Market district, another Craigslist hookup. His destination was the Caribbean island of Dominica, but lying on the beach and snorkeling were not his primary objectives. He planned to spend two weeks in Dominica to qualify for the country's economic-citizenship program, which allowed foreign nationals to obtain a second citizenship and passport for a fee of $75,000 and completion of some paperwork.

After the scare with the Homeland Security agents at his door, Nate had decided that it was time to finalize an escape plan—and execute it. A Commonwealth of Dominica passport provided visa-free or visa-on-arrival access to more than 115 countries around the world, including the entire European Union, which made it the perfect accessory for any fugitive's well-stocked go bag. As an added bonus, he could sock away millions of dollars of his Kyte profits in Dominica's banks without attracting the attention of the IRS or the FBI.

Nate was on his laptop until the boarding gate was about to close for his flight out of SFO, but FrostyImp was still battling the hackers, and Kyte was still down. He didn't dare use in-flight Wi-Fi to access his Kyte account because he couldn't risk a fellow passenger viewing his screen, so he would have to endure an agonizing radio silence during his cross-country flight to his first connection in Atlanta. Nate wished that he had chartered a private jet for the trip to Dominica (he certainly could afford it), but he knew that was another move that might attract unwanted attention.

Adding to his stress, DPain's followers in Kyte's health-and-wellness forum were starting to notice his absence and ask about him. Nate had responded using a generic Kyte administrator ID, stating that DPain appeared to be taking a break, but that the drug advice provided in the forum would resume shortly. He didn't want CaptainMal making any statements about DPain in public forums; they might serve as evidence against him later. He needed to recruit a new moderator for the drug-advice forum so that the users would move on and forget about DPain.

As soon as the plane landed for his ninety-minute layover in Atlanta, Nate found a quiet corner of the terminal and booted up his laptop to get a damage assessment.

FrostyImp reported that Kyte was back in operation, but the hackers appeared to be maintaining a persistent presence on Kyte's servers. The attackers had upped their demand to $25,000, and if they didn't get paid in the next two hours, they promised to resume their attacks on the site.

I can't let my pride get in the way here. Pay the $25K, Nate messaged FrostyImp. *We're losing more than that in sales every hour the site is down. Let's see if they keep their word.*

Aye, Captain. Talk to you when you get to Puerto Rico.

Nate was never able to sleep on planes, so he was bleary and stiff when he disembarked for his next layover in the San Juan airport. Fortunately, FrostyImp had paid the hackers, and the truce appeared to be holding. They'd taken their ransom and seemed to have moved on to other targets. Kyte was back to business as usual.

Maybe he would actually be able to enjoy his sojourn in Dominica. Operating Kyte was an exercise in 24-7 stress, and he could really use a little time to depressurize and get himself centered.

The last bumpy leg of his trip was on a Windward Islands Airways puddle jumper that sounded like it was powered by twin lawn mower engines. The small plane traced a lazy circle over the capital city of Roseau with its candy-colored tile rooftops, rocky shoreline, and impossibly blue water.

Walking across the tarmac to claim his bag, Nate was exhausted and couldn't wait to lie down on the crisp white sheets in his luxurious room at the Fort Young Hotel. Nate felt like he could sleep for days, sleep like he hadn't slept in over a year. Maybe it was the enervating, endless series of flights. Maybe it was the heat and the humid, fragrant air.

But probably it was the fact that he was finally in a country from which he could not be extradited.

———

Analyzing the data from Kyte's Reykjavík server provided a wealth of information about CaptainMal, but nothing that led directly to his identity or location. After reading hundreds of hours' worth of chats and messages between Mal and his various admins, as well as his libertarian philosophizing in the Kyte forums, Lisa felt that if she ever met him, she could practically finish his sentences for him.

In her darkened office, Lisa pored over Mal's most recent private messages on the Icelandic server. One brief exchange caught her attention.

CAPTMAL: Ever been to Dominica?

FROSTYIMP: Don't even know where that is. Why?

CAPTMAL: Just heard a friend talking about it. Sounded nice.

That was innocuous enough, but then Lisa noticed another exchange later the same day between Mal and the manager of one of his shipping hubs.

BRAZOS: I should be able to have all of the backlogged product shipped by Saturday. You want to have that conversation about shifting inventory then?

CAPTMAL: Nah, I'm taking a little downtime. Reboot.

BRAZOS: Someplace nice?

CAPTMAL: Yea, white sands, blue water, rum drinks.

BRAZOS: Sounds nice. You'll bring your laptop, right?

CAPTMAL: But of course.

BRAZOS: Ok. Had me worried there for a minute.

Another relatively innocuous conversation, but taken together with the earlier one, it was easy to draw the conclusion that CaptainMal was going to be visiting Dominica. After rereading the exchange, she noticed that Mal actually said that he was *taking* a little downtime, rather than *going to take*. He might already be on the island.

So why would CaptainMal visit Dominica? She did a little online research. Aruba had better beaches. In fact, Dominica's shoreline was fairly rocky. San Juan and Curacao had better nightlife. Virgin Gorda and Barbados had greater natural beauty. Then Lisa found a website of the Commonwealth of Dominica outlining its Citizenship by Investment Programme, and she understood how the tiny island had learned to compensate for its shortcomings and why it had attracted CaptainMal's interest. He was laying out his escape plan. Perhaps he sensed how close the FBI was to apprehending him.

Lisa immediately called SAC Gilbertson, and after convincing her that she wasn't just trying to scam a tropical vacation on the FBI's dime, she booked a flight and began packing her bag. Her boss was going to request that the Commonwealth of Dominica provide the FBI with a list of the American citizens who were currently applying for a passport.

In the US, Mal could be almost anywhere. In Dominica, he would almost certainly be in the capital of Roseau, which had a population of about sixteen thousand. And within that small town, she figured that a recently minted millionaire would want to stay at the city's most luxurious resort, Fort Young Hotel. So she was looking for a rich young American staying at the Fort Young Hotel, who would be visiting the Commonwealth of Dominica's Citizenship by Investment Unit in the Ministry of Finance on Kennedy Avenue. Within those parameters, Lisa suddenly liked her odds of coming face to face with the elusive CaptainMal.

During his two-week stay in Dominica, Nate studiously completed and submitted the paperwork necessary to obtain his passport, which included tracking down some old friends for character testimonials and having a medical exam. He suspected that the two-week residency requirement was primarily designed to bolster the local tourist economy. Nate also spent more time than he would have liked occupying a private corner of a dingy internet café near the hotel, where he continued to manage his criminal empire. He didn't trust his hotel's Wi-Fi, which was an attractive target for hackers looking to exploit wealthy tourists and businesspeople.

But after he had met his business obligations, Nate still had plenty of time on his hands to explore the pleasures of the so-called Nature Island. He hiked with a guided group to Boiling Lake in Morne Trois Pitons National Park, the world's second-largest hot springs. The strenuous trek had Nate gasping a bit as they climbed along trails hacked from the rain forest and then down into the volcano's crater. Spending so many hours in front of the keyboard had taken a toll on his conditioning. As he stood on an outcropping of rock over the boiling gray-green lake, watching the steam rise and fade against the brilliant greens of the jagged mountains, Nate marveled at how much his life had changed in the past year.

In that moment, Nate decided that he wanted to live in Dominica, or someplace like it, where he was safer and could feel more at ease. He would regret leaving his family and friends behind, but they could always visit him. It was time to begin putting his escape plan into motion. He resolved that after he got back to the States, he'd take two weeks to wrap up some loose ends with Kyte, and then he'd take his new Dominica passport and find a nice quiet beach somewhere in the world where CaptainMal could devote his full attention to making Kyte a global force. Perhaps someday, when attitudes had changed and more drugs were legalized for recreational use, he might even be able to return to the US and finally be recognized for what he had accomplished.

As Nate turned to hike back up out of the volcano's crater, he was full of plans for a new life.

Two weeks, and he would be free.

Back at the hotel, Nate made a few friends among the locals. He spent his time kicking around a soccer ball on the narrow beach, smoking weed, and drinking rum and Cokes late into the night with Gerard and Romy, a tatted-up, sunbaked couple who worked in the hotel restaurant. Spending time with the young couple made him wish that he and Ali were still together and that she were with him on the trip. He knew she would have loved the island, but she would not have liked how much time he spent in the internet café.

Nate eventually tired of being a third wheel to Gerard and Romy, and he grew a bit lonely. As he gazed out at the blue Caribbean, Pointe Michel, and Champagne Beach from his hotel room balcony, Nate realized that he missed his people, the Kyte community. And he had an inspiration for how to reconnect: the first Kyte movie night.

The following evening at eight p.m. eastern standard time, Nate and thousands of other Kyte customers from around the globe all simultaneously pressed play on a download of the movie *V for Vendetta*, which he had posted to a Kyte forum the day before. Naturally, the download was pirated. CaptainMal had informed the Kyte faithful that the movie was about a fascist police state and a masked vigilante, known only as V, who fought against the government's oppression. Some of the lines spoken by V sounded exactly like things that Lorenz Mayrhofer might say—or CaptainMal.

Nate didn't feel lonely anymore as he lay on the white sheets of his canopy bed, watching a movie in a room lit only by his laptop screen, with thousands of his sort-of friends. The curtains billowed with the ocean breeze. The forum that he had opened up on Kyte for the event was blowing up with comments and wisecracks as the movie progressed, some expounding libertarian theory, others just silly snark. The scene in which Natalie Portman's head was shaved was especially popular.

Nate was experiencing that peculiarly modern feeling of being both alone and with his tribe in the very same moment. As much as he loved his IRL (in real life) friends, Nate realized that this was the communion that he had really missed. Kyte seemed to be on its way to becoming a movement. Nate had never thought of himself as someone who could change people like that, but it appeared that maybe he was.

———

Lisa spent her days in Dominica holding down a table in a café across the street from the Ministry of Finance office that administered the economic-citizenship program. She drank sodas and picked at platters of barbecue, plantains, and rice, her eyes always on the entrance to the office building, waiting for a young American who might be CaptainMal. The sinewy woman who was the proprietor remained indulgent as long as she kept the money and tips flowing. Her task would have been much simpler if Dominica had produced a list of the US citizens currently applying for passports, but the government had not yet responded to the FBI's request.

At night, she hung around the pool and bar of the Fort Young Hotel, looking for likely young Americans. She fended off a lot of unwanted advances and allowed a lot of Americans to buy her drinks, but she encountered no one who fit her profile. As a week and a half slipped away, the only thing she had to show for her expensive, government-funded road trip was a painful sunburn.

With three days left in her stay in Dominica, Lisa lay on a beach chair at sunset, watching a three-on-three soccer game being played nearby on Champagne Beach. She was wearing a floppy white sun hat, an extralong San Francisco Giants T-shirt over a bathing suit, and large sunglasses and was completely slathered in 45 SPF sunblock. The Caribbean sun somehow managed to penetrate these defenses and scorch her pale skin.

After an errant kick, the soccer ball arced toward her chair and landed in the sand near her feet. She sat up and picked it up as a tall, good-looking, shirtless guy in his midtwenties and wearing bright-green board shorts jogged toward her.

She tossed him the ball.

He studied her for a moment, perhaps deciding whether or not to flirt, but Lisa was so effectively shielded against the sun that she probably appeared to him as nothing more than a hat, sunglasses, and a few inches of sunblock-shiny ankle.

"Thanks," he said. The voice was American, no discernible regional accent. In response to her T-shirt, he added, "Go Giants."

He started to turn away to return to the game.

"You from the Bay Area?" she asked.

"Nah. Texas. Austin."

She had no reason to doubt him, but she thought the response took a fraction too long.

"What brings you here?" she asked.

"Just vacation. Hanging out. You?"

"Business," she said.

"Well, have a good one," he said, already jogging back to the game. "Thanks again," he said over his shoulder.

She briefly considered whether the Texan could be her CaptainMal, but she had no real reason to make him a suspect. As far as she knew, he wasn't staying at the hotel. He appeared to be well entrenched with the locals, judging by the soccer game. If he was to be believed, he wasn't even from the Bay Area. Simply being a young American in Dominica wasn't enough by itself to arouse suspicion—there were plenty of those.

Before she left the beach to take up her now-regular seat at the hotel bar, she had an idea. Kyte was such a demanding business that she figured CaptainMal was probably still staying in regular contact, overseeing his crew of admins and distributors. He wouldn't want to use hotel Wi-Fi to access Kyte because that wasn't anonymous enough. CaptainMal would probably set up shop in an internet café.

When she had first arrived on the island, she had canvassed all of the internet cafés in Roseau, looking for someone who fit CaptainMal's profile. She decided to try again by asking the hotel's concierge for a list of nearby internet cafés. Only one piqued her interest.

"Well, it's more of a café café than an internet café, but they offer free Wi-Fi, and they're right around the corner."

Lisa arrived at Zebo's the next morning as it was opening up. The manager, who looked to be about eighteen, was brewing a pot of coffee, and the place was still empty.

"I'm looking for someone who's probably been here a lot in the last week or so. A guy. American."

"Yeah, we get a lot of Americans in here," he said as the coffee began to sputter and hiss. "That doesn't narrow it down."

"He probably would have been here a lot. With a laptop. Working really intensely. Very careful not to let anyone see what he was working on."

The manager started nodding. "Oh yeah. I think I know who you're looking for. He always sits in that corner with his back to the wall. He's here for three, four hours at a time. Drinks green tea."

"Was he here yesterday?"

"No, he hasn't been in the past two days."

"Do you have his name or credit card information?"

"We respect the privacy of our customers, lady."

"This is a US law enforcement matter. I'm with the FBI." She flashed her badge.

"I'm not sure you have jurisdiction here. But he just paid cash for his tea and used the Wi-Fi. We wouldn't have anything on him."

"What did he look like?"

"I don't know. Brown hair. Tall, six two, maybe."

Lisa was now fairly certain she knew where this was headed.

"Do you remember what he wore?"

"He'd come in without a shirt a lot, like he was coming straight from the beach."

"What else? Swimsuit? Shorts?"

"Yeah, board shorts."

"What color?"

"Green. Bright green."

The young man she had tossed a soccer ball to on Champagne Beach, in all likelihood, had been CaptainMal.

Lisa spent most of her remaining two days in Dominica staking out Zebo's without any luck. She assumed that CaptainMal must have left the island.

But her trip to Dominica had not been a complete waste of tax dollars. She was fairly certain that she now knew what CaptainMal looked like.

28

After a meeting of the interagency task force at the DOJ's San Francisco office, Sanjay Srinivasan of the IRS invited Lisa to compare notes on the investigation over coffee. She was still jet lagged from her flight back from Dominica, and she was waiting for Homeland Security to produce the passport photos of every American who had flown there in the past few weeks.

Lisa grew impatient waiting in line for her cup.

"I saw that," Sanjay said. Today, he was wearing a dark trim-cut suit with a pocket square.

"What?"

"The eye roll. You think this is totally pretentious, don't you? So San Francisco." At Philz Coffee, each cup was individually brewed from a dizzying assortment of exotic roasts.

"I didn't say that, but it is a little leisurely." She suppressed a small smile. "I guess it's what you would call . . . artisanal."

"Ouch," Sanjay said, pantomiming removal of an arrow from his chest.

When their coffees finally arrived, they sat down at a sidewalk table, watching the Financial District's lawyers and tech workers hurry past. "I asked for some nonfat milk for my coffee, and I swear the barista didn't want to give it to me."

Sanjay nodded. "Oh yeah, they're coffee snobs here. They think you can't fully appreciate the subtleties of the flavor if you add milk or sweetener. I once mocked too," he added. "But now I'm mainlining Aromatic Arabica, and I mock no more." He pursed his lips and took a sip from his cup, steam rising into his face. "So kudos to you on cracking the case, finding the server."

"Don't congratulate me just yet. We still don't have Mal. We've identified a port with an encrypted connection used by Kyte admins, and some of the IP addresses linked to it are not masked by Tor because we're behind Kyte's firewall. There's a backup server in Atlanta, a VPN in Czechoslovakia, and a hosting proxy server in London." Lisa still wasn't ready to share the lead that had taken her to Dominica.

"You think Mal is here in the Bay Area?"

"Probably. The times when he's online suggest that he's in this time zone. Also, when we studied the Reykjavík server, we noticed that CaptainMal had erased one of the Kyte servers. However, he failed to delete the IP address of the place where he logged in to do the erasing—Ground Zero coffee shop in the Mission."

"That's not that far from here. For all we know, he could be sitting at the next table."

"Yeah, I really think CaptainMal is somewhere here in San Francisco."

"Sounds like progress. I've also found something, but I'm not sure what to do with it, and I'm not sure it amounts to anything."

"I'm all ears. But why aren't you taking it to the full task force?"

"Because I know that you have access to the Kyte server data, and you might be able to make a connection with what I have—and I don't think you would cut me and the IRS out of the loop. I can tell that those guys from Homeland and DEA don't take me seriously. I don't think they even wanted to include the IRS in the task force."

Lisa took a sip of the strong, bitter brew. "Sure. Of course we have a deal. What do you have?"

Sanjay reached into his messenger bag, produced a short stack of screenshot printouts, and laid them on the table, using his smartphone as a paperweight against the breeze.

"So—what am I looking at?"

"These are screen grabs of Reddit posts trying to stir up interest in the very first iteration of Kyte, all dated about fourteen months ago. I figure that if we concentrate on the very earliest posts involving Kyte, we're more likely to find CaptainMal or someone in the inner circle."

"I think I saw some of these, too, but they didn't get me anywhere. Have you been able to identify anyone?"

"Maybe, but I don't know how significant it is, and that's where I need your help. The person could be just some random Kyte associate. Or maybe an early fan of the site."

Sanjay pulled several pages from the stack and handed them to Lisa. "Take a look at these, and tell me if anything jumps out at you."

Lisa examined the screen grabs, which at first seemed completely unremarkable. They consisted of an anonymous poster encouraging the denizens of a druggy message board to check out the prices for psilocybin mushrooms at Kyte. This was a mark of Kyte's earliest days because promotion had quickly become unnecessary once the site had connected with its drug-seeking audience.

"Being an early fan of Kyte isn't a crime."

"Keep looking," Sanjay said.

Then she saw the handle that the online barker was using—Yeti.

Yeti was the name of a server that was at the center of much of Kyte's admin activity, but it was always associated with a Tor-masked IP address. The person currently using the Yeti server was clearly one of the key administrators of Kyte, perhaps even CaptainMal himself. Lisa knew this because she could see the complete access rights that Yeti enjoyed on the Kyte systems, as well as the level of online activity—which sometimes bordered on twenty-four hours a day.

"Lisa," Sanjay said. "You're not saying anything. You've seen something, haven't you?"

"I've seen the name Yeti before."

"Okay. Don't keep me in suspense." He was already beginning to smile in anticipation of the answer.

"Yeti is also the name of a server associated with CaptainMal. That server handles lots of Kyte's most sensitive internal communications. It's either linked to Mal or at least to one of the site's key admins."

"Yes!" Sanjay said. He raised a hand for a celebratory high five, but Lisa left him hanging.

"What's wrong?"

"I don't have an IP address for Yeti."

Sanjay awkwardly lowered his hand and then stroked his chin. "Well, I don't have an IP address, either, but how about a name? Would a name do?"

"I thought you just had the name Yeti."

"Well, Yeti slipped up just once in one of his very earliest posts." Sanjay pulled a sheet from the bottom of the stack, where he had clearly been saving it.

He pointed to a post that read, If you're looking for safe, quality drugs, reasonable prices and reliable delivery, then the new Dark Web site Kyte is going to rock your world. Check it out if you're looking to get high as a—well, you know. The post was attributed to Yeti.

"So?" Lisa said.

"Note the time—5:05 p.m." Sanjay produced another sheet, which looked like an exact duplicate of the one she had just reviewed but was time-stamped 5:02.

Sanjay was grinning now. "He originally posted under a username that looks like a real name. Three minutes later, he deleted the message and reposted it using the name Yeti. He forgot that he was using his real Reddit account and that the username would show."

"That's very interesting." She scanned the email address, her pulse quickening when she saw the original username, NateFallon.

Sanjay sipped his coffee. "Isn't it, though? In those very early days, Yeti had a momentary lapse when he wasn't quite careful enough. He probably thought no one was paying attention to him and his little site yet."

Lisa nodded. "He realized his mistake almost immediately and reposted using the Yeti username, but it was too late."

"Because the internet never forgets," Sanjay said. "We subpoenaed Reddit's audit logs for the posts and found this."

"This is good," Lisa said. "Of course, Nate Fallon could turn out to be just another alias. This could still just be another dead end."

"But then why would he cover his tracks so quickly when he put it out there?"

"I was thinking the same thing. Just trying not to get my hopes up," Lisa said. "But I may have a way to confirm that Nate Fallon is the name we're looking for."

She told Sanjay about her trip to Dominica, her likely encounter with CaptainMal, and the passport information that would be arriving soon from Homeland.

When she was done, Sanjay said, "It feels like we're getting close."

"Maybe," Lisa said, gazing at the passing throng on Market Street. "All I know is Nate Fallon better have that escape plan of his finalized, because we're coming for him."

29

When the black van pulled up alongside him, Brian Hardwick was walking to his apartment on Hawthorne Avenue in Palo Alto. He had just completed office hours as a teaching assistant for a Stanford computer science class. It was a clear, crisp day, and he was looking forward to a beer and watching the Stanford-Cal game on TV. He was thinking about a disagreement that he'd had with a disorientingly attractive red-haired student, trying to parse whether the friction between them was a form of flirting.

If it had been flirting, he felt guilty for not shutting it down more quickly. Things were getting serious with his girlfriend, Janine, and he was definitely not interested. In that moment, Hardwick's situational awareness, never terribly acute in the best of circumstances, had been nil.

He looked up at the telephone wire overhead and the starlings arranged along it like notes on a musical staff. The birds suddenly scattered at the sound of a car pulling up close at hand.

When the side door of the van slid open for him, he knew he was in grave trouble, but by then it was too late.

Two men came up behind him, grabbed his arms, and shoved him inside the van. He bumped his knee hard on the runner and fell forward into the cabin, unable to protect his face.

The next few moments were a blinding blur of pain and confusion, his senses a video set to fast-forward.

Hardwick barely had time to be scared before he found himself upright and staring at three young, hard-looking Latinos as the van squealed away. They were all carrying guns. Two were sitting on the bench seat in front of him, and the other was next to him, jabbing a muzzle into his ribs.

"If you want . . . my wallet . . . you can have it." He had trouble getting more than a few words out at a time because there didn't seem to be any breath in his lungs.

He made a show of reaching slowly for his back pocket. "Let me get it for you."

The man sitting next to him said, "We don't want your money, *güero*. And keep your hands in front of you, or I'm going to start breaking your fingers."

He couldn't have been more than twenty-one, but a puckered scar on his neck made him seem older. So did the fact that a sizable notch had been crudely carved out of the top of his left ear. He appeared to be the leader of the war party.

Hardwick struggled to calm himself. He remembered an exercise that Janine had taught him from her yoga class. He drew in long, jagged breaths through his nose and let them out through his mouth. He repeated the exercise until he felt that he could speak without quavering and gasping.

"Okay, then," Hardwick finally said. "You don't want money. That's good because I don't have any. Who do you think you've got here, anyway?"

"Brian Hardwick."

"Well, okay, you're right about that. That is my name. But what do you think I've done? Whatever this is, it's some kind of huge mistake. Are you sure you've got the right Brian Hardwick?"

"There's no mistake, and you're gonna need to shut the fuck up until we get you across the border."

"What border? You're taking me to Mexico?"

"Don't be stupid, *güero*. Yes, the Mexican border."

"I don't have much money in my wallet, but if you pull over at an ATM, I can withdraw everything I've got in my account. No problem."

"I think I just told you that we don't want your money."

"What do you want, then? Just tell me, man, because I'll give it to you."

His seatmate, the human cutting board, just fixed him with a nickel-plated stare.

For the first minutes following his abduction, Hardwick had been able to entertain the notion that this was a robbery. That was bad, but it might have been survivable.

He now realized that whatever was happening was something far worse.

The panic started rising again as his eyes seemed to move involuntarily from the faces of the men to the guns to the neck scar to the hacked ear and back again. He needed to stop staring at them.

Hardwick desperately flashed through the events of the past few days, searching for the incident that might have brought him to this pass. These people clearly knew who he was and wanted something specific from him, but they weren't authorized to tell him what it was. That questioning was probably being reserved for their boss after they smuggled him across the border.

Had he done anything out of the ordinary recently?

Hardwick stared out the window of the van, watching people pass on the sidewalk, people who were not in danger, people who were just living their lives as part of the world that he had belonged to only minutes earlier. They had no idea of the terrified person behind the van's tinted glass who was wishing he could rejoin them.

After a while, the realization struck him like a small object dropped from a great height. Only after the impact did he realize how long it had been accelerating toward him.

He had included his phone number in the coding that he had provided to Nate for his website. That had to be what had brought these thugs to his doorstep.

Before he had handed over the coding, he had asked Nate if there was anything about his business that was not legit.

Nate had told him that there was nothing illegal about what he was doing.

His friend had lied to his face.

Hardwick could have handed over a version of the code that did not include his phone number, but he had trusted Nate to tell him the truth.

Nate's lie was most likely going to get him killed.

30

Nate felt guilty about leaving Hardwick in the dark about Kyte, particularly now that he was making so many valuable contributions as a coder. He had decided that he wanted to tell Hardwick everything because, even though he could be a harsh critic (one of the drawbacks of having a working moral compass), he also would fully appreciate what Nate had accomplished. Nate also felt he owed Hardwick an explanation before he fled the country and disappeared off the grid.

Hardwick would have made a great partner—a Page to his Brin, a Woz to his Jobs. And it would have relieved some of Nate's stress to share this adventure with Hardwick, would have made him a little less isolated and paranoid.

But in many ways, Nate was doing Hardwick a favor by not telling him that he was CaptainMal. Hardwick still had plausible deniability.

Still, once Nate left town, he couldn't be certain that Hardwick wouldn't put two and two together, connecting him with Kyte. He'd decided to cut him loose now—at least then, if a prosecutor ever tried to get to Nate through him, Hardwick's only knowledge would be outdated.

As Nate approached the apartment building on Hawthorne Avenue, he noticed that Hardwick's window was dark. That was uncharacteristic. He wasn't a partier and was usually home by ten.

Maybe he was napping. On the front steps, Nate pushed the button for Hardwick's apartment several times, but no one buzzed him up.

He'd have to catch him another time—he'd be in town for at least another week and a half. But as he walked away across the brown, drought-sparse lawn, his foot kicked something that responded with a metallic rattle. He saw that it was a set of keys and picked them up.

There was a tiny flame-haired troll doll attached to the keychain. These were Hardwick's keys, including the key to his apartment and his beater car.

Nate knew immediately that something was wrong. If Hardwick had lost his keys, he would have recognized it within minutes—and certainly by the time he attempted to either open the door to his apartment or start his car. The keys were in the middle of the yard and would have been plainly visible in daylight.

Maybe Janine had picked him up? Or maybe Hardwick had gone for a walk? Nate dialed his friend's cell phone but got no response.

He looked up and down the silent tree-lined street, but he didn't see anything out of the ordinary, just the lighted windows of apartments behind which Stanford students were studying for the next day's classes.

Using Hardwick's keys to enter the building, he climbed the stairs to the third floor landing and tried various keys from the keychain until he found the one that worked. If it turned out that Hardwick was in there, Nate would simply say that he was there to return the lost keys.

But the air in the apartment was stale, and the place felt abandoned. Nate felt increasingly uneasy. He was careful not to touch anything, including the light switches, because if something had happened to Hardwick, as he feared, then he didn't want to become a suspect.

He moved like a specter through the apartment, looking for any notes or other clues to Hardwick's whereabouts. He found nothing useful.

Nate considered waiting in the apartment for Hardwick's return but thought better of it. For all he knew, someone might be watching the building.

He exited the apartment and quietly shut the door so that the neighbors wouldn't hear. Although he had very little evidence, he couldn't escape the ominous feeling that something bad had happened to Hardwick—and that he was the cause.

31

Lisa had a name now—Nate Fallon—and it didn't take long to pick up his trail. When more information arrived from Homeland Security about US citizens who had recently traveled to Dominica and she saw the passport photo of Nathan Fallon, she knew she had the right guy. It was the face of the young man she had encountered on the beach in Dominica.

She located his LinkedIn account, which was rife with libertarian rhetoric. He had favorited YouTube videos from the Mayrhofer Institute. She also got a surprising hit when she searched law enforcement databases. A Nathan Fallon had been questioned about purchasing a batch of fake passports on the Dark Web. Buying fake passports would be something that CaptainMal might do to prepare an exit strategy if he felt that the Feebs, as he called them, were getting too close.

The DHS agents had had no idea who they were speaking with. They hadn't taken Fallon into custody because he'd denied that he had placed the order, and their mission was to bring down professional passport forgers, not the forgers' customers. But they'd noted that he seemed to be using an alias with his housemates and had placed his name on a DHS watch list. In the end, they had simply confiscated the forged passports and given Fallon stern federal-agent glares. Apparently Fallon had even made a point of mentioning Kyte to them, explaining to them how the Dark Web site made it easy to purchase illicit goods like the fake passports.

The cocky bastard.

Lisa could even imagine the barely perceptible eye roll that he must have given them as he said it.

CaptainMal had been right in front of them, and they had allowed him to just walk away. She wouldn't make that mistake when her chance came.

Finally, a small but telling detail removed any possibility of doubt. In his Facebook and Reddit posts, Fallon always spelled the word *yeah* as *yea*. As in, "Yea, these shrooms are Grade AA, choice, and trippy AF."

Lisa had read hundreds of messages from CaptainMal taken from the Reykjavík server, and they always displayed that very same spelling tic—*yea* rather than *yeah*.

Nate Fallon was CaptainMal.

Lisa drove out to the house in the Richmond district where Fallon had received the package of fraudulent passports. She assumed that he had probably been spooked by the DHS agents and had moved out, but there was at least a possibility that he was still living at the address. If Fallon showed, she would be able to spot him based on the photos used in the passports and others that she had assembled from the DMV, the Stanford student directory, and social media. The face that stared out at her from the various photos was no one's idea of a criminal kingpin.

Fallon looked young (which he was—twenty-five, according to his legitimate driver's license), with straight brown hair that fell carelessly over his forehead. He was handsome, with a long face, a strong chin, and deep-set brown eyes.

He looked like some sort of sensitive graduate student, the type who was vegan and backpacked across Thailand. Maybe she was reading too much into the photo, but he seemed to have that aura of invulnerability that good-looking people had when they were young.

She had pulled the phone number for the address, and after staking out the house for an hour from a parked car down the street, she dialed it.

"Hello?" A male voice.

"Is this Nate Fallon?"

"No. This is Dave. Who are you looking for?"

"Nate Fallon."

"You must have the wrong number."

"I think he was living with you about a month ago. He was visited by federal agents, I believe . . ."

"Oh, you must mean Shane. Shane Price."

"Okay. Is Shane there?"

"Who am I speaking with?"

"Another one of those agents. FBI. So I recommend that you tell me what you know."

"He moved out the same day that those agents came by. He's done something, hasn't he?"

"Do you know where he moved to?"

"No, he just picked up his bag and walked out. Didn't even leave a forwarding address. Of course, he only received one piece of mail the whole time he was here. When someone is living off the grid like that, it usually means they're hiding from something, right?"

Even though Fallon wasn't there, Lisa still wanted to take a look and see what she could learn from his former housemate. "I'm just down the street, so I'm going to come over. We can finish this conversation in person."

"Cool."

Lisa knocked on the door and was greeted by a pudgy, shirtless young man in board shorts.

"Dave, I presume?"

"Indeed. Aren't you supposed to show me your badge?"

She produced the badge, and Dave leaned forward to study it admiringly. Lisa snapped it shut, and he flinched.

"I just wanted to see it, you know. I expected it to be shinier."

"Did he leave anything behind?"

"Just some groceries. A lot of that MorningStar Farms fake-meat stuff. No one here ate that shit but him. Soy will kill you. It's still in the refrigerator, if you want to see it."

"That won't be necessary." A pause. "Oh, and Dave?"

"Yes, Agent Tanchik?"

"That thing you're doing here?" She made a rotating motion with her finger to indicate the light banter between them.

"Yeah? That's just Dave being Dave, Agent Tanchik."

"Well, stop it, Dave."

"So you called first because you thought he might still be here, right? What would have happened then? I'll bet you would have used that," he said, nodding at the Glock she wore in a holster on her waist.

Lisa sighed and forged ahead. "What was Shane like?"

"Just a chill dude. A good housemate. Always did his chores. Liked to get high." Dave paused. "Of course, I don't condone that sort of thing."

"Of course."

"He was just a fun guy to have around the house."

"Did he seem preoccupied at all? Like he was hiding something?"

Dave rubbed his belly contemplatively. "Well, he was on his laptop a lot, working on some project. We thought he was a day trader. I'd often see the light on in his room when I got up in the middle of the night. I'd hear those keys clicking."

"Did you ever ask him what he was working on?"

"Yeah. He said it was his physics graduate thesis. He said he was taking a break from school but was still working on it. I know he told me what it was about, but as soon as he started talking about neutrinos and alpha particles, I zoned out. I'm a right brainer."

"Anything else that you can tell me about him? Anything at all unusual?"

"He was a libertarian. When he was high, sometimes he would go off on these riffs about this Austrian economist."

"Mayrhofer."

"That's right. You a libertarian too?"

"No."

"Was Shane some sort of libertarian terrorist? Is that a thing?"

"I'd like to take a look at his room."

"Sure."

Dave led the way to a back bedroom of the house that was largely empty aside from a tired-looking futon in the center of the floor. There were no signs of Fallon other than some crumpled PowerBar wrappers and a CD case on the crate next to the futon that served as a night table.

Lisa picked up the CD case by the edges. Ben Harper's *Fight for Your Mind*.

"See?" Dave said. "What'd I tell you? A chill dude."

32

February 4

Brian Hardwick's abductors had driven all night, heading south on the I-5, and had barely spoken during the entire trip. They took turns driving, while the ones in the passenger cabin slept. Hardwick had watched carefully for an opportunity to grab a gun, but it had not presented itself. That was probably just as well, because his chances of getting the better of four armed cartel soldiers were slim to infinitesimal.

For the first couple of hours after his abduction, Hardwick's thoughts had raced as he'd tried to deny the reality of his predicament. His mind couldn't accept what was happening to him, like a body rejecting a mismatched transplant organ. After twenty-six years of quiet upper-middle-class life spent largely studying and teaching mathematics, he did not belong here in the midst of these violent young men.

This was the stuff of Tarantino films. This was not his life.

He had done nothing to deserve this.

It should not be happening.

But it was.

By the time they hit Bakersfield, Hardwick had managed to achieve some semblance of calm. It was the only way that he was going to solve this problem, if it was solvable. In order to get to that place, he had to accept that it was likely he was going to die. Once he stopped struggling against the unjustness and finality of his predicament, the panic subsided a bit, and he was able to focus his thoughts.

Hardwick's adrenaline spiked when the van came to a sudden stop. He was dragged out of the van into bright sunshine behind a dying strip mall somewhere in the greater San Diego area. One of the thugs shoved him toward a Prius that was parked nearby, its trunk popped and yawning like a hungry mouth.

It was a perfect, balmy day in SoCal. He stood before the open trunk, looking around and letting the sun warm his face, no longer taking a moment for granted.

"A Prius?" Hardwick kept trying to get some kind of human response out of his captors.

"Not my ride," the scarred man said, stubbing out the glimmer of a smile. During the long drive, Hardwick had learned that his name was Javier. "Get in."

"We're going across the border now?"

"Yes."

"Aren't you worried that a border guard is going to inspect the trunk?"

"That's not going to happen. We've made sure of that. But if you try to make noise or signal anyone, you're dead."

"If you were allowed to kill me, I think you would have done it by now."

"Shut up, *güero*."

Hardwick just stared at the trunk, not sure how to get in with his hands bound by a zip tie without losing his balance. Hardwick glanced around, hoping to spot a CCTV camera that might capture the scene. There were cameras, but they were all off their axes, lenses smashed. His abductors probably knew this spot and had disabled the cameras themselves. They were relaxed about their work. Like it was something they had done before.

"I think I need my hands for that," Hardwick said.

"Don't make us lift you," Javier said.

Hardwick leaned forward and put his upper torso inside the trunk, and then he felt his legs launch as he was shoved inside like a carpet.

The trunk lid slammed shut, extinguishing the sun. The darkness was relieved only by the pale-red light that filtered through the taillight. Even if he managed to get his hands out of the zip ties, he saw that the emergency lever that opened the trunk from the inside had been disabled.

The Prius began moving with an electric hum. Fortunately, the trunk had vents that were connected to the car's air-conditioning, so he wouldn't die of heatstroke.

Hardwick tried to stay awake in case some sort of opportunity presented itself—maybe the chance to cry out and be heard. But after a while, the heat, the monotonous sound of wheels on pavement, the postadrenaline crash, and the need to blot out the reality of his circumstance got the better of him, and he fell asleep. He was awakened by the pop of the trunk and dazzling sunlight.

Two of the men reached in and hauled him out, scraping his back on the bumper and roughly depositing him on sticky, hot asphalt.

One of the men cut the zip ties that bound his hands as he looked around, blinking hard. He must already be across the border. They were in some sort of compound ringed by a high chain-link fence topped with barbed wire. The heat coming off the pavement was blistering.

"Come on," Javier said. "Boss wants to meet you."

He was led to a large building that looked like an airplane hangar. A bay door was open, and they stepped through it into the shade. When his eyes adjusted, he saw they were approaching a Mercedes sedan idling in the middle of the hangar.

When they were in front of the car, a door to the back seat opened, and a tall man with a gray-flecked beard and a mustache emerged.

"Brian," the man said in a tone that was not unkind, "welcome to Mexico. How was your trip?"

"Unconsented."

The man nodded and smiled sympathetically. "Sorry about that. But we need to talk."

"You could have called."

"You've got some *huevos* on you. But you make any more jokes, and I'm gonna think you're disrespecting me. I want to know about your relationship to Kyte."

"Kyte?"

The man glanced down at his expensive-looking oxblood loafers. "Is that how it's going to be, Brian? Really?"

"I'm serious—what is Kyte?"

The man shook his head gently. "Okay, we can do it this way for now. Kyte is a Dark Web site that sells drugs—the same kinds of drugs that my organization sells."

"So they're the competition."

"I wouldn't say competition, but they've become a nuisance."

"What makes you think I have anything to do with them?" Hardwick was pretty sure he already knew the answer to the question.

"Your phone number was contained in the website's coding. So there is clearly a connection. I just need to know what it is."

Hardwick wasn't about to send these brutal drug dealers after his friend Nate.

Even though Nate had used him and lied to him.

But if he wasn't going to give Nate up, then he wasn't sure what he could say to the man.

"I can see you're struggling with this," the man said. "Listen, I know that Kyte is not your operation. I can tell that just by looking at you. But you must have an idea about how your phone number ended up in that line of code."

Hardwick recognized that when lying, a slightly tweaked version of the truth was always more persuasive.

"Actually, I do. I'm a teaching assistant in the computer science program at Stanford, which means that I don't make much money. I've been supplementing my income by doing some coding for hire on the side through a Dark Web site. I got the impression that the site was selling my coding to third parties at a markup, and I wanted to cut out the middleman. I figured that the best way to do that was by embedding my phone number in the code. That way, whoever was ultimately buying my work could go directly to the source, and I could start getting paid retail rates instead of wholesale. The phone number was like my business card."

When Hardwick was done speaking, the man studied him for a long moment.

Finally, he said, "That's a pretty good story, Brian. Plausible. If you're a liar, you're a good one."

"It's plausible because it's true."

"Let's say it is for the moment. Did the person you were selling your coding to ever reveal his identity in any way? Did you get an indication of what city he was in? Habits, preferences?"

"No, the transaction was completely anonymous, and he never got chatty with me. It was strictly business."

"Was there ever anything to suggest that he was with Kyte?"

"No."

"How many times did you sell your work through that Dark Web site?"

Hardwick considered his answer carefully because he sensed that a trap was being laid. "I don't know. Not that many times. Two or three."

"Two or three, huh? That's often enough that you should remember the site pretty well." The man walked back to the car and leaned into the back seat.

He returned with a piece of paper and a pen. "Here. Tell me how to find that site. I'll take a URL or a name that I can search for. But you're going to have to get me there in one move. I'm not going to do a search and let you pick from the results."

"You have Tor?"

"Yes," he said, nodding toward the car. "My associate in there has a laptop with Tor."

The man produced a pen and a piece of paper and handed them to Hardwick.

Hardwick tried to keep his hands from shaking as he took the items. He placed the paper on the trunk of the Mercedes and racked his memory for a Dark Web coding exchange. He was certain that he had seen one when he was surfing, but he couldn't come up with the name.

The rising panic didn't help matters, but he simply could not remember a specific site.

Finally, he handed the paper and pen back to the man. "Sorry, I can't remember. My memory goes out the window when I'm nervous."

The man shook his head and rubbed the graying beard on his chin. "That is the wrong answer, my friend."

33

Nate searched for Hardwick at all of his regular haunts—the math-department teachers' lounge, his favorite carrel at the Terman Engineering Library, the coffee shop where he sometimes worked on his laptop—and his anxiety grew with each location that he ticked off the list.

Hardwick was a creature of habit, and his daily routine followed a familiar orbit. Since there were few options left, Nate dialed Hardwick's girlfriend, Janine, from the sidewalk outside the coffee shop. He had hoped that he wouldn't have to resort to calling Janine because he didn't want to alarm her if Hardwick wasn't with her.

"Hi, Janine, this is Nate."

"Hey, Nate. What's up?" There was already a note of concern in her voice.

"Nothing really. I was just trying to catch up with Hardwick. Thought he might be with you."

"No, I haven't seen him all day. He didn't return my texts this afternoon, but he does that sometimes if he's coding or grading exams. He turns off his ringer."

"I'm sure he's fine. Like you said, he's probably zoning out somewhere, oblivious to the world."

"Yeah, he does that." After a pause, "Do you know something that I don't?"

"No, no. I just need to run something by him. Hardwick usually answers his cell."

"How long have you two known each other?"

"Since middle school really."

"You might try calling him by his first name."

"Yeah, you're right. I guess it's a guy thing."

"The bromance that dare not speak its name."

"Something like that."

"You guys should really talk to each other about things other than computers, sports, and music. I'm getting a little tired of being the dude whisperer around here."

"But you're so good at it."

"I know, right?"

Nate was relieved that at least he had managed to ask his questions without causing Janine to be overly alarmed. "When he shows up, have him give me a call, okay?"

Nate made another lap of the Stanford campus, hitting all of Hardwick's haunts—some of them for the third time—but he was no longer very hopeful that he would find his friend. Walking around and around the campus just made him feel like he was doing something, and it also helped him organize his scattered thoughts.

By ten thirty p.m., there were fewer students on the sidewalks crisscrossing the campus, and Nate realized that he was better off at home with his cell phone on.

He drove back from Palo Alto to the Mission District and the spare room that he had found on Craigslist after fleeing Casa de Dave. He passed through the living room, where a retinue of beefy, tatted-up guys was sprawled over a couple of vinyl couches, absorbed in an ultraviolent Korean crime movie.

After drawing a couple of perfunctory nods from his new housemates, Nate retired to his room so that he could check up on Kyte.

Logging in as an admin, he saw that Kyte had racked up some impressive sales numbers for the day, continuing an upward trend over the past month. The site was an e-commerce juggernaut, with nearly $3 million in revenues per day.

Nate frowned when he saw that there were about two dozen unanswered messages to his Kyte admin account. He had been so preoccupied with Hardwick that he hadn't checked in a full day. Scrolling through the inbox, he saw

- an invitation to speak to a libertarian student association at Washington University in St. Louis (via pixelated webcam, of course)—he flagged for response;
- a flaming screed from a Kyte customer who felt that she had been shortchanged by a seller of LSD—opened without response;
- an interview request from a *Wired* reporter who had been after him for months—flagged for response; and
- a message from El Chingon.

Nate sat bolt upright on his bed and hesitated before opening the message. When he finally clicked on it, it simply included a link accompanied by a message:

THIS IS WHAT HAPPENS WHEN YOU IGNORE US.

Recognizing that the mysterious link could be a delivery system for malware, he moved the message to a secure, sandboxed server before clicking.

The link led to a Dark Web site that was hosting a grainy video feed. It took him a few moments to realize what he was seeing.

The image fractured with static and then resolved itself.

It was a bunkerlike room with gray, unpainted concrete walls and a concrete floor.

There was a male figure in the center of the frame.

Bound to a chair with duct tape.

With what looked like a rubber tire resting around his neck.

The man's head was down, and Nate couldn't make out the face, but there was something about the figure that filled him with dread.

He felt like some sort of sick voyeur watching a snuff film, but this tableau was clearly being staged for his benefit. He could not look away.

Suddenly, he knew why the image hit him so hard. It was the shirt.

The man was wearing a checked short-sleeve shirt that looked exactly like one of Hardwick's favorites.

Then the man's head rolled to one side, and he made eye contact with the lens, confirming what Nate had already realized.

It was Hardwick.

There was a sign scrawled in Magic Marker and clipped to Hardwick's shirt, which read:

CALL ME AT (555) 887-9252 BY MIDNIGHT OR YOUR FRIEND BURNS. THE TIRE IS SOAKED IN GASOLINE.

Nate leaped up, knocking over his chair, and let out some kind of guttural cry. He took a couple more steps backward, his eyes still locked on the computer as if it were an animal baring its teeth and coiling to attack.

He literally couldn't believe what he was seeing. Maybe his tired brain was manifesting his obsession with finding Hardwick, transposing his friend's image onto some Dark Web horror show. Maybe it was a flashback to the nightmares he'd been having since El Chingon had threatened him with necklacing.

Nate picked up the chair and sat down again before the computer. He moved with the deliberate pace of someone who had just suffered head trauma.

Some part of Nate wanted to prolong the moment when he could still deny to himself what he was seeing.

But it was Hardwick. He didn't appear to have been harmed, but his eyes looked wild and panicked. His affect and movements were all wrong and foreign, but there was no doubt that it was Hardwick.

Hardwick's lips were moving, but Nate couldn't make out what he was saying. He turned up the volume on the computer, but there was no audio. Maybe he was speaking to his captors, who were out of frame.

Or maybe Hardwick was talking to himself. Maybe he was drugged or in pain.

If he dialed the phone number, Nate was fairly certain that he would be speaking with a representative of the Zeta cartel. El Chingon or one of his colleagues would probably demand that Nate relinquish control of Kyte to the cartel in exchange for the life of his friend.

Then Nate remembered the words of the ultimatum and checked his watch.

Ten thirty.

He wasn't going to dial the number just yet. He still had an hour and a half to try to save his friend's life.

34

In Lisa's mind, it was indisputable: Nathan Fallon was the founder of Kyte. And after pulling all available public—and some not-so-public—records, she knew a great deal about his personal history. The one crucial thing that she didn't know was his location at that moment.

FBI agents were observing the Palo Alto house of Fallon's parents. They were also watching the house of his girlfriend, Allison Nunn, whom they had identified through Fallon's Facebook posts. She might be an ex-girlfriend at this point for all they knew.

If those Homeland Security agents hadn't blundered into the picture, confronting Fallon with the fake passports he had purchased, then he might still be living in that house in the Richmond District. Now he had probably moved on to some other under-the-radar house-sharing arrangement.

Lisa was in her apartment, bathed in the soft blue light of her computer. It was ten forty-five p.m. on a Wednesday night, and she was picking at a salad while randomly checking the Kyte message boards in a vain attempt to glean any information that would be helpful in tracking down Fallon/Mal. There had been no sign of him on the site for the past few days. Even the most wonky discussions of libertarian philosophy hadn't drawn him out.

Perhaps he had sensed that the net was closing on him and had walked away from Kyte at precisely the right moment. Maybe they would never catch CaptainMal, and he would become even more of an outlaw folk hero of the internet, the D. B. Cooper of cybercrime. Lisa could think of nothing that would piss her off more.

One of Lisa's messaging-app accounts pinged. It was the account reserved for her online persona Rodrigo, the genial independent drug dealer from Mexico.

Lisa nearly dropped her fork when she saw that the message was from CaptainMal.

CAPTMAL: Rodrigo, you there?

Lisa didn't want to seem too anxious, so she let a couple of minutes creep by before replying, in the meantime getting herself into character. Finally, she responded.

RODRIGO: Hey, Captain. Been a while. Que pasó?

CAPTMAL: I need your help.

RODRIGO: Ok.

CAPTMAL: Can I trust you?

RODRIGO: I thought we were past that.

CAPTMAL: You said you know people in the cartels.

RODRIGO: Yeah, I grew up with people who are deep in the Cali cartel and the Zetas. What's your point?

CAPTMAL: I'm being threatened by someone in one of the cartels, probably the Zetas. They have leverage on me and I don't know what to do.

RODRIGO: What sort of leverage?

CAPTMAL: That's not important right now.

That response suggested to Lisa that Fallon still didn't entirely trust Rodrigo. However, he was also clearly desperate.

RODRIGO: What do you want me to do?

CAPTMAL: I want you to help me figure out how to reach out to the Zetas. I want to know how I can open up a backchannel and give them something without getting myself killed.

RODRIGO: Let me get this straight. You're actually talking to the Zetas?

CAPTMAL: Yea. Their idea, not mine.

RODRIGO: Mierda.

CAPTMAL: Can you help me?

RODRIGO: What exactly are you trying to do?

CAPTMAL: I want to hand over my username and password as Kyte's system admin, along with all other admin rights. I need to call the Zetas by midnight tonight, and when I do, I want to be able to tell them that my plan is in motion.

RODRIGO: You're handing over Kyte to the cartel and walking away? They must really have something on you.

CAPTMAL: They do.

RODRIGO: What's the play?

CAPTMAL: I've put the usernames and passwords on an encrypted smartphone, but I have the ability to wipe it remotely. I'd like to put that phone in the hands of someone with the Zetas, someone local here in San Francisco. Someone who doesn't know what this is about. Someone who won't be lying in wait for me at the handoff.

RODRIGO: And you brick the phone unless they release the collateral they're holding?

CAPTMAL: That's right. First I give them the encryption keys, and they unlock the data, so that they can see what they're getting. Then they release the collateral while I observe them with the phone via a live video feed. When I know that the collateral is safe, I let them extract the usernames and passwords without wiping the device.

RODRIGO: This collateral is a person, isn't it?

CAPTMAL: That's not your concern. Can you help me?

Lisa saw an opportunity to finally pinpoint Fallon in the physical world. And possibly even a chance to strike a blow against the Zeta cartel. While some of her bosses at the bureau still didn't fully appreciate

Kyte's significance, everyone recognized the Zetas as a high-value law enforcement target. This had the potential to be a career-making bust.

RODRIGO: Maybe. I know someone in San Francisco who has connections to the Zetas. Someone on the fringes, like me.

CAPTMAL: I don't have much time. I need the information in about a half hour. RODRIGO: Jesus, Captain! You really think I can put something together that fast?

CAPTMAL: I don't have any choice. And I just can't imagine any scenario where I make this exchange directly and walk away.

RODRIGO: Let me make a call. I'll get back to you.

CAPTMAL: Don't leave me hanging. Someone's life depends on it. And—this is very important—you can't tell the cartel contact what this is about or who he will be meeting. If you do that, he'll speak to the people who are threatening me, and I'll be done.

RODRIGO: I understand. I'll just tell him I've got a business proposition for him. A limited time offer.

Lisa immediately picked up her cell phone and dialed her special agent in charge, who would have access to the bureau's latest intelligence on the Zeta cartel and its members. She told Gilbertson that she was going to have an opportunity to pass along an item, a smartphone, that would probably be taken directly to one of the leaders of the Zeta cartel in Mexico. Lisa needed to know that there was a reliable channel for handing over the phone to the cartel that would not tip them off that law enforcement was involved. She would also need a team formed to figure out how to follow that phone to its destination.

She had to call her boss at home—never a good career move—but Gilbertson was excited about the prospect of orchestrating a strike against the cartel and was going to immediately start assembling a team. Lisa went back online with Fallon.

Lisa did not tell her boss that she also had an opportunity to locate Fallon. That was going to need to happen too fast to involve backup, and she felt that she could handle that part of the operation on her own. Lisa could tell from Fallon's urgency that if the meeting didn't happen immediately, there might not be another opportunity. There was no time to wait for backup.

RODRIGO: My man insists we do this face to face, and I have to be there with him. This could be dangerous for him too.

CAPTMAL: I didn't even know you were in San Francisco.

RODRIGO: Never said I wasn't.

CAPTMAL: You know this sounds like a setup.

RODRIGO: You're just going to have to trust me. Like last time.

Lisa waited as Fallon considered the proposition.

CAPTMAL: Ok. What's your contact's name?

RODRIGO: Arturo Garza.

Another long pause, and then:

CAPTMAL: Let's meet at Fog Town Diner. Do you know it?

"Gotcha," Lisa whispered.

If Fallon wasn't under some sort of terrible pressure, he never would have agreed to such a risky meet up.

RODRIGO: 24th Street in the Mission.

CAPTMAL: Get a booth near the window and be there with Garza.

RODRIGO: Got it.

CAPTMAL: Can you be there in twenty minutes?

Lisa checked her watch. It would be close.

RODRIGO: I'll do what I can. Might be a few minutes late.

CAPTMAL: I'm putting my life in your hands, and I don't even know you.

RODRIGO: It's a little late for trust issues, isn't it? Not after the last job I did for you. But it's your call. I've got other things I could be doing tonight.

CAPTMAL: Twenty minutes.

Lisa went down the hallway and knocked on the door of her neighbors Benny Alomar and Carlos Perez.

"Hey, girl," said Benny, sleepy eyed. The TV was playing low in the background, some cop show.

"I have a big favor to ask, but I'll buy you a late dinner."

"At this hour, it's going to have to be something good. What do you have in mind?"

"I just need you and Carlos to sit in a booth at the Fog Town Diner. It's FBI business . . . and there will be pie."

"Is this dangerous?"

"Maybe, but hopefully not. Probably not."

This gave Benny pause, but then he added, "You really need this, don't you?"

"I do."

"You'll have to tell Carlos what you just told me."

"Of course."

"Sure, I'm in. To be honest, you had me at pie."

Carlos appeared behind Benny in a robe and knee-length basketball shorts.

"Oh, hi, Lisa," Carlos said. "What's up?"

Benny opened the door wider. "Our little FBI agent wants to use us as bait in some kind of sting operation."

"But doesn't the bait get eaten?"

"Not this time," Benny said. "That's right, isn't it, Lisa?"

"Definitely," Lisa added a little too quickly.

"And there'll be pie," Benny said.

———

It took some hustle, but Lisa got Benny and Carlos installed in a booth at the diner with a few minutes to spare. The diner was a boxcar-size relic from the fifties with scuffed chrome counters and tattered red-leather stools. There were only three other people inside, and they all looked like they were hunkered down for the long haul.

She needed to lure Fallon out so that she could follow him back to his new residence and set up surveillance. And she needed a couple of people who might plausibly be taken for Rodrigo and his cartel contact.

It was vital that Fallon at least enter the diner, rather than scoping out the location from a distance and bolting.

Lisa set up across the street in a laundromat with a good sight line on the diner. A light rain began to fall, blurring the windows and obscuring her view.

She bought a pack of cigarettes at the bodega next door to give her a pretext for standing outside in the doorway. She hadn't smoked since college, but the char of the smoke and the bitter taste of tobacco brought back a surprisingly acute sense memory of junior year at Northwestern and her brief, failed stab at bohemian cool.

Lighting another cigarette, she nearly missed the tall, wiry figure crossing the street to the diner. As he pushed inside, the light over the front door illuminated his face for an instant.

It was Fallon.

Lisa watched him advance down the center aisle of the diner to the booth where Benny and Carlos were sitting. Fallon said something to them. Benny said something back. And then Carlos said something. She hoped that they were sticking to the script.

Fallon reached out and handed over an item, which Benny placed in his pocket.

Fallon stared at them for a moment, said something else, and then disappeared.

Lisa took a step or two into the street to get a better view, even though she risked exposing herself. Then she heard a metal door slam. Fallon was leaving through a rear exit.

She moved laterally down the street to gain a better vantage point and caught sight of Fallon power walking away.

Lisa gave Fallon a one-block lead, stubbed out her cigarette, and set out after him. She wasn't going to take him into custody that night, but she swore that he would not escape her again.

35

When he saw the video of Hardwick bound in the bunker/torture chamber of some Mexican drug cartel boss, Nate's first reactions were horror, revulsion, and resignation. He felt the free fall panic of knowing that every step that had led him to this moment had been a horrible mistake, and there was no going back—for him or his friend.

In that instant, he resolved to do anything in his power to save Hardwick. The Kyte experiment was over. Let the drug cartels have it. He was now officially and irrevocably out of his depth.

He couldn't imagine what Hardwick must be going through, and it was all his fault. It was Nate's hubris that had brought them to this pass.

How could he have ever thought that he could control a huge segment of the US drug market without ending up in jail or dead—or, worse still, getting his friends and associates jailed or killed?

As he approached the Fog Town Diner in a light rain, Nate could make out two male figures in a booth by the window. They were Latino and, he figured, must be Rodrigo and Arturo Garza, the Zeta cartel contact.

He fingered the smartphone in the pocket of his jacket, which he intended to deliver to the cartel contact. The encrypted phone contained instructions on how to assume control of the operations of Kyte, including admin credentials for all of the site's key functions—the keys to the kingdom. Once the data was decrypted, Kyte's future revenue stream could immediately be diverted into a Zeta bank account. Nate would still walk away with millions in Bitcoin. Enough to support him wherever he wanted to travel with his Dominican passport. And perhaps Hardwick would be allowed to live.

As he neared the front door, he slowed his pace a little and tried to catch his breath and settle his nerves. He was breathing hard.

Nate pushed inside as the waitress behind the counter looked up and stifled a yawn. He walked down the aisle that bisected the boxcar diner to the booth where the men were sitting.

He approached the two men and spoke to the one who was facing him.

"Rodrigo?"

The man looked up from his pie and coffee. "No, he's Rodrigo."

Nate stepped forward and turned to face the other man in the booth. He was in his late twenties, maybe early thirties, with a light stubble, thick black hair, heavy-lidded eyes, and a wary look.

Rodrigo, more or less how Nate had pictured him.

"Didn't think I'd ever meet you in person," Nate said.

"Me neither," Rodrigo said in a husky voice. "This is Arturo," he added, nodding to the other man in the booth.

Arturo nodded with a jerk. He looked tense.

"As much as I'd like to hang out, Captain," Rodrigo said, "we don't have time for that. Arturo doesn't feel safe here, and I'm not going to argue with him. You got the item?"

Nate handed over the cell phone to Arturo, who examined it.

"Has GPS been disabled on this?"

"Yes," Nate said.

"Show me," Arturo said, handing the phone back. Nate opened up "Settings" and "Location Services" on the phone and demonstrated that GPS had been turned off.

"You have to deliver this to one of the heads of the Zeta cartel, a man who goes by the name El Chingon online. He must get it within twenty-four hours. You can reach him at this phone number." He handed over a slip of paper. "No later. Can you do that?" Nate said.

"I will," Arturo said.

"Okay," Rodrigo said. "I think we're done here. You leave first."

Nate looked around at the patrons to see if anyone was casting a surreptitious eye their way. No one seemed to be paying any attention. Given his odd-sounding exchange with the two men, that in itself was suspicious. Surely someone had overheard their conversation in the cryptlike silence of the late-night diner.

"No one knows you're here, right?" Nate asked Arturo.

"That's right," Arturo said.

Nate looked out through the rain-streaked windows but could see nothing beyond the lights of the diner reflecting off the glass. He felt like an insect specimen in a glass case and wondered if Arturo's cartel friends would be waiting for him when he left the diner.

He gave a final nod to Rodrigo, then asked the waitress, "Is there an exit in the back?"

She pointed down the center aisle. "Next to the bathrooms. But that's not for—"

Nate was already halfway to the bathrooms, and then he was through the door and back in the cool, rainy night. He heard the waitress hailing him from behind the counter, telling him to stop, but her heart wasn't in it.

In his haste, he pushed too hard on the door, and it bounced off a metal railing before slamming shut behind him with a metallic clang. If someone was pursuing him, he hoped they hadn't heard the noise.

Nate hurried down the alley that ran beside the diner. When he emerged onto the next block, he paused and looked back the way he had come but saw no one trailing him.

He crossed the street and ducked into another alley, putting as much distance as possible between himself and the diner. He still felt certain that he was being followed, so he picked up a piece of rebar from an apartment building that was under construction, hid behind a dumpster in the alley, and waited.

A light rain continued to fall, bringing out the full fragrance of the dumpster, a heady brew of sour milk, rotting food, and, and—he stifled a retch—some sort of toxic paint thinner. Nate felt simultaneously foolish and frightened.

After a few endless minutes of crouching behind the dumpster, he was ready to emerge and head home when he heard a set of footsteps approaching on wet concrete. It was a lone person.

The wet footfalls stopped a couple of yards away, like the person was looking for something, or someone.

He heard a match strike.

Nate tightened his grip on the rebar until he could feel its stippled ridges imprinting on the palm of his hand. He crouched down, ready to spring.

More footsteps, and the person was beside the dumpster and in view.

It was a young woman, cupping her hand to protect her cigarette from the rain, dark, wet hair matted and framing a pale face, a purse slung over her shoulder. He didn't know what he had been expecting—someone who matched his idea of a cartel thug or a law enforcement officer. This woman in sneakers and a dark-blue hooded rain poncho didn't look like any sort of threat.

No matter how scared he had been a moment ago, there were some things that he still could not—would not—do. He slowly lowered the rebar, but it scraped slightly against the dumpster as he brought it down.

It wasn't a big noise, but it was enough to make the woman turn.

She stared at him, saw the rebar in his hand.

"I don't have any money," she said. She dropped her cigarette and raised both hands in front of her. "Well, I have a twenty and some small bills. I'm going to reach into my purse to get them, and I'm going to lay them down here and back away, okay?"

"I don't want your money," Nate said. "Who do you work for?"

She pointed back up the alley. "I wait tables at Beretta. It's a restaurant on Valencia."

"Yeah, I know Beretta. Why were you following me?"

"I was just going home after a shift. I wasn't following you. How was I even supposed to see you back there?"

"Are you alone?"

"Of course I'm alone. I wish I wasn't, believe me. I wish I had a big boyfriend with me who could beat the crap out of you." When she'd seen him lurking with the rebar in hand, he'd seen the electric spark of fear in her eyes. Now she just seemed annoyed.

If she was lying to him, she was doing a very persuasive job of it. He couldn't imagine that this person was affiliated with a cartel. However, she might be with the FBI or one of the many other agencies that were undoubtedly pursuing him. She didn't look like an FBI agent, but then again he didn't really know what one was supposed to look like. He doubted that they resembled the models and heartthrobs who portrayed them on TV.

There was something in her eyes, some glimmer of recognition that made him think twice about her. When someone was truly afraid, all their emotions and thoughts rose to the surface, transparent. But he got the sense that there were things going on beneath the surface with this woman, a counternarrative playing in her head. Was he imagining that?

But why would anyone send one young woman with no backup?

"Look, like I said, if you want money, I'll give you some money," she said. "I just need to get home and out of the rain, okay? I'm going to reach into my purse and take out my wallet now. Is that okay?" She saw that he was wavering, so she was trying to defuse the situation by talking.

"Stop," Nate said. "You might have a gun in there."

"Who do you think I am? I hate guns. How about if I set my purse down on the ground here, and you can take some bills out of my wallet?

Go ahead and take what you need, just don't take it all. That's my tip money, and I worked hard for it. And leave me the purse, okay? It's got my phone and my driver's license. My whole life's in there."

"Step away from the purse, and I'll take a look—at your ID."

Nate fished the woman's wallet out of her purse, searching for a law enforcement agency badge or ID. He found little more than a wad of sandwich shop coupons and a driver's license with the name Lisa Tanchik.

"Satisfied? Who do you think I am, anyway?"

Nate took one last long look at the unhappy, irritated, bedraggled young woman standing in the dank alley. The rain was picking up, and he could hear it pattering on her poncho. Her hair was now so wet that it was clinging flat and helmetlike to her cheeks.

"Sorry to have scared you—Lisa. I thought you were someone else." After a pause, he added, "I'm not a thief."

"Whatever you say," she said. "Can I pick up my purse now?"

"Yes, take it," he said. "Go."

He watched her walk quickly away down the alley and around the corner.

Once she was out of sight, he looked back in the direction from which he had come. He had stopped watching for pursuers while his attention was focused on the woman.

There was no movement on the street. If someone was actually following him, they were well concealed.

Nate checked his watch. Eleven thirty.

He began walking quickly, nearly running, back to the house he was sharing and his laptop. He didn't feel the rain anymore, even though it was falling harder. Even if he were being trailed, there was no time left for evasive measures.

Nate's sneakers slapped wetly on the sidewalk as he ran, his thoughts roiling.

Although Nate was using Garza as an intermediary, he was still going to have to call the cartel boss before midnight to assure him that he was cooperating and that the Zetas would soon have operational control of Kyte.

Nate looked up and saw that he was now in front of the apartment house where he lived with his housemates. The rain-slick street glistened dully under a streetlamp, and fog was rolling in, sliding malevolently, graspingly, over the rooftops and between the brick apartment buildings, like fingers closing into a fist.

He opened the front door and made his way to his room, ignoring the greetings of his house bros.

He sat down at his laptop and found that, at last, he knew what he had to do.

It was like a physics equation. Once you solved for X, there was only one answer.

36

When Lisa left Nate Fallon standing in the rain in that alley in the Mission, she felt his eyes on her back as she walked away. And as soon as she turned the corner onto Twenty-Second Street and was out of his sight, she breathed a sigh of relief that she'd carried her badge in her back pocket and worn her gun in an ankle holster tonight. Then she ducked into the doorway of a hardware store to resume her surveillance, more cautious this time.

There were only two ways out of the alley, and she figured Fallon was unlikely to return in the direction of the diner. She assumed that he would follow the same path that she had, emerging from the alley onto Twenty-Second Street. If he took some other route, then he would escape, and she didn't relish the thought of returning to scrutinizing Craigslist housing ads for leads on his new residence.

She stood in the doorway as a puddle of water formed at her feet. She ran her hands through her black hair, wringing some of the water out. But she kept her eyes fixed on the alleyway, willing Fallon to appear.

Clearly, her surveillance skills were a little rusty, or she never would have allowed him to get the drop on her like that. She wasn't an experienced field operative, but every agent had strengths and weaknesses in their game. Lisa's adeptness at lying was what made her online identities so convincing, and it was what had preserved her cover in the alley.

She'd let herself fall into a character, the annoyed, hardworking waitress at Beretta. The prior weekend, Lisa had been waited on by a young woman who had displayed the same pissed-off demeanor. Online, she had the luxury of time to thoroughly invent the backstories of her identities before trying one on. In that alley, she had been forced to create one on the spot, and it had played surprisingly well. It made her wonder if she might have the temperament for undercover work.

Clearly, Fallon hadn't recognized her from their brief encounter on the beach in Dominica because she had been cloaked in more UV-protective gear than a nuclear–power plant worker.

But now that she'd encountered him face to face, knowing who he was, she realized that she'd unconsciously bought in to some of his online mythmaking. She had expected someone bigger somehow, more charismatic—CaptainMal.

Aside from the fact that he was fairly good looking, he seemed just like any other twenty-something bro man that she might encounter at the supermarket. But looking him in the eye, she was sure of one thing.

Nate Fallon was scared. And he was scared of something more than the FBI and the host of law enforcement agencies that were pursuing him. He was afraid for the life of someone he cared about. Someone the cartel had kidnapped.

It couldn't be his sometimes-girlfriend Allison Nunn because she was under surveillance and accounted for.

So someone else that he was close to. Perhaps a Kyte associate? Maybe he really wasn't the site's sole system admin.

Just when she was starting to think Fallon must have taken another route, he emerged from the alley, looking up and down the street before taking a right on Capp Street.

Lisa set out after him, maintaining a cautious distance. It was far more difficult to trail someone who might recognize you, and even harder when they were on guard. She tried to remember every surveillance trick she had learned in her classes at Quantico, using the reflection off plateglass windows for an oblique view whenever possible.

The fog diffused the illumination from the streetlights, making everything lighter and whiter than it should have been—a day-for-night effect, like in the movies.

The strange, hazy brightness made Lisa feel exposed. So did the fact that almost no one was out on the sidewalks in the rain. If Fallon simply stopped in his tracks and turned, she was pretty sure that he would see her.

But Fallon didn't turn. At least not until he had run up the steps of a brick apartment building on Capp Street. From the top step, before placing his key in the lock, he turned to survey the street, but Lisa had seen that move coming and was safely concealed behind a parked SUV.

Once he was inside, Lisa relaxed. She had finally located the new apartment that Fallon was sharing. And this time there would be no surprise visits from DHS to scare him away.

37

It was ten minutes until midnight, and Nate was back in front of his laptop in his bedroom. He caught his reflection in the obsidian surface of the laptop screen, looking desperate and broken. He was still soaked from the rain, and his eyes were wild with panic.

Everyone had a line that they could not, or would not, cross. Nate's line was drawn at a place that he never could have imagined when he was a graduate student, and it had permitted him to order the hit on DPain. But he felt that now, finally, he had reached his limit. He could not allow his best friend to be gruesomely murdered.

But what if gaining control of Kyte wasn't enough for them? What more was he willing to do to save his friend?

Nate already felt sick turning over admin rights to Kyte, making it the latest, online branch of the Zetas' criminal empire. They would probably keep the CaptainMal identity to preserve the brand and as a sign of continuity, but they would subvert everything that Kyte and Mal had stood for. They would subvert everything that *he* had stood for. Kyte would cease to be a proving ground for libertarian ideals and a living example of how much could be accomplished outside the grasp of government. CaptainMal, if he continued to exist online, would become some sort of hollow shill for the cartel's product, the Ronald McDonald of methamphetamine and crack.

Kyte would become a ghost of its former self. The cartel would eliminate Nate with the brutal murder of his best friend. Under new cartel ownership, Kyte would bring its murderous, drug-fueled reign of terror to the internet. Say what you will about less-than-inspired late-eighties Apple products like the Macintosh Portable; they never caused anyone to be beheaded or burned alive. Under the cartel's stewardship—if Nate could call it that—Kyte would only be about selling drugs for profit and perpetrating any violence or moral hazard necessary to maintain those profits.

But if the cartel insisted on learning Nate's identity, wouldn't they be able to obtain it anyway? Wouldn't Hardwick give him up?

Nate could barely imagine the sort of punishment that the cartel was expertly administering to his friend. How would Nate hold up if it were him duct-taped to that chair? What would he be willing to do or say if someone flayed his skin? Pulled his fingernails? Connected jumper cables to his tender parts?

But Hardwick was different. Nate had always known him to do the loyal thing, even when it was difficult. And nothing was more difficult than this. But while Nate had never experienced it firsthand, he recognized that pain was the ultimate solvent. At some point it dissolved all personality, all resistance.

Nate couldn't even pretend to have the sort of physical courage that would allow him to stand up to that. He could think of a handful of small but telling incidents where he had been given the opportunity to display that sort of bravery. In each instance, he had remained frozen in place, unable or unwilling to put himself at risk. In the third grade, he could have stopped Craig Harper, a schoolyard bully who was pummeling a friend, but he had done nothing. In the fifth grade, he had stood paralyzed in his swimming trunks on the ledge of a primordial-looking sinkhole near Lake Tahoe. He simply hadn't been able to jump, no matter how many of his friends had made the leap, and no matter how much he had been taunted.

But Nate did have another kind of courage, and he thought that maybe it was just as honorable, just as valuable. He had always had the ability to commit to an idea and follow it through to realization. When other people gave up and lost focus, Nate doubled down. Anyone who had ever founded a new venture had to endure these fraught moments when the future of the enterprise was at stake.

Starting a business was like starting a war to carve out a bloody patch of turf in the marketplace. And no war could be fought without casualties.

Nate's thoughts were so disordered that it took him a moment to realize that the clock had nearly struck midnight and the video feed was live again. Hardwick looked worse than before. His right eye was purple and swollen shut, and his face was smeared with blood from what looked like knife gashes on his left cheek.

Hardwick's lips were moving rapidly, but again there was no audio. Nate couldn't tell if he was trying to speak to him or to his captors.

They were waiting for him to call.

Nate dialed the number, and his call was answered on the first ring.

"I was starting to think you weren't going to call." It was a calm male voice with a slight Mexican accent.

"Who is this?"

"You can call me Ernesto. Last time, I called myself El Chingon. You were very rude to me. Do you remember?"

"Yes. You're with the Zeta cartel."

"That's right. I hope you've learned some manners since then."

"Yes. You should let that man go."

"*That man*? That's no way to talk about your friend."

Nate couldn't be certain how much Hardwick had told them. It was probably best to start from a position of complete denial. "I don't know that guy," he said. "Who do you think he is to me, anyway?"

Nate wanted to see Ernesto's face, but the video only showed Hardwick, staring into the camera, his mouth moving with no soundtrack. Did he know that Nate was watching? Did he think that Nate had the power to save him?

"His phone number was included in the coding of your website."

"I don't know anything about that. We hired dozens of coders to help build out the site. They were all just part-time contractors."

"What do you mean *we*? You're the boss of Kyte. It's your operation."

"We're a collective. I'm just one of the admins."

"You're CaptainMal."

"No, that's a name that several of the admins use. There is no CaptainMal."

"That was the devil's best trick, wasn't it? Convincing the world that he doesn't exist."

Nate couldn't believe that a cartel boss was quoting *The Usual Suspects* to him.

"Are you saying that I'm the devil?"

"Maybe we both are. Think of this as one devil giving another devil his due. You know, I've read the forums on your site. Who else but a real person would spout all of that libertarian horseshit?"

"There's one of us who specializes in that. That's not me."

"I have to hand it to you. It's a brilliant pile of *mierda*. You actually managed to figure out a way to let those privileged, white *güeros* feel self-righteous about buying drugs." The man gave a genuine-sounding chuckle. "It's a beautiful con, my friend. I have to give you credit for that."

"You've got it wrong."

"Look at your friend here," he said, anger flaring. "Does it look to you like this is some fucking game?"

Throughout the conversation, Nate stared at the video feed of Hardwick taped to the chair, bruised and bloody. His lips were still moving.

"What did he say? Did he tell you that he was my friend?"

"He hasn't said shit. He says that he's just a contracted coder. He says you hired him off of some Dark Web coding site."

"You should believe him. He's telling the truth."

"No, he's lying. That's obvious. But your friend has got some balls on him. He's held out longer than some of the Sinaloan *putas* we did this to last week. And *they* were soldiers. I can already tell that you don't deserve that kind of loyalty."

"I'm prepared to make a deal with you, if you let that man live and release him."

"I'm listening."

"You want control of Kyte, right?"

"Yes."

"I've already taken steps to send you the usernames and passwords that will grant you full admin rights to Kyte. You'll be able to take over the operation and start diverting Kyte funds immediately."

"When will I receive this?"

"Soon. Within twenty-four hours."

"And how are you making the delivery?"

"Through a man named Arturo Garza."

The line was silent for a moment. "I don't think I know anyone by that name."

"He knows how to reach you."

"Does he work for you?"

"No, I know someone who knows him, and it's our understanding that he knows you, or at least how to reach you."

"And if you've already put that in motion, what do you have left to bargain with?"

"Two things. First, I have the ability to delete the contents of the phone remotely. When it's in your possession, I'll give you a password to unlock it. You will then be able to view the contents while I watch you on this video feed. Once you have confirmed that I've given you what you want, you release him. If you do not release him, I'll wipe the contents of the phone."

"And what's the other thing?"

"After you take over Kyte, you'll need help understanding how the site works. You'll want a smooth transition. I'm willing to help you do that by consulting with you. Anonymously."

Another silence. "And you're willing to do all of that to spare the life of a stranger."

"I know him," Nate said. "But he had nothing to do with Kyte. He never would have put his phone number in the code if he had known."

"Those terms are acceptable. But I must receive the phone within twenty-four hours, or there is no deal, and your friend dies."

"I understand."

"I'm glad you've stopped lying to me. It was insulting. Do you see your friend's eyes? He looks scared, doesn't he?"

Hardwick's left eye, the one that wasn't swollen shut, widened, and he turned his head to say something to his offscreen captor. Hardwick began shaking his head violently. He could see something coming that Nate couldn't.

"Do you know what I'm doing now? I'm about to use this knife to sever your friend's Achilles tendon." A hand came into the frame, wielding a slender silver knife that resembled a scalpel. "It hurts like a bitch, and after it's done, he won't walk. I'm doing this because you lied to me at the beginning of our call."

The hand disappeared from the frame, and a moment later Hardwick struggled against his restraints and screamed through the gag, his face hideously contorted.

Nate felt a wave of nausea.

"Of course," the cartel boss continued, "that assumes that he has someplace to walk *to*. That assumes he's going to leave that chair alive."

Now Ernesto's voice was coming from the phone and Nate's computer. The audio accompanying the video feed had been turned on. It was clear that Ernesto was in the room with Hardwick, but he was still offscreen. Nate had not gotten even a glimpse of his face.

"You know that your friend has already admitted that he knows you," Ernesto said to Hardwick, "but he says you didn't know the business he was involved in. That doesn't sound like something a good friend would do, does it?"

"I don't know him!" Hardwick shouted, sticking to his story. His voice was hoarse, probably from screaming. Maybe he was so addled from the pain that he didn't understand what Ernesto was telling him.

Then Hardwick added, more softly, "I never knew you."

Even in the moment that those words left Hardwick's mouth in that grainy video feed, Nate knew that he would be hearing them forever.

"You have twenty-four hours," Ernesto said.

The image of Hardwick disappeared, and the phone went dead.

38

After watching Fallon enter the apartment building on Capp Street, Lisa stood outside on the street to make sure this wasn't a temporary stop. There was no way that she was going to lose him again.

Lights went on in a couple of third floor windows. One of them must be Fallon's. It felt safe to assume that Fallon wouldn't be sleeping tonight.

Desperation had caused him to make the mistake that had led her to his apartment. With a little luck, it would lead to another mistake, the one that would put him behind bars.

———

Before three a.m., reinforcements arrived from the FBI's field office—a two-man team of young agents who would be on the first shift of twenty-four-hour surveillance, Ben Robison and Eldon Flynn. They brought her a large coffee from the bodega down the street.

"Thanks, but it took you long enough," Lisa said. She needed to be relieved from the stakeout as soon as possible so that she could meet with an FBI-and-DEA team to develop a plan for using the delivery of the phone to strike at the cartel.

"We got here as quickly as we could," said Robison, who was whippet thin and wearing skinny-legged jeans and a western shirt with pearl buttons. He blended in nicely in the Mission. "We just got the call, what—an hour and a half ago?"

"Hour and fifteen," Flynn interjected. He also looked like he was fresh off the Quantico campus and hadn't yet added the extra pounds that tended to follow completion of the boot camp–like training.

The first agent cleared his throat. "I just wanted to say that it's an honor to meet you. We've been briefed a little on the case, and we've heard what they're saying about you."

"Oh yeah? And what are they saying?"

"They're saying that you've generated just about every major lead in this case. That you're in this guy's head."

"If that was true, we'd have him locked up by now." Even though she had located Fallon, she couldn't just move in and arrest him. He needed to be apprehended while he had his laptop open and was acting as Kyte's administrator. Otherwise, it might not be possible to prove that Fallon was CaptainMal.

"So you think this is where he's living now?"

"It looks that way. There's a rear exit, but I couldn't watch both doors. I doubt he's used it in the past three hours, though."

"We'll get it covered," Flynn said. "Boss said the task force is meeting at six a.m."

Lisa checked her watch. "Then I'd better get out of here."

"If we encounter him, do you think he's armed?" Robison asked.

"You two *do not* encounter him, okay? Keep your distance. This is purely a surveillance assignment. And no, I don't think he's armed. He's dangerous, but not like that."

———

After catching a fitful hour of sleep at her apartment, Lisa was getting dressed for the task force meeting when she got a call from her boss.

Lisa fumbled with the phone. She had never gotten a call at home from Gilbertson.

GILBERTSON: Special Agent Tanchik?

LISA: Good morning, boss.

GILBERTSON: You're doing some good work on the Kyte investigation.

LISA: Thank you. I really appreciate that.

GILBERTSON: I've gotta say you've surprised me. Even in the midst of that shit-show joint task force, you've managed to distinguish yourself. And now we have an opportunity to not only bring down Kyte but also hurt the Zeta cartel. So I've decided that I'm going to make things a little easier on you. I've spoken with Constantine at the DEA and a couple of the other agency representatives. You're going to have a freer hand going forward.

LISA: Does that mean I'm leading the investigation?

GILBERTSON: For all practical purposes, yes. But not officially. Don't try to take over any meetings. No standing at the podium. And for heaven's sake, don't mess with Constantine's laser pointer. But you should be able to do what you want in the field with little interference. You'll be able to pick who you want to work with. But play nice, because I don't want to have to attend a deconfliction meeting over this.

A deconfliction meeting was a sort of mediation conducted by someone high up in the government to resolve a conflict between two agencies.

LISA: Thank you. I appreciate the vote of confidence.

GILBERTSON: *Confidence* is a strong word, Tanchik. Let's just say that you've earned this opportunity. Don't screw it up.

LISA: Thanks. And I won't.

For the first time in quite a while, Lisa felt like she might have made the right choice when she'd passed on a career in IT.

———

Lisa was surprised at how many members of the task force were able to show up at the meeting on such short notice, even many of the ones who had to travel to get there. They could sense that the hunt was nearing its end, and they all wanted to be in on the takedown.

As Lisa surveyed the room from the doorway, Sanjay appeared beside her. "So I guess the old saying is true," he said. "It takes a geek to catch a geek."

She smiled. "Hi, Sanjay. Thanks again for that lead."

"So what was it like meeting the guy face to face? The dreaded CaptainMal."

"He seemed—kind of normal."

"Aside from the fact that he nearly cracked your skull with a piece of rebar."

"Yeah. Apart from that."

"Well, you are now officially the CaptainMal whisperer. Everyone is saying that Constantine may be running the meetings, but you're running the show."

"If that's true—and I'm not saying it is—it would be more trouble than it's worth."

"This is your moment. Own it. Time to be the special special agent that we all know you can be."

Lisa cringed and snort-laughed. "Please stop."

Sanjay nodded to indicate that Constantine was approaching. "And on that note . . . ," Sanjay said before withdrawing to the conference room.

"Excuse me, Agent Tanchik." Constantine motioned down the hallway. "Can I speak with you for a minute?"

When they were out of earshot of the conference room, Constantine said, "That was some fine work you did locating Fallon."

"Thank you. We caught a break there."

"But it also was not smart. You should have had backup. I can't decide if you were just foolish or if you were greedy for credit."

"There wasn't time. The opportunity for a meet up came out of the blue. I barely got there in time myself. I'm happy to run through the entire sequence of events for the group."

"You certainly will. But from now on, we operate as a team—period. No freelancing."

"Got it."

"That said, I think we all have to recognize that you seem to have a . . . knack . . . for this case. I recognize it, and the people that I report to recognize it. So I want us to be partners on this as we bring it home. Does that work for you?"

Lisa wanted to smile at the thought of Constantine trying to buddy up to her now that she was having some success in the investigation, but she maintained a poker face. "Works for me."

Back in the conference room, Constantine called the meeting to order around a long table. Behind him was an easel with a pyramid diagram in black Magic Marker with lines connecting various IP addresses and servers that were now linked to Kyte. "We're here today because we now have a fix on Fallon. We've got the address where he appears to be living—thanks to the fine work of Special Agent Tanchik."

Someone clapped, and the rest of the agents grudgingly joined in an anemic round of applause.

Lisa was called up to the podium and described the events of the night before, from the exchange of messages with Fallon as Rodrigo to the ploy at the diner, the encounter in the alley, and the surveillance that had led to the Capp Street apartment. And, most importantly, the twenty-four-hour deadline to deliver the smartphone.

Randall Perry, a prematurely gray DOJ agent who was more bureaucrat than field agent, raised a hand at the end of her talk. Perry was such a gray visage that Sanjay referred to him as Agent Walker because he resembled one of the zombie walkers from *The Walking Dead*.

"Wait a minute," Perry said. "Are you telling us that you involved two civilians—your next-door neighbors—in a sting operation to bring down a dangerous fugitive?"

"I had to improvise. There was no time."

"But couldn't you have just waited outside the diner for him to show and followed him from there—without using your neighbors?"

"I thought about that, but I don't think he would have shown himself and entered the diner unless he saw someone who looked like he could be Rodrigo. That's why he chose that location. He knew he'd be able to see us from a distance. Besides, I don't think they were in any real danger." She regretted that statement as soon as the words left her mouth.

"And why is that?" Perry leaned forward with a smile that was screwed on tight.

"Because I don't think Fallon is capable of physical violence. I just don't think that's who he is."

"So he's not capable of violence, but he can order a hit on one of his associates?"

"That's different because it was online, and he was removed from the act itself. He's able to rationalize violence when he thinks it's a necessary business decision. But AFK, he's too much of a well-bred suburban kid to kill someone face to face."

"AFK?"

"Away from keyboard."

"And what about the fact that he nearly brained you with a piece of rebar?"

"But he couldn't do it," Lisa said. "That's my point."

"You sure seem confident that you know this guy."

Constantine came to her defense for once. "I think we can all agree that the tactic was unorthodox. But it worked, there was no harm done, and it will not be repeated. Right, Agent Tanchik?"

Lisa nodded. "That's right."

Constantine stood at the head of the table. "Right now we need to concentrate on making the most of this opportunity to hit the Zeta cartel. We've already identified a DEA undercover agent who can be responsible for getting the phone to someone in the Zetas. It will be the end of that agent's undercover assignment, but we think it's worth it for this opportunity to pinpoint the location of Ernesto Bonilla. He's a member of the cartel's *Junta Directiva*, or executive committee."

"How do you propose to follow the phone?"

"We'll use GPS to track."

"They'll spot that immediately," Lisa said.

"I don't mean the phone's standard GPS. That will be turned off. We can open up the smartphone and place a micro-GPS transmitter inside. They won't want to tear the phone apart for fear of losing the data. And even if they do, this transmitter is so tiny it's damn near invisible."

"Won't the cartel be able to detect the transmitter's signal with a scanner?"

"Highly unlikely. The transmitter will only send a brief GPS signal once every hour. The odds of them scanning at the right time to catch the signal are low."

Lisa wouldn't let it go. "But if they get lucky and scan at the right time, the hostage is dead."

"We're going to do our best to extract the hostage, but getting him out alive is going to be difficult regardless of the approach we take."

"Can't you use satellite surveillance? Wouldn't that be safer?"

"We're going to use that, too, but combined with the GPS tracker. They'll be using evasive measures and may be able to lose the satellite coverage." She could see that Constantine was getting angry. "Listen, Special Agent Tanchik, the cyber portion of this investigation is your strong suit. But this part is what the DEA does best. We have very little time to get this organized, we need to coordinate with Mexican law enforcement, and you need to let us do our job."

"Put me on the strike team," Lisa said. She wanted to make sure there was someone on the ground who was actively trying to get Fallon's colleague out safely. She sensed that might not be a priority for the DEA team.

"Wouldn't you be able to play a more valuable role sticking to the cyber investigation, keeping an eye on Fallon?"

Lisa put her elbows on the table and leaned forward. "I'm a trained field agent, this opportunity wouldn't exist without my work, and I'm going with the team to Mexico to see this through."

"All right, Tanchik. You're in. Be careful what you wish for."

39

Lisa sat in the back seat of an SUV filled with DEA agents as it barreled down a dusty road outside Nuevo Laredo at ninety miles per hour, shaking as it hit the potholes like it was about to come apart. They were all wearing tactical vests, with night vision goggles dangling from their necks and Rock River Arms LAR-15 semiautomatic carbine rifles resting muzzle down between their knees. The dispensing DEA agent had kindly issued one to Lisa, saying, "You'll want the firepower out there."

Unlike the operation in which her FBI team had taken down DPain's crew, there was no laughing or joking. The Zetas were a paramilitary outfit, and everyone seemed to know that they were, quite literally, heading into battle.

The smartphone with the GPS tracker had led them to an imposing villa in the scrub-covered hills about ten miles outside the city. The DEA knew that it would be impossible to surprise the Zetas if they approached solely by car, so three helicopters full of DEA agents made up the first wave of the assault. The plan was for the agents in the choppers to pin the Zetas down and keep them from running, while six more SUVs full of agents rolled in to provide support.

Because these sorts of cartel hideouts were often equipped with escape tunnels that emerged hundreds of yards away from the house, one helicopter was going to roam the perimeter with a thermal scope once the agents had established their positions.

Lisa had never been in a firefight. She had never even discharged her weapon in the field. So it took all of her willpower to calm herself as they approached the villa and saw the muzzle flashes of a pitched battle.

A fireball rose into the night sky as one of the DEA helicopters exploded and crashed in the courtyard. She gripped the butt of her rifle tightly so no one would see her hands shake.

Finally one of the DEA agents, who had a blond crew cut and a crooked nose, broke the silence. "I guess they have rocket launchers," he said matter-of-factly.

The agent leading the team added, "When we reach the courtyard, you all need to exit the vehicle immediately and spread out. The SUV will be a target."

The house drew closer and closer, and it was all happening too fast. The cabin of the SUV had been dark as they'd driven through the night, but now it was fully illuminated by the floodlights from the house and the flames from the burning helicopter.

The SUV stopped in the villa's courtyard with a shriek of brakes, the panel door flew open, and the agents leaped out. As Lisa exited the car, she could hear the bullets caroming off the concrete and pinging against the bulletproof SUV. Bodies of cartel soldiers and DEA agents were everywhere. It was impossible to tell who was winning.

As instructed, Lisa started running from the SUV as soon as she was out. She had only made it four or five strides toward the nearest corner of the villa when she heard and felt a whoosh of displaced air. Then the SUV exploded.

A moment.

Of quiet.

Oblivion.

And then her vision, hearing, and other senses all returned like water finding its level. She was covered in bits of windshield glass. She was able to move her arms and legs. She had not been shot or injured by debris, but bullets were still pinging around her. She didn't know where her rifle was, but it was no longer in her hand or within reach.

Lisa looked up to see a Zeta soldier, a hard-looking man in faded Mexican Army fatigues. He was about five yards in front of her, getting to his feet and looking for his weapon. He was not moving quickly, and he seemed to be nearly as stunned as she was.

The Zeta saw her, and he saw his rifle, which was about midway between the two of them.

They both lunged for it. Lisa was too far away to grab the rifle, but she was able to get one hand on it and push it with all her strength, sending it skittering across the concrete, where it came to rest about ten yards away.

Bullets were no longer whizzing past. The most intense part of the firefight seemed to have moved to the other side of the courtyard. This moment seemed to be just between the two of them.

Instead of going for the rifle, the Zeta stepped forward and punched Lisa in the face. She didn't black out, so she was able to see the boot coming as he kicked her in the head.

Lisa might have been unconscious for an instant, but she managed to pull herself back from that brink. The Zeta had turned his back to her as he went for the rifle so that he could finish the job.

She knew everything came down to that moment.

She grabbed his ankle and pulled him backward, hard. The Zeta went down face first on the pavement.

Lisa scrambled onto the man's back, grabbed two handfuls of his greasy hair, and began smashing his head into concrete.

Once, twice, three times.

Until he stopped moving.

Lisa stood up unsteadily, picked up the rifle, and staggered away from the courtyard to the side of the villa and out of the line of fire.

She took a moment to assess the damage. Her right eye ached, and so did her left temple, but there was only a little blood. She was going to be okay.

Lisa realized that the helicopter that had been destroyed by the rocket was probably the one that had been assigned to roam the outer perimeter of the grounds looking for tunnel escapees. She decided to assign herself that task, pulling on her night vision goggles and walking away from the villa.

She could still hear the gunfire, but it grew fainter as she walked out through the scrub and down a rocky hillside behind the house. She released the safety on her rifle and traced a broad circle about two hundred yards distant from the villa.

With her goggles on, everything was radium green and glowing. Far off in the distance, she could see the headlights of cars streaming down a highway, white hot in night vision.

Lisa walked and walked around the perimeter. She felt dizzy and wondered if she had suffered a concussion.

As she walked, the intervals between the gunshots increased. She wasn't ready to speculate on what that signified. It reminded her of the sound of a bag of popcorn that was nearly done popping.

While Lisa considered that incongruous observation, she saw movement twenty yards ahead. Something was alive in the scrub. She thought it might be a coyote, but it grew larger, man shaped. The figure was emerging from the ground, climbing out of a tunnel, shutting the hatch, and covering it with a fallen branch.

She crouched down and readied her weapon. The moon was out. The man would probably see her if he looked her way.

"Move and I'll shoot," she said.

The figure froze. She could see that he was holding a pistol. "Drop the gun. Now!"

He dropped it.

"Turn around. Slowly."

Lisa drew a bit closer.

"Okay," he said. "I surrender."

"Raise your hands. Now!"

"I said I—" The man made a sudden move for a weapon that must have been tucked behind his back, and Lisa fired. The report seemed unbelievably loud, echoing down the hillside.

The figure went down, and Lisa hurried forward, ready to fire again.

She had hit the man in the right shoulder. The pistol was on the ground, and she kicked it away, then picked it up.

"I think you killed me, agent," he said.

She recognized his face from the DEA's photos. It was Ernesto Bonilla, one of the leaders of the Zeta cartel.

"No, you'll live," Lisa said. "You're not that lucky, Ernesto."

40

Nate didn't want to wait until the midnight deadline to contact the cartel. He didn't want to risk a misunderstanding that could cost Hardwick his life.

He dialed the phone number again. After three rings, Ernesto answered.

"Do you have the smartphone?" Nate asked.

"Yes. It got here a few hours ago. Click on the link I sent you before. The video feed is live again."

Nate accessed the video feed. Hardwick was still in that bunkerlike room, strapped to a chair, a tire around his neck.

"Now, the password please."

Nate read the first three digits of the password, but he was interrupted by the sound of gunshots on the phone. Ernesto fully entered the video frame for the first time. He was staring at something off camera. The cartel boss looked surprisingly ordinary, like a businessman on casual Friday—a carefully trimmed, gray-flecked beard and mustache, an expensive-looking watch, black pants, and a tan shirt.

Then Ernesto turned to the lens and pointed his finger. "You betrayed me, and you're going to pay with your life for that. And then your family is going to pay. And then everyone that you love will pay. But first, your friend's going to pay."

"I don't know what's happening!" Nate said.

On the other end of the line, Nate heard a metallic *shing* and then: *Snick, snick.*

Whoosh.

Because Nate's father was a sometimes smoker, he instantly recognized the sounds—the metal lid of a lighter flicked open, the turning of the spark wheel, and the flame igniting.

"No," Nate said. The first time, he murmured it to himself, a private, terrible recognition. Then he screamed it into the phone: "NO!"

But it was too late.

Ernesto touched the lighter to the gasoline-soaked tire around Hardwick's neck. It happened fast, but there was still time to see Hardwick's eyes register the horror. Then Hardwick shut them tight and screamed.

And he kept screaming.

The tire ignited instantly, and the flames shot up around Hardwick's face. Through the veil of fire, Nate watched as his friend's hair disappeared and skin blackened and peeled away like old wallpaper to reveal the skull of his forehead. As the gasoline dripped down the front of his shirt, his entire torso caught fire.

For a few horrific moments that seemed so much longer, Hardwick's screaming continued, feral as a wild dog and insistent as a car alarm.

Then the cries ceased.

Then Hardwick stopped writhing against his bindings.

And finally, there was only the sound of the flames hungrily licking and consuming what remained.

In that crazed, sickening moment, Nate knew that he was responsible for the death of his best friend in the world.

"I hope you watched all of that," Ernesto said, the sound of gunfire louder now in the background. "Because I'm going to get out of here. And when we finally meet in person, you're going to be sitting in that chair."

41

There are times when only a consciousness-obliterating blackout drunk will do. After watching the live video feed of Hardwick's death, Nate had paced manically around his rented room like his brain was on fire with a flame that only alcohol could quench.

And when he wasn't thinking about Hardwick, he was thinking about how law enforcement had been tipped to Ernesto's location, which had to be linked to the delivery of his smartphone. That meant Rodrigo was not who he appeared to be and must be working with the FBI or DEA. At least Nate had managed to brick the smartphone—the federal agents wouldn't be able to take control of Kyte.

He scavenged the shared kitchen and found a bottle of tequila, careful not to wake his housemates. Returning to his room through the darkened apartment, he groped for the wall at the end of the hall like a swimmer looking to make the turn in a lap pool.

For two days, Nate continued drinking. He knew he had drunk enough when he stopped hearing Hardwick's animal screams. Then he drank some more to erase the image of the flames shooting up from the gasoline-soaked tire and engulfing his face, igniting his hair. But no matter how much he drank, he couldn't obliterate the sound of Hardwick's last words to him.

I never knew you.

———

Nate awakened to the marimba ringtone of his smartphone.

He groped to silence the phone, but thankfully it went to voice mail.

A minute later, the phone rang again. This time, he managed to answer.

"Hello."

"Nate, where are you?"

"Who's this?"

"This is Hannah. *Your mother.*"

"Can I call you back?"

"No, you can't call me back. It's your sister's wedding day. Everyone's here. Where are *you*?"

He mouthed a silent *fuck*. He had completely forgotten that Amanda was getting married that day. He had been receiving planning emails from his family for the past week but hadn't been able to focus on them in the midst of his crisis.

Nate swung his feet out of bed and felt his stomach lurch. "I'm on my way."

"Are you?"

"Yeah, Mom. Well, I will be soon. The ceremony isn't until four thirty." He checked his watch—twelve thirty—and performed the mental calculation. "I can be in Half Moon Bay by three fifteen, no later than three thirty. No problem."

"She's already asking where you are. Thank god we didn't entrust you with the ring, or she'd really be freaking out."

Nate took a quick, hot shower to draw some of the tequila out through his pores. Moving as fast as his aching head would allow, he donned his rented tux, which had been delivered days ago. In order to avoid any screwups, his mother had taken his measurements and made the arrangements a month ago. As he left the apartment, he was trailed by the shouted mockery of his housemates commenting on his monkey suit.

Driving south on the 101 to Half Moon Bay, he tried to calm his thoughts, concentrating on the road as he wound through the traffic. He wondered if this was going to be his last opportunity to see his family before he fled the country. In his own emotionally muted way, he would miss them.

When he reached the venue, there was a line of cars waiting for the valet. The Ritz-Carlton, Half Moon Bay, was a rambling, New England–style structure occupying a stunningly beautiful promontory over the Pacific.

It was 3:35 p.m. While he'd probably created a little unnecessary anxiety for the bride and family, no one could accuse him of ruining the wedding.

The hotel clung to the cliff in tiers. He took an elevator down to the wedding site, a green hillside overlooking the ocean not far from the hotel's outdoor dining area. The scene was one of nature domesticated, with surf pounding a rocky shore that was as curved as a scimitar and only a short distance from the immaculately manicured eighteenth green. Hotel guests in golf clothes huddled around firepits, sipping drinks and smiling as they watched the wedding party assemble. In a final pretentious touch, a bagpiper in a tartan kilt paced the lawn, warming up for his daily sunset performance at the cliff's edge.

As Nate made his way through the patio area toward the wedding site, he sensed a white blur bearing down on him like a ballistic missile designed by Vera Wang. He turned to face his sister and braced for impact.

Lisa and Sanjay followed Nate Fallon's Audi down to Half Moon Bay. They had already found an announcement of Amanda Fallon's wedding online, so they knew where he was headed as soon as he began driving south. Lisa figured that Fallon needed to be under surveillance at all times because there was no telling when he might run.

"He's cutting it a little close," Sanjay said.

"I'll say," Lisa replied. "I don't care whether you're a criminal kingpin or not, you don't screw up your sister's wedding."

She had returned from Mexico only the day before. The strike against Bonilla and the Zetas had been a success, but it came with a heavy toll. Six DEA agents had been killed in the attack. SAC Gilbertson had encouraged her to take some time off, but there was no way she was going to sit out Fallon's capture. An MRI had confirmed that she didn't have a concussion, and the bruises to her face were passably hidden by makeup and concealer.

But they hadn't been able to save the hostage. They'd found the still-smoldering corpse in a basement underneath the villa. The smell when she had entered the room had made her sick. The medical examiner was still trying to identify the body.

"Are we going to crash the wedding?" Sanjay asked.

"I don't think I should. He might recognize me from that night in the alley. Do you know how to operate the parabolic mic?"

"I'm an IRS agent, remember? This is the first time I've ever been out in the field."

"It's okay; I was trained on it. I can show you how."

It took a while to get through the line of cars for the wedding, which stretched all the way back to the security guard's kiosk at the border of the property. They saved some time by veering off at the first opportunity onto an access road that ran past the golf course and led to some guest cottages that adjoined the main building.

Lisa parked the car at a vantage point across from and below the hillside where the wedding party was assembling, white folding chairs standing out against the green grass like golf tees.

Sanjay pulled out a pair of binoculars and scanned the crowd. "The visuals should be good from here, but I doubt we'll be able to get any usable audio."

"They'd have to be out on the edge of the cliff for that," Lisa said. She tried to focus the mic on a couple of kids chasing about near the cliff's edge. Some knob twiddling brought the children's shouts into sharp focus, along with their mother's stern warning as she grabbed arms and led them back to the wedding party.

"What are the odds of that happening?"

"Not very good," Lisa said. "Why don't you go on over and mingle with the guests? See what you can get."

Sanjay was screwing a long lens onto his camera and testing the focus on the wedding crowd. The camera whirred and clicked as he squeezed off several shots. "I'm not dressed for it," he said.

"That's okay. The wedding is so close to the patio. They'll assume you're a guest of the hotel looking to score some appetizers."

Sanjay climbed out of the car. "Well, I wouldn't say no to one of those little crab cakes."

———

"Where the hell have you been?" Amanda said. "Are you trying to freak me out? Because I'm already freaked out enough, okay? I'm getting married in . . ." She checked her watch. "Thirty-five minutes."

"Sorry, sis. I didn't mean to be late, but traffic was terrible on the 101."

She noted her skepticism with an arched eyebrow but didn't bother to challenge his lie.

"Come on, let's get away from here." She led him to the edge of the cliff, away from the gathering wedding party. "People aren't supposed to be seeing me in the dress before the ceremony."

"It's a beautiful dress, and you look amazing in it. And I don't mean that in a Jaime Lannister sort of way."

"Thank you. And ick."

They walked out on the crayon-green grass and gazed down at the waves crashing and frothing on the rocks below. She studied his face. "You look like shit, Nate. Are you okay?"

"Yeah, I'm fine. Just had a few too many last night."

"I've seen that before. This looks like something else."

"All appearances to the contrary, I'm not here to make this about me."

"Nate, I don't have a lot of time here, but I want to know what's going on with you. At least the short version. Then after I'm a married woman, I want to hear the long version too."

"It's not easy to talk about."

"Are you in some sort of trouble?"

Nate stared at a golfer lining up a putt on the green below because it was easier than looking at Amanda. He couldn't say no, but he didn't want to say yes.

"Is this about that start-up of yours? The one you won't talk about?"

"Yeah."

"And you're realizing that it's not going to be as perfect and successful as you had hoped it would be."

"Oh, it's been successful."

"Okay, then. Anything worth doing has a price." She smiled ruefully. "Now that I'm getting married, I'm trying to sound more like an adult. How was that?"

"Very convincing. If I didn't know better, I could have sworn that I was talking to Mom."

She drew a breath and tried again. "Does this have something to do with the breakup with Ali? Because Mom told me about that. I was sorry to hear it. She seemed like a nice girl."

"Yes, she was. She is. But no, it's not that either."

"Don't make me work for it, Nate. I don't have that much time."

He felt something loosen and go liquid in his chest. She was perhaps the only person to whom he could tell his story. Even if he revealed everything, including his role in the deaths of DPain and Hardwick, he knew that Amanda would not freak out and report him to law enforcement. She was family, and she was a steely pragmatist. She would hire him a good lawyer and fight tooth and nail to keep him alive and out of prison. He didn't have to worry that the news would crush her, at least not in the way it would crush his parents.

Still, he couldn't bring himself to tell her about Kyte and his predicament. He didn't want to make her a part of his nightmare. It would be easier if she didn't learn what he was doing until it was over and he was in another country. In many ways, things would be simpler then.

He certainly couldn't tell her at this moment, when she was about to walk down the aisle.

"What do you do when the best thing you've ever done is also the worst thing you've ever done?" His voice trembled, and the words came out clenched. Whatever had come apart in his chest was now black and vile in the back of his throat.

"You're my brother." She leaned forward to look him in the eye. "I know you. What, did you have to fire someone? And now you think you're a bad person? Well, you aren't. You're just not capable of it."

"Yeah, that's what I thought too."

She laid her hand on his forearm, a gesture that wouldn't telegraph that something was wrong to the wedding attendees who were starting to cast glances their way from the folding chairs. "Whatever this is, it's not as bad as you think right now. There are people who have your back, and I'm one of them."

Nate just stared at her, appalled and embarrassed that he was no longer able to govern himself.

"You need to go back over there with Mom and Dad and enjoy the show. Have a glass of champagne. Or two." After studying him for a moment, Amanda added, "But not three. Then get a good night's sleep tonight."

"I'm sorry," Nate said. "I never meant to do this."

"It's okay," she said. "Truly it is. We've both gotten so busy that we've stopped talking, haven't we? We're going to do something about that. When I get back from the honeymoon in Costa Rica, we're going to have dinner, we're going to drink an unhealthy amount of wine, and we're going to talk about everything."

"I'd like that," Nate said, forcing a smile. "I may take a little time off myself, go away for a while. Maybe a long while. Now go get married, doofus."

Amanda put on her beaming-bride game face and returned to the wedding party. Nate stayed on the cliff for a bit longer, drawing deep breaths of the brisk sea air until he felt that he could speak without his voice trembling.

Lisa pulled off her headphones when Amanda left Fallon standing on the cliff. After a little bit of garbled reception at the beginning, she had managed to record most of the conversation.

When Fallon had started to open up to his sister, Lisa had begun to hope that she might luck into obtaining an admission. In the end, he hadn't really said anything that was useful as evidence, but it was still illuminating.

She knew now that Nate Fallon was not some hardened criminal mastermind. Overhearing the conversation with his sister made Fallon seem more human, but somehow that made his actions even more appalling.

If Fallon were some sadistic cartel boss, she would know how to understand him, how to place him in context. Without discounting the crimes, it was no mystery how poverty, a culture of addiction, and a cycle of violence could produce someone capable of climbing the bloody ladder to the top of a criminal empire and maintaining that position by slaughtering everyone in his path.

But she didn't know how to understand someone seemingly like herself ordering murder for hire and brokering hundreds of millions of dollars in illegal drug sales, with all of the addiction, death, and sickness that were the byproduct of that business. A well-educated, middle-class kid choosing to enter the world of the cartels and organized crime was an anomaly. Maybe he thought that adding a web interface somehow made the business cleaner—Cartel 2.0. If he really thought that, then he was in for a rude and violent awakening, and he had apparently gotten it. At the end of the conversation, Fallon had sounded scared and vulnerable.

Maybe Fallon had finally figured out the fundamental flaw in his business model—that conventional drug dealers were better at brutality and murder than he could ever be. Perhaps she was reading too much into the conversation, but Fallon seemed to recognize that everything was coming to an end.

But she was most concerned by his comment about going away for a long while. She suspected that Fallon was about to execute his escape plan.

42

As Nate drove back to the city from Half Moon Bay, his phone began pinging with text messages. He pulled off the freeway at the next exit. The texts were from Ali.

ALI: Is Hardwick with u?

ALI: U need to respond. This is serious.

Nate tapped out a response.

NATE: He's not with me. Is something wrong?

ALI: He's missing. Call me.

Nate dialed Ali's number, and she picked up on the first ring. "Nate, Hardwick has gone missing. No one has seen him in three days. We think something has happened to him. Something bad."

"Have you checked with Janine? Maybe he's with her."

The FBI had probably just notified Hardwick's parents of his death, but Ali hadn't yet heard. Nate had to keep pretending that he didn't know what had happened to his friend.

"That was the first place I looked," Ali said. "When was the last time you saw him?"

Nate paused. He might have been the last person to see Hardwick alive. And if that was the case, he would be a suspect. If the police began digging into his activities, they might uncover his role in Kyte. They might even confiscate his laptop. Although he had implemented strong encryption to protect his Kyte documents, he did not want to test the technical capabilities of the Palo Alto PD. He had been thinking about leaving the country immediately after the wedding, but he wondered if that would make him even more of a suspect in Hardwick's death.

"I think it was about a week ago," he said. "I've been busy."

"Wasn't he helping you with your project?"

"Not lately. I had lunch with him—a week ago Wednesday." That much was true. They'd discussed a coding assignment over carnitas.

"You didn't go by his apartment?"

Had someone seen him when he'd found Hardwick's keys and entered his apartment? That was the same day that Hardwick had gone missing. He needed to choose his words carefully.

"I think I went by his place once, but he wasn't home."

"What day was that?"

Nate paused. "I'm not really sure. I'm going to have to think about that, reconstruct my schedule. I've been so busy lately that everything is a blur."

"Was this for one of your tech projects?"

"No, it was just to hang out. But he wasn't around."

"Nate, do you know something that you're not telling me?" She knew him well enough to know when he was lying.

"Of course not."

"Well, you're going to need to think about that timeline and figure out exactly when you last saw Hardwick and when you went by his apartment. That's the kind of thing that the police are going to want to know."

"The police are involved?"

"Yeah, Hardwick's family filed a missing persons report yesterday."

"Does anyone have any idea what happened?"

"Not really. But there's a lot of street crime in East Palo Alto, and the police officer said that sometimes extends to Hardwick's neighborhood. Can you come down to the police station to give a statement to the officer in charge of the case?"

"Sure."

"It's the Palo Alto station on Forest Avenue. Officer Markham. I've given him your cell number."

Ali had included that last statement because she didn't expect him to show. She was clearly suspicious of him.

"He's going to turn up soon, Ali. I know it. Probably holed up somewhere on a coding jag."

"Yeah, maybe. I hope so."

"So how are you doing?"

"I'm okay. How about you?"

"Okay. It'd be great to get a cup of coffee with you sometime."

A moment of staticky silence as Nate watched the cars zip by on the 101 overpass.

"Yeah, I don't think that's such a good idea."

"Why not?"

"It's just too late, Nate."

"What if I changed? I can, and I will." He did want to try again with Ali, but he also wanted to get her on his side in the investigation of Hardwick's disappearance.

"We're past that. I'm out of the trying-to-change-Nate business."

"I'm sorry to hear that."

Another pause. "Nate, if you know something about what happened to Brian, you need to go to that police station and tell Officer Markham everything. For your sake, as well as his."

"I'll do that. I don't think I have anything very useful, but I will definitely do that."

"Goodbye, Nate."

They both knew that Nate wasn't going to meet with the police. Not unless they called him and insisted. And even if they insisted, they would still have to find him. Nate figured that this sort of missing persons case probably wouldn't get the full attention of the police. If he was lucky, Markham would never call. The real question was whether

Ali would tell the police that she suspected that Nate was involved in Hardwick's disappearance. He supposed that would be the real test of whether she had any remaining feelings for him.

Judging by the tone of Ali's voice when she said goodbye, Nate expected to receive that call from Markham.

43

Lisa and Sanjay were in a car two blocks back, trailing Nate Fallon, who appeared to be walking to his favorite coffee shop, Ground Zero. It was on Valencia Street and always crowded with overcaffeinated young people on laptops. Another team consisting of a DOJ and a DEA agent were following in tandem on the street behind the coffee shop in case Fallon tried an evasive maneuver.

They had been following Fallon for two days, and patterns were beginning to emerge. He spent a lot of time in the apartment he shared, but when he went outside, he visited the Safeway supermarket down the street and the gym. Yesterday, he had sat in the park and drummed on his djembe, which had provided rich comedic material for Sanjay. When Fallon carried his gray vinyl laptop bag, he was heading for the public library or Ground Zero to access Wi Fi.

"So Constantine and the DEA expect us to just keep tabs on Fallon," Sanjay said. "Where's the fun in that?"

"The thing is I know Constantine's plan just won't work. As soon as Fallon hears that SWAT team knocking down doors and windows, he'll close his laptop, and it's game over."

Lisa knew that once the laptop went to sleep and the hard drive was encrypted, the only way to access the data was by knowing Fallon's password. Cracking the password through a brute-force attack would not be possible because the laptop was undoubtedly configured to self-destruct after a few failed password entries.

"But in a setting like the café or the library, we might be able to get in close."

"I know exactly what you're thinking," Sanjay said. "And it would be a singularly bad career move. I just want to say that, for the record."

"Just running some scenarios, Sanjay. I have to keep my mind occupied, don't I?"

Fallon did indeed enter Ground Zero, so Lisa parked the car a half block down the street.

"Go inside and see what he's doing," Lisa said. "I shouldn't go with you because he might recognize me from the alley."

"Okay. Maybe I'll get a coffee while I'm in there. You want anything?"

"Text me if he sits down."

"What do you have in mind?"

"Just text me if he sits down. If he does, we might want to put some other agents in position."

Sanjay shook his head as he climbed out of the car.

Lisa watched as Sanjay crossed the street and entered the coffee shop after Fallon. A few minutes later, Fallon emerged with a cup of coffee and continued walking down the street.

Sanjay emerged a moment later and returned to the car.

"Well?"

"He looked around like he was trying to find a place to work, but no luck. The tables were all occupied, except for one that was in the middle of the room. He wouldn't take that one."

"He probably likes to sit with his back to the wall. Otherwise someone could see his screen."

Lisa texted the other team to let them know that Fallon was on the move again; then she started the engine. "If he does the same thing tomorrow, maybe we can make sure he gets a table along the wall."

44

February 10

No matter how hard Nate tried to immerse himself in Kyte business, the image of Hardwick burning to death in that grainy video feed kept coming back to him. The scene never entirely vanished from his consciousness, like a ghost image burned onto a computer monitor. All he had to do was shift the focus of his vision a little, and there it was again.

Lately, when he managed to sleep, he dreamed of the room in which Hardwick had died, with its cinder block walls, bare concrete floor, and large industrial drain in the center. As a physics student, he knew that all objects vibrated at a certain frequency, even if it was inaudible. When those inaudible frequencies were translated into the audible spectrum, most objects vibrated at frequencies that had whole number mathematical relationships between them, meaning that they produced harmonious, almost-musical tones. Nate always found that fact strangely comforting, a sign that there was some underlying order to the universe.

In Nate's dream, Hardwick was gone, but the empty chair remained in the center of the room, along with the charred, melted tire. Nate could hear every object in that room screaming like a demon choir, and he awoke with a start.

Better to remain awake than be revisited by that dream, even though each blink of his dry eyes felt like it was scraping his corneas. The primary light source in his room was his laptop screen. He'd pulled the shades on his window and turned down the lights so that he lost all sense of the time of day, sunk in undersea half light. He had his headphones on and was listening to something quiet that didn't detract from his concentration.

His roommates knocked on his door occasionally, an uncharacteristic show of concern. He waved them away. Every minute of the day, someone somewhere in the world was buying drugs on Kyte, and Nate was determined to deliver that product faster and with better quality than any competitor.

Although he had been willing to turn over Kyte to the Zetas in order to save Hardwick, that moment had passed. Now he was determined to continue with business as usual, even if he had to operate Kyte from outside the US. Kyte was thriving: sales, already robust, continued to rocket. The chart tracking Kyte's revenue growth was a hockey stick, and the site was now on pace to exceed $1 billion in annual revenues. If he wasn't so distressed, he would have celebrated that milestone.

As Nate combed his Kyte messaging account, he noticed another message from a reporter at *Wired* named Jonathan Egan. He was once again seeking an interview, but this time with a different angle.

The message read:

> Dear CaptainMal—As you've seen from my previous messages, I would love to interview you about the success of Kyte. I'm particularly interested in your views on Kyte as a laboratory for libertarian ideas. But if you choose not to respond, I want you to know that I plan to schedule an interview with the founder of Planetary, a new Dark Web site that seems to be influenced by Kyte.

Are you familiar with Planetary? Here's a link to their new ad. I think it's kind of clever. You may have also heard that the spokesperson for Planetary, who calls himself Heisenberg, conducted a group chat with some reporters where he called Planetary the "Facebook to Kyte's Myspace."

Kyte is still clearly the big player in Dark Web commerce, but I have an assignment to write an article—with or without your participation. If the founder of Planetary is willing to speak to me and you're not, then they will be the focus of my piece.

I would need to speak with you by COB Wednesday. Thanks for considering the request. I really hope we get a chance to talk.

Despite their cute YouTube video ads, he wasn't worried about Planetary—yet. He had to admit that the comparison to Myspace was a nice bit of shade throwing, but it would take a lot more than that to make Planetary a serious threat to Kyte's market share. So why not give the journalist his interview? Sure, it would further enrage the law enforcement agencies that were pursuing him, but they were coming for him anyway. In the short run, the added publicity would only bolster Kyte's profits. Nate would take as much as he could get for as long as he could get it.

Nate responded to the journalist's message.

Ok, he wrote. I'll do the interview. By email.

EGAN: Great. My editor told me this might even be considered for the cover. When would you like to do it?

CAPTMAL: How about now?

EGAN: All right, diving in. What inspired you to start Kyte?

CAPTMAL: I was excited by the ability of Tor and bitcoin to enable truly anonymous transactions. Suddenly, people had the ability to operate entirely beyond the reach of government regulation and interference. I don't think that possibility has existed since the time that we stopped being hunters and gatherers and began forming villages and governments.

EGAN: So you really are a pure libertarian?

CAPTMAL: As pure as you can be in this world. We've created a community of people who are discovering what it feels like to be truly free in this one aspect of their lives—free of taxes, free of government regulation, free of warrantless wiretapping and surveillance.

EGAN: Some would say that Kyte is free of morality, too, selling illegal drugs, automatic weapons, and other illicit goods.

CAPTMAL: Free of whose morality? On the first day that Kyte went live I posted some guiding principles. One of them was that we sell no products that inherently harm others. What you choose to do with your own body is your business.

EGAN: Isn't an AK-47 inherently designed to harm others?

CAPTMAL: People have a right to defend themselves. That's what the Second Amendment is for.

EGAN: I actually don't think that's what the Second Amendment is for, but let's not go down that path. So you're saying that guns don't kill people, people kill people. Don't you think that's being disingenuous?

CAPTMAL: No, I don't.

EGAN: Aren't you just creating another form of government at Kyte—a dictatorship?

CAPTMAL: I don't think anyone who has bought or sold through Kyte would say that. While the experience is designed to be as open as possible, no business can exist without some structure and some rules. I've tried to impose those rules with the lightest touch possible, and always with the objective of creating a safe environment.

EGAN: How does Kyte resemble other disruptive business models?

CAPTMAL: Why do you think guys like Jobs, Gates, and Zuckerberg changed the world? It wasn't because they wanted the world to be a better place—no matter what Jobs said. They did it because they could. When Shawn Fanning and Sean Parker created Napster, their music file-sharing site flagrantly violated every copyright law ever written. But they saw how transformative MP3 technology could be. Did they spend a lot of time trying to predict how that technology would affect the record industry and musicians over the next 20 or 30 years? No. They saw something that would change the world—and so they changed it.

EGAN: Do you see parallels between you and someone like Sean Parker?

CAPTMAL: I hope so. Napster was shut down by the recording industry, but is Sean Parker viewed as some sort of criminal today? No, he's considered a visionary, and Napster wasn't the end of his career in Silicon Valley. Not by a long shot. He went on to be the first president of Facebook and an early funder of Spotify. Kyte is illegal today, but who's to say how it will be viewed in ten years, particularly as more states legalize recreational use of marijuana? Sean Parker wasn't afraid to violate copyright laws, and I'm not afraid to violate drug laws. At the end of the day, Silicon Valley respects those who have the vision and the skill to disrupt an established industry— because that's where value is created, and that's where people get rich.

EGAN: Do you worry about being arrested?

CAPTMAL: Sure. I'd be a fool not to worry about that. But I'm not going to change what we're doing at Kyte to protect myself.

EGAN: Why not?

CAPTMAL: Because if I succeed in staying out of custody, it's going to empower other people to stand up to government interference. Also, I think if I can stay out of jail long enough, the tide is going to turn in our favor. Every year more states are decriminalizing recreational marijuana, and that's our best-selling product.

EGAN: But you also seem to sell a lot of cocaine, heroin, and meth. I don't think anyone's going to decriminalize those drugs in our lifetime.

CAPTMAL: Maybe not. But sometimes society changes faster than we ever imagined it would, like with the legalization of marijuana. You need catalysts to create that sort of change, and that's what Kyte is about.

EGAN: What about your idea of applying minimal rules to keep people safe? Shouldn't not selling a highly addictive drug like heroin on Kyte be one of those rules?

CAPTMAL: Like I said, we prohibit the sale of products that are inherently designed to harm or exploit others, like child pornography. Heroin is something that people buy for personal use, and I believe individuals should have the freedom to make that choice if they want to. Would I make that choice? No. Would I defend someone else's right to make that choice? Absolutely.

EGAN: You make Kyte sound like a pretty altruistic enterprise, but not everyone sees it that way. What about the people who've died of overdoses from drugs that they've bought on Kyte?

CAPTMAL: I'm not aware of any incidents, but I have to assume that they exist given our sales figures. But that same question could be posed to the CEO of an auto manufacturer or a distillery. It's a sad reality that some people abuse drugs and die. We didn't create that problem and we can't be expected to change it. But we do have resident experts in our community forums who provide advice on the proper use of drugs. We also have community members who test certain sellers' product for purity and potency and post the results so that buyers can make a more informed decision. If anything, I believe we're reducing the number of deaths related to drug use.

EGAN: Tell that to the family of David Ellroy. He was a 15-year-old boy from Evanston, Illinois, who purchased the synthetic opioid fentanyl through Kyte, had a heart attack, and died. According to one of his friends, he had never taken any form of drugs, and didn't even know what fentanyl was, until he discovered Kyte. I'm sure Kyte is making it easier for a lot of young people to buy drugs.

CAPTMAL: I think history has shown that if people want to buy an illegal substance, a market will always emerge and it will be available to them, despite the best efforts of law enforcement. If people are going to buy drugs—and clearly they are—then at least Kyte allows people to purchase those drugs safely from their home without having to go out in the street and expose themselves to potential violence. You have to figure that's saving a few lives. I have to admit that this wasn't the interview that I was expecting from WIRED.

EGAN: What were you expecting?

CAPTMAL: Maybe a little more appreciation of Kyte's disruptive business model.

EGAN: About that. Have you encountered any resistance from what you might call the "brick and mortar" drug business?

CAPTMAL: I can say that I know for a fact that they've been "disrupted" by what Kyte is doing.

EGAN: It seems to me that you're in a dangerous business, CaptainMal.

CAPTMAL: If it was easy to be first, then everyone would do it.

45

When Nate Fallon emerged from his apartment building, Lisa fervently hoped that he was heading for Ground Zero. His laptop bag was slung over his shoulder, and that was a good sign.

The DEA SWAT team was prepared to storm Fallon's apartment building later that day, when he returned home. But if Lisa and her team, in the course of their surveillance, happened to corner Fallon while he was working in his favorite café, then who could fault her for seizing that opportunity?

Harold Constantine, for one.

Lisa was on foot, maintaining a full block between herself and Fallon because, after their encounter in the alley, he might recognize her if he got a good look. It was a cool, overcast day, and the clouds were banked across the sky like surf breaks. Fallon walked fast, and he never looked back. Poor situational awareness. On a surveillance assignment, it was the gift that kept on giving.

Lisa texted Sanjay: He's on the way. 5 minutes out.

Sanjay texted back a unicorn emoji. Lisa wasn't quite sure what that signified, but at least it confirmed receipt.

After receiving her text, Sanjay was supposed to give a prearranged signal to the other members of the team, who had already taken up positions in the coffee shop. He was going to conspicuously drop his newspaper.

Fallon was headed down Valencia Street, but Lisa wasn't satisfied until she saw him push through the front door of Ground Zero. Then she slowed her pace, giving Fallon time to order his coffee.

She circled around to the rear of the shop so that she could enter by the back door near the restrooms. That way, Fallon wouldn't see her right away. When she turned the corner past the restrooms and looked into the main room, Fallon had already gotten his coffee. He was looking around for an open table, but once again, the coffee shop was crowded with students, and there were no openings.

And then Sanjay rose from his perfectly positioned table along the wall.

Fallon saw Sanjay getting up and quickly slid into the vacant seat. So far, so good.

At the table next to Fallon was a young woman with a blonde pixie cut and an enormous backpack. She was beautiful, with porcelain features, green eyes, and a persistent half smile. Fallon's eyes lingered for a small but unmistakable moment.

This was not some random student; it was FBI Academy trainee Sandra Powell. Lisa had found a couple of recruits from the academy for this assignment, and Sandra was one of them. Lisa had needed a couple of fresh faces who could blend in with the young clientele. Nothing would be more suspicious to Fallon than walking into his favorite coffee shop to find it overrun by older customers emanating that distinctive, steely-eyed law enforcement vibe. You could muss them up, give them different clothes and hairstyles, but you couldn't change the look that was in a veteran agent's eyes. The trainees still had the vaguely stunned look of harried undergraduates.

After an appreciative glance at Trainee Powell, Fallon removed his laptop and booted up.

Lisa hovered at a rack of newspapers at the back of the room, making a show of trying to pick out some reading material. There was no need to make much of a show, however, because Fallon had his back to her.

In fairness to the DEA team, Lisa thought it was time to text Constantine to alert him to the situation.

LISA: We have Fallon cornered in Ground Zero coffee shop on Valencia. He's on his laptop.

CONSTANTINE: DO NOTHING. DEA SWAT is on the way. We can be there in 10 minutes tops. Your assignment is surveillance. Remember that.

LISA: Got it.

The clock was ticking now. She could practically hear the squeal of tires as the DEA SWAT team headed for her location at top speed and in full tactical gear. It was time to make a move.

She studied the arrangement of the room and the team's positioning.

Sanjay looked like a businessman, with a *Wall Street Journal* tucked under his arm. He was scanning emails on his phone while he waited in line for another coffee, about ten feet away from Fallon.

Another of Lisa's young recruits, John Beattie, was even closer, positioned on a bench at a communal table just five feet to the right of Fallon. Beattie was clearly of the method-acting school of surveillance because he looked like he hadn't shaved or showered in more than twenty-four hours—the cramming-for-an-exam look.

She needed to make sure not only that the laptop was open, but also that it was fully powered up and logged in to Kyte as an administrator. Grabbing Fallon's laptop only to gain access to his Facebook home page would be a disaster from which their case, and her career, might never recover.

Fallon's fingers began to move over his laptop keyboard.

Lisa texted Agent Adam Lytle, who was at the Thor Data Center in Iceland monitoring current activity on the Kyte server.

LISA: Is Kyte admin online?

LYTLE: Just logged in to the Yeti server. You have eyes on him?

LISA: I think so.

Beattie had an angle that might allow him to glimpse Fallon's laptop screen.

Lisa texted Beattie: Can you see his screen?

Beattie leaned forward in his chair to get a better angle.

LISA: Don't stare!!

BEATTIE: It's not Facebook or Twitter. Don't think it's a commercial site. He could be logged in at Kyte. Can't be certain.

Lisa hesitated, wishing that she could be absolutely positive.

Her deliberations were interrupted when she heard someone behind her say, "Is that you, Nate?"

Fallon looked up at a sandy-haired young man who was winding toward him between the tables. He was wearing jeans, a faded plaid short-sleeved, button-down shirt, and Warby-Parkerish black-framed glasses.

Fallon lowered his laptop screen but didn't close it. "Rob!"

Lisa cursed to herself. If this conversation dragged on, her team would miss their chance, and the coffee shop would be overrun by the heavy-handed SWAT team.

"I almost didn't recognize you. Haven't seen you around the physics building in at least a month," Rob said.

"Longer than that, actually. I'm taking a little sabbatical."

"You're coming back, though, right?"

"You know, I'm just not sure."

"Got something else going?"

"I'm doing a little work for a tech start-up. We'll see how it goes."

"If they're offering, take the options, man."

"Words of wisdom. How's your dissertation going?" Fallon didn't seem to like lying about Kyte, so he was changing the subject.

"Done. It's under review as we speak." Rob raised two crossed fingers. "Like I need coffee right now. I'm anxious enough."

Lisa feared that Fallon and Rob were going to leave the coffee shop together, in which case her plans would definitely be ruined.

"Well, good luck," Fallon said. Thankfully, he was trying to wrap up the conversation. "It was great seeing you."

"Great seeing you, too, man. Whatever you decide to do, you're going to be awesome at it."

"Thanks, Rob. I appreciate that. See you around."

Rob went to the counter to order a coffee.

With Rob out of the picture, Fallon returned to his laptop. Lisa allowed a few minutes to pass to make sure that Fallon had time to log in and get down to business.

Lisa sent another text to Beattie.

LISA: Can you see his screen?

BEATTIE: He's definitely not surfing the web. He's got a couple of screens open. One's an Excel spreadsheet. He's coding! I think he's in!

Lisa sent a text to Powell: NOW.

Powell drew a couple of audibly shallow breaths; then she reached into her backpack and produced an asthma inhaler. She shook the inhaler, and it made a noisy, empty rattle.

Finally, Fallon looked up from his keyboard and met her gaze.

Powell gave Fallon a panicked look and said in a constricted voice, "Empty."

Fallon looked concerned, but before he could do anything, a young man sitting behind her produced his own inhaler and said, "Here. Use mine."

Then, instead of waiting until the mock health crisis was completely averted, Fallon did something unexpected. He looked back down at his laptop. He was doing something online that seemed to command his full attention.

Lisa felt certain that this was the moment. If Fallon was so absorbed in his work that he wasn't even tempted to go to the aid of beautiful, blonde, seemingly asthmatic FBI trainee Sandra Powell, then he must be attending to his criminal empire at Kyte.

She gave a nod to Sanjay and then stood up herself.

Lisa approached Fallon down a path between the tables, heading for the counter. He didn't look up to see her coming, but she saw his shoulders tense slightly at the sound of her approaching steps.

"Hi, there," she said.

Fallon looked up at Lisa, causing him to face toward the front of the shop. When he recognized her, it took a moment for him to process the information. She saw his eyes flit as he tried to remember where he had seen her before. Another moment passed as he made the connection—she had looked different in the alley that night, drenched, her hair plastered around her face.

But eventually he got there.

"You," he said.

"Yeah, me," she replied lightly. "What a coincidence, huh?"

Her breezy demeanor also seemed to buy another second, long enough for Fallon to briefly consider whether she might actually be a waitress at Beretta, as she had said that night. She saw Fallon's expression cycle from confusion to suspicion to alarm.

The clack of a coffee cup against a saucer seemed to bring them out of their frozen moment and back to real time.

But by then it was too late.

While Fallon was looking at Lisa, he didn't see Sanjay advancing on him from the back of the shop. Sanjay grabbed the laptop—still open—with both hands. Fallon managed to clutch it with his left hand, and there was a brief tug-of-war.

Fallon was gripping the keyboard half of the laptop with all the strength that he had in his fingertips, but his one hand was no match for Sanjay's two.

Sanjay ripped the laptop away, careful that its clamshell remained open.

Fallon glanced around frantically and then grasped the large cardboard cup containing his coffee.

In a quick-handed motion worthy of a shortstop making the turn, Fallon hurled the cup at his laptop, no doubt hoping it would short out the motherboard and ruin it.

Lisa and Sanjay both stared in frozen horror, helpless to prevent what was happening.

An agonized shout rang out. The other FBI trainee, John Beattie, was standing in the space between Sanjay and Fallon, his T-shirt soaked brown with coffee, hopping up and down.

"Damn, that's hot! Damn!"

Lisa let out the breath she'd been holding, then came up behind Fallon, pulling his arm behind him for the cuffs and shoving his head down on the scratched wooden table.

As Powell pressed fistfuls of napkins to Beattie's chest to take the sting out of the coffee burns, Lisa got Fallon fully cuffed.

"Can I see my laptop for just a second?" he asked. "I just need to close out of a document I was working on."

Lisa sighed. "Who do you think you're dealing with here?"

"Had to ask," he said.

She followed Fallon's eyes and saw that he seemed to be staring at the laptop of the person sitting next to him. The MacBook had a slit of white light on its side that pulsed when it was closed to show that the power was still on.

Lisa could hear Fallon's ragged, adrenaline spiked breathing settle. He was fixing his eyes on the slowly pulsing light, trying to calm himself, trying to calculate his next move. She realized that the pulse had the unmistakably even rhythm of a person's breathing, a Jobsian design grace note.

"I want my lawyer," he finally said, his cheek still pressed into the table.

"We'll get to that soon. First I'm going to read you your rights, and then we're going to take you in." Lisa pulled Fallon upright in his chair, and they had an opportunity to study each other.

She noticed that Sanjay was still gingerly holding the laptop. "You need to touch the touch pad, Sanjay."

"Are you sure?" he asked.

"If the laptop powers down from inactivity, it'll encrypt. Don't type anything; just keep touching it."

Sanjay did as instructed and held up the screen, which was still on and open to what appeared to be the Kyte system-admin account.

"Is he logged in to Kyte?" Lisa asked.

Sanjay examined the screen. "Definitely. He was using an account called—I love this—Mastermind."

"Who are you, anyway?" Fallon asked.

"FBI special agent Lisa Tanchik. We met before, but we weren't properly introduced."

"Right," Fallon said. "In that alley in the Mission."

"Yes, and before that," Lisa said.

"I'm not sure what you mean."

"You can call me Rodrigo. You had me arrange that hit for you, remember?"

Lisa watched that statement register in Fallon's eyes. He looked like he had just been slapped. While she had felt like actually slapping the smug off his Mayrhofer-quoting face, she decided that just saying those words to him was far more gratifying.

"I'll say it again. I want my lawyer."

"I'm sure you do."

Lisa had just finished reading Fallon his Miranda warning when several cars braked sharply outside in unison. This was followed by the sound of heavy boots on pavement as an entire battalion of DEA SWAT agents stormed through the front door of the tiny coffee shop, led by an apoplectic Harold Constantine.

Before he could get started, Lisa said, "We apprehended Fallon while he was logged in as Kyte's admin."

"Well . . . good," Constantine said, momentarily brought up short. "But you're going to have to answer for this cowboy shit. You were not authorized."

"I don't think I've ever been called a cowboy before," Lisa said. "Strange words coming from a SWAT team in full tactical gear. I think I'm going to have to take that as a compliment."

46

February 13

Three days after his incarceration at Manhattan's Metropolitan Correctional Center, Nate was allowed to receive visitors other than his attorney. When the inmates were led into the large, institutional visiting area, he was expecting to see his entire family, but there was only his father.

Davis was standing with some other visitors against the opposite wall, all of them anxiously shifting from foot to foot like wallflowers at a high school dance. When he saw Nate, his eyes lit for a moment, but he didn't wave. Nate didn't wave either. That was the sort of spontaneous human gesture that you tamped down behind bars. He was only three days in, but he had already learned that much.

They had not spoken at all since his arrest at Ground Zero. Nate couldn't read the expression on his father's face, but he had to assume that it reflected disappointment. Disappointment was a given.

He took a seat across from Davis at the round metal table, which was bolted heavily to the floor. "Hi, Dad. It's good to see you. Where's Mom and Amanda?"

"I thought I should visit you first. Hear what you have to say."

"I understand." He wanted to be able to filter the story for the rest of the family. Protect them from the truth, as if that were possible. "How are they holding up?"

"Well, they're upset. Of course. The question is how are you holding up?"

"I'm okay. I haven't had to deal with the other inmates too much yet. It's quiet in here. They let me have books. So there's that."

"Is there anything I can do?"

"Well, it would be great if you could fund my incidentals account. It would give me a few dollars to spend at the vending machines."

"Sure, of course. I'll talk to the lawyer about how we do that."

"Just like the old days when you used to give me an allowance."

Davis winced at the memory. "Are you going through withdrawal in here?"

"No, no. No matter what you've heard, I was never addicted to anything."

"For as long as I can remember, you've always had your nose in a device."

"Let's just say that it has been really strange being unplugged for three days straight."

Davis was a person who smiled a lot; it was his ingratiating default setting. He began a tentative smile but then quickly erased it. It was not the message that he was there to send.

"My lawyer said he's spoken with you," Nate said.

"Yes, but it was hard to get any sort of explanation out of him that made any sense. He doesn't want to tell us anything that might compromise the defense."

"Carlton's just doing his job. Thanks for finding him. He seems to know what he's doing."

"So I'm going to have to ask you the question I asked him."

"What's that?"

"Is it true? What the FBI is saying? That you're this CaptainMal character? Some kind of internet drug kingpin? It's completely absurd."

"I'd like to tell you everything, Dad. I really would. But you may be asked to testify. Carlton says that he's the only one I can tell everything to right now because then we know it's privileged."

"Is that what your attorney wants, or what you want?"

"I need to be smart about everything I do now."

"You've always been smart, Nate. That has never been the problem."

"My life's at stake here, Dad. Carlton says this case is the first of its kind, so it's hard to say how the sentencing might go. A life sentence is not off the table. Under this federal kingpin statute, the death penalty is even a possibility."

Davis winced. "That's not going to happen," he said.

His father's eyes drifted away and made a circle of the gray-green walls of the visitation room like he was searching for something familiar that he could anchor himself to.

When he returned his gaze to his son, Davis said, "You don't have to say a thing, Nate. I certainly don't want to make your situation any worse." A pause. "But I also need to know. Your mother and Amanda need to know too."

He placed both hands palms down on the table. "I'd like you to look me in the eye, and I'm going to ask you again. And you're going to look me in the eye, and I'll know your answer. You don't have to say it."

Nate really did not want to play this game. He wished the buzzer would sound, marking the end of visiting hours.

Davis looked at him directly and asked again, "Did you do what they're saying?"

Nate stared back at his father, and despite himself, he felt a rising anger. Anger that the FBI had destroyed the business he'd created, the thing that had given his life significance, the tool and weapon that he had used to make his dent in the universe. Anger that his father would never understand why he had done it because he had never taken a real chance in his entire life. And of course, there was also the guilt, horror, and anger he directed at himself for allowing himself to become what he had become.

Most parents knew how to read their children, but Davis was going to have to have Jedi skills to glean all of that from Nate's expression.

But he seemed to understand enough.

Nate watched the realization come over his father like a wave of nausea. Davis removed his lined hands from the table and placed them in his lap. He leaned back a bit in his molded plastic chair, and the metal casters scraped slightly on the tile floor. It would have been too much to say that he recoiled.

Davis studied the pattern in the floor tiles for a long moment. When he looked up again at Nate, it was with the expression of someone who had just been gut shot, someone who needed to carefully hold himself together for fear of what might come spilling out.

"Can you at least tell me why you did it, Nate?" His voice was constrained and small. "You had so much."

"I know it probably seems that way to you." Nate didn't want to insult his father. Or maybe he did.

"What do you mean by that?"

"Nothing."

"No," Davis said. "I really want to know. What we gave you, was it so little?"

"No, you and Mom gave me a good home, a good family, put me through Stanford. This isn't your fault. Is that what you want to hear?"

Davis's expression started to change. He was getting angry too.

"I think you have something that you want to tell me, so I want you to say it. Forget about all that father-son crap. We've been doing that all our lives. You're twenty-five. You're a man now, and you're going to have to pay for this like a man. So now that we're here—at this place—we might as well finally get to know one another a little. I mean, why not, right?"

Nate didn't think that his father had ever spoken to him with this tone before. Finally, he said, "I didn't want to live my life the way that you lived yours."

"And what does that mean?"

"It means I wanted to do more than just follow that path—degree, job, marriage, kids, retirement. I was willing to put myself at risk to have a life that was bigger than that. I bet big, and yeah, I lost. But at least I tried. I never wanted to be someone's employee all my life, someone who never really had any skin in the game."

"Is that really what you think of me?"

Nate was silent.

Davis continued. "I had skin in the game." He leaned forward over the table. "It was you. *You* were my skin in the game."

47

Two Years Later

Lisa stepped to the podium in a small auditorium at Quantico. The FBI's investigation of AlphaBay, the Dark Web marketplace that was the successor to Kyte, was getting underway, and she was leading it.

Outsiders could take a pessimistic view and say that nothing had changed since the arrests of Nate Fallon and Ernesto Bonilla. Both on the streets and on the Dark Web, the drug trade continued taking lives. But she preferred to think that some wars were worth waging, even if they were never ending.

Like her battle with depression, her black dog. She no longer carried a water bottle full of vodka with her to work, and that helped. She wasn't kidding herself; there was no cure for what she had. But there was the work, and her colleagues, and that helped too.

Lisa thought about how far she had come since her early days at Quantico, when none of her bosses had known what to do with her. Now no one remembered the video with the Russian, or if they did, it was merely a footnote to the often-repeated story about the security-camera footage that had been retrieved from the cartel villa in Nuevo Laredo, in which she had overcome a much-larger Zeta soldier without a weapon. The trainee who'd had her ass kicked every day at Quantico now had a reputation as a badass. Who would have imagined that?

She surveyed the eager faces of the agents in the first few rows and was pleased to note that there were several young women on the team. Most of them looked to be a couple of years younger than her, about the same age she had been when she'd started the Kyte investigation.

As she scanned the room, she thought for just a moment that she saw the face of her sister. And she wasn't scowling this time. She was smiling.

Lisa blinked, looked again, and saw that it was just a dark-haired agent in the back row who looked a bit like Jess. Maybe taming the black dog didn't necessarily mean dimming Jess's presence in her life.

Lisa tapped the microphone.

"Okay. Let's begin."

———

At first glance, the Metropolitan Correctional Center—or MCC—located in lower Manhattan near city hall and South Street Seaport, resembled an unfortunately authoritarian-looking office building. MCC was a gray concrete monolith pocked by tiny windows and ringed by fences topped with razor wire. This was the same facility that had been home to infamous felons such as Bernie Madoff and Joaquín "El Chapo" Guzmán Loera. It seemed like a fitting address for the headline-grabbing internet drug kingpin Nate "CaptainMal" Fallon.

When Fallon had asked for a meeting with Lisa two years into his life sentence at MCC, she had initially dismissed the request. But finally, her curiosity got the better of her. She had never stopped trying to solve the Rubik's Cube of contradictions that was Nate Fallon. On the one hand, he was so similar to the blandly chill dudes that she had taken college classes with, even dated. And yet, from reading every word that he had publicly posted as CaptainMal, combing through his private messages after they seized the Reykjavík server, and trading messages with him as Rodrigo, she knew that he was like no one else that she had ever encountered. The Fallon that she knew could be naive, idealistic, and occasionally inspiring but also brutally pragmatic and ruthless. He was a libertarian icon to the Free Nate movement that had sprung up among cypherpunks and in certain geeky corners of the internet. He was a dangerous drug kingpin to the law enforcement community and the mainstream press.

Fallon was also the cornerstone of Lisa's newly resurrected career at the FBI. He was her calling card. If he wasn't in the first sentence of her bio, then he was certainly name checked by the second. The investigation and capture of Fallon, along with the arrest of the Zeta cartel boss Ernesto Bonilla, would probably define her for the rest of her professional life. It was the reason she had become something of a role model and ringleader for a group of young female agents who were the FBI's next generation of cyber investigative talent. It was a role that she had never imagined that she would play when she was getting her ass kicked on a daily basis as an academy trainee. If she was always going to be spoken of in the same breath as Fallon, she felt the need to better understand who he was and what he meant. If he meant anything at all.

Lisa couldn't help but feel a chill as she proceeded through chamber after chamber of steel doors, each one announcing itself with a metallic clang and a harsh electric buzz like a live power line. A civilian couldn't penetrate this stronghold without feeling a creeping claustrophobia. She felt the weight of each ring of security as she passed through it like fathoms of seawater pressing down on a deep-sea diver.

She was led to a small room with a table, two metal folding chairs, and white fluorescent lighting that illuminated every corner. Nate Fallon was sitting at the table in pale-brown prison scrubs, watching her approach with a slight smile. He seemed calm. Lisa supposed that he had been inside long enough now that he was fully acclimated to his new reality.

There were no restraints on his hands or feet, so he stood as she approached, presumably out of courtesy. At six feet two, he towered over her, but she didn't feel particularly threatened by him.

"Special Agent Tanchik sounds so formal. Mind if I call you Lisa?"

"That's fine."

"I'd shake your hand, but . . ." He nodded to the security camera in the corner. "They frown on that sort of thing."

"I understand."

"Thanks for coming. I really appreciate it."

"I saw your mother last month at a conference."

"Right. She's out there speaking at hacker and cryptography conferences against abusive government prosecution tactics. The cypherpunk crowd loves her. She's like a mom to all these black hat hackers and crypto-geeks. Funny where life can take you. When I was growing up, I don't think I ever saw her in front of a computer. You didn't introduce yourself, did you?"

"Oh no."

"That's good. You're not her favorite person."

Lisa nodded.

"Do you know how DPain, I mean Jason, is doing?"

"He's doing well. He owns a marijuana dispensary in Oakland. We always suspected that he hid some of the money that he made from Kyte to buy the business, but that's water under the bridge now. Do you mind if I call you Nate?"

"Yes, please. Doesn't it feel weird to be so formal? I feel like I know you, and you probably *really* feel like you know me."

"True."

"Do you mind if I call you Rodrigo?"

She gave a mock grimace. "Please don't."

"Sorry. Bad joke." Then he added, "I've been good for your career, haven't I? You could probably leave the FBI and get some big job with a security consulting firm. I'm surprised you haven't done that."

"Please don't make it sound like you did me some sort of a favor. The only favor you did me was making enough dumb mistakes to get caught."

"You're right, of course."

"Since I came here as you requested, can I ask you a question?"

"Sure."

"What really happened to Brian Hardwick? How did he end up in that basement in Nuevo Laredo? You obviously had something to do with it, but it's never been clear how it happened. During your trial you denied all responsibility, but that clearly isn't true, is it?"

It couldn't have been a complete surprise, but she still noticed that Fallon's eyes widened. There was some reservoir of raw emotion there.

"Such a terrible thing," he said.

"He was your best friend, wasn't he?"

"Yeah, I'd say he was."

"Some of your other friends have told us that Hardwick was working with you on some mysterious project. Was that project Kyte?"

"I'd rather not say."

"So you didn't get Hardwick involved with Kyte?" She paused. "Ernesto Bonilla and the Zeta cartel were directly responsible for his death. But you had something to do with it, didn't you? You told Rodrigo that the Zeta cartel had abducted one of your people. You were obviously referring to Hardwick."

Fallon shook his head in disbelief. "Now I get it. This isn't just about satisfying your curiosity. You want to hang a murder charge on me. Or at least make me an accomplice. I answered those questions during my trial."

"I want to understand what happened to your friend. Don't you think his family deserves that? Or his girlfriend, Janine?"

"If you had just delivered that smartphone to the cartel like I asked, then Brian might be alive right now."

"It wasn't my decision to put a tracking device on the phone," Lisa said. "But we had to take down Bonilla when we had the opportunity. And it was you who put Hardwick in that position, not the FBI."

He ran a hand through his hair and looked like he wanted to stand, but thought better of it. "I can't help you. I think this is where I'm supposed to end the conversation and ask for my lawyer, right?"

Lisa shrugged. "Yeah, that's probably what your attorney would tell you to do. But you're already serving a double life sentence with no opportunity for parole. You've already asked an FBI agent to commit murder for hire—"

"That wasn't me. There were several people who had admin rights and played the role of CaptainMal."

"I know that was your defense. But we were never able to identify any others. We found thumb drives in your apartment with tens of millions of dollars in Bitcoin on them."

Fallon shrugged. "That doesn't prove anything. And no one was actually murdered, right? It was all a big entrapment scheme anyway."

"If that's the conversation that you want to have, then I'll leave right now."

Fallon took a breath and seemed to calm himself. "Sorry, but I still get upset thinking about the prosecution, especially the sentencing. Do you really think it was fair for me to get double life without parole? Major drug dealers, cartel guys, are put away for twenty years or even less. How is that fair?"

"You're asking the wrong person, Nate. I just make arrests. I don't play judge and jury."

Fallon leaned forward across the table. "Look, here's what I will say. I was really glad to hear that you brought down Bonilla. I'm glad he's paying for what he did to Hardwick. I just wish he had paid with his life. Thank you." Through an arrangement with the Mexican government, Bonilla was serving a life sentence in a maximum-security prison in Colorado.

"I didn't do it for you," Lisa said.

"My lawyer thinks that eventually I'll start getting parole hearings, once people get some perspective on this whole thing."

"Is that why you wanted to talk to me? If you're looking for someone to help put your case in perspective, you definitely came to the wrong person."

"I guess I wanted to talk to someone who understood."

"What is it that you think I understand?"

Fallon leaned forward and looked into her eyes like the earnest grad student that he had been not so very long ago.

"You were probably watching Kyte every day for months. You saw the community that developed in the forums. The way we tapped into something."

Lisa resisted the impulse to insert a sharp comment there. Best to hang back and hope for some oversharing.

"I want to ask you something," Fallon said.

"Okay."

"I'll bet you read Mayrhofer, if only to get inside my head. What'd you think of it?"

"Nate, I'm an FBI agent. I believe that the federal government helps people, at least on the good days. And the day I arrested you in that coffee shop, well, that was one of my good days."

"Have you seen AlphaBay?" Fallon was referring to the new Dark Web site that had picked up where Kyte had left off. "And Planetary had a decent run for a while."

"Yeah. Are any of your former associates involved with AlphaBay?"

"I really don't know. Are you working on that case?"

"I can't say anything about a pending investigation."

"I'll take that as a yes. You know, when you shut down Kyte, you didn't really stop anything. What I started with Kyte is just the beginning."

"Well, I stopped *you*."

Fallon acknowledged that with a nod and a shrug. "I met a guy in the yard who has been here for twenty-eight years, and he gave me a good piece of advice. He said that you have to embrace what happened to you, go ahead and mourn the life that you lost, and feel the grief and the sadness. He said to do that for a few days; don't try to hide from it. Let it sink all the way in. And then you get on with your life in here."

"And you've reached that stage now?"

"I think so. I'm even teaching yoga to some of the inmates. The guys in here are so obsessed with pumping iron and building strength. Flexibility is just as important."

She leaned forward and said, not unkindly, "I have to admit I still don't really understand why you asked me to come here."

"Talking to Rodrigo helped back in the day. I enjoyed it, thought we could have another chat like that."

"That wasn't actually me, Nate." Lisa began to gather herself to leave.

Fallon leaned back in his chair. "If it wasn't a little bit you, you wouldn't have been so good at it. I think we're both pretty good at putting on a persona."

Lisa couldn't deny that, so she sat silent, still waiting for an explanation that made sense to her.

Fallon offered a wan smile and looked down at his prison-issue shoes. "I guess I wanted to talk because you're the only person I know who really understood."

"Understood what?"

"How much fun we had."

48

If you know how to see it, it's all right there from day one in the garage or the dorm room or wherever. Every great company starts with the vision of one person, the founder. Whether it's Gates, Zuckerberg, or Jobs, that person is the single cell that contains the DNA of the business.

To do something amazing, something that really disrupts the status quo and transforms the way we live in some small or large way, you have to have the ability to see something that wasn't there before, and then believe it into existence. That kind of vision doesn't come from a committee, or a board of directors, or even from a team of coders.

But along with the vision, you also get that person's flaws, their blind spots, and that becomes another tangled strand in the company's DNA too. Sometimes those flaws can be turned into strengths. Other times those imperfections just bring everything down and blow it all up.

We're all more than just one thing, right? I guess my friends and family have learned that the hard way now. But I can't renounce what I did with Kyte as CaptainMal. That's a big part of who I am too.

Does that sound egotistical of me to say that Kyte was something that I did? I'm just being honest. Sure, there were admins, programmers, and logistics managers who contributed their time and talents, and they all played valuable roles, but the business started and ended with me. I know my lawyer doesn't want me to say that, but it's true.

I'm not blind to what happened. I know what I did, and I understand I have to pay. I get that. But as I look back over how it all went down, I'm still having trouble figuring out, realistically, where I would have done something differently, changed the narrative.

I guess if I had to name a role model it would probably be Steve Jobs. I've been using my downtime to reread the Walter Isaacson biography.

Jobs said that we're here to put a dent in the universe. If you're lucky, you get to feel that way at least once in your life. And if you're really lucky, you get to feel that way when you're young.

But it doesn't last forever. Because the universe has one hell of a counterpunch.

When I was running Kyte, it was like living in a fever dream. Now that I'm here at MCC, I feel like the fever has broken and I have to somehow carry on with my life in here with what's left of me. I have to try to do small, good things. Like when I had just been in for a week, I got a new cellmate, Augie, who was going through heroin withdrawal. He was practically out of his mind and I don't think he probably understood or remembered a word I said. But I crouched down next to his bunk, and I just said, as much to me as to him, "We got this."

Yeah, I got this.

But, just like my friend Augie, you never forget that electricity in your brain, the pinball machine with all the lights blinking and bells ringing. Because once you've really done something in this world, you can't go back to being a small person, not forever. Someday I'll be out of here, I truly believe that. And I'll get another opportunity to use my talents. The right way, this time.

So many of the giants of the tech industry failed in their first ventures, often their first several. But they didn't give up, and I won't give up.

That's what it means to be a serial entrepreneur.

Acknowledgments

Although writing is essentially a solitary act, it always amazes me how many people I'm deeply grateful to by the time a book sees print. My sincerest thanks to the following:

- My agent and friend, David Hale Smith at InkWell Management, for his unflagging support for the idea of this book.
- Megha Parekh, my wonderful editor at Thomas & Mercer, who, along with my developmental editor, Caitlin Alexander, steered the manuscript in all of the right directions.
- The entire team at Thomas & Mercer, especially Gracie Doyle (who listened to me pitch this book more than once), but also Carissa Bluestone and Sarah Shaw. I'm so pleased to be working with T&M again on this new series and very appreciative of the way they got behind this book.
- Joseph Lopez, for being a smart and insightful beta reader.
- Ben LeRoy, for reading an early version of the manuscript and providing astute and thoughtful notes.
- The renowned security technologist and author Bruce Schneier, who read an early version of the manuscript and provided technical advice. Runa Sandvik also contributed valuable guidance on data-security matters. Any remaining errors regarding security or technology are definitely on me.

- My wife, Kathy, for her tolerance and support while I obsessed over this story, and for being my first and best reader.

As the disclaimer goes, this book is a work of fiction, but it was inspired by the true story of Ross Ulbricht and the rise and fall of Silk Road. There are events in this book that parallel the Silk Road story, but there are also enormous variations and departures from that narrative, from characters (both major and minor) to key incidents. This book should not be read as a commentary on or portrayal of Ross Ulbricht, Silk Road, or anyone else associated with that investigation—it is an invented story inspired by those events. Nevertheless, I owe a debt to the journalists who reported on Silk Road, including the *Wired* magazine series "The Rise & Fall of Silk Road" by Joshuah Bearman, *American Kingpin* by Nick Bilton, and the reporting of Andy Greenberg in *Wired* magazine.

ABOUT THE AUTHOR

Photo © 2013 Sarah Deragon

Reece Hirsch is the author of five thrillers that draw upon his background as a privacy attorney. His first book, *The Insider*, was a finalist for the 2011 International Thriller Writers Award for Best First Novel. His next three books, *The Adversary*, *Intrusion*, and *Surveillance*, all feature former Department of Justice cybercrimes prosecutor Chris Bruen. Hirsch is a partner at the San Francisco office of an international law firm and cochair of its privacy-and-cybersecurity practice. He is also a member of the board of directors of the Valentino Achak Deng Foundation (www.VADFoundation.org). He lives in the Bay Area with his wife. Find out more at www.reecehirsch.com.